DARK NATION

Escaping Anarchy

Enduring Anarchy

Surviving Anarchy

www.relaypub.com

ESCAPING ANARCHY

DARK NATION BOOK ONE

BLURB

They're trapped inside a prison when the power goes out…

Molly is determined to get the troubled teens she teaches back on the right path and is convinced a trip to a local prison will show them the consequences of bad behavior. But when an EMP blast knocks out all power across the country, Molly and her five students, along with their former-Marine bus driver, Colton, are locked in with the prisoners with no safe exit.

The guards are little help against clever convicts, and when a riot throws everything into chaos, Molly and Colton must find a way to get to freedom with their charges, even if it means trusting a prisoner who is using them for his own gains.

Prisoners aren't the only danger in the suddenly powerless world. Escaping the prison may be more dangerous than staying inside as it becomes clear to everyone that the power isn't coming back, and society is about to crumble.

CONTENTS

1

MOLLY

Molly O'Neil swept a flyaway strand of strawberry-blonde hair from her face and stifled a yawn. She'd been up since before sunrise and was already flagging. Behind her, the busload of school kids she was in charge of for the day was becoming restless, but she couldn't bring herself to confront them. Not yet.

"How much longer?" She bent forward and put her hand on the back of the bus driver's seat.

Colton shrugged his thick shoulders at her and pointed to the ugly red line on the satnav that indicated heavy traffic. "Who knows?" he replied, drumming his large fingers impatiently on the steering wheel. "Could be an hour or more."

Molly looked at her watch and sighed. It was unseasonably warm, and the musty smell of the school bus was making her feel a little car sick. Taking a long sip from the flask of lukewarm coffee she was holding, she wondered—not for the first time that day—why she, as an English teacher, had been roped into this.

The school's annual "Scared Straight" trip was usually handled by their brash and bulky gym teacher, Mr. Jones. However, this year, the principal had wanted to switch things up. She'd volunteered, not actually expecting to be picked. Now here she was, stuck on the highway on the way to Fairfield Prison with five disgruntled teenagers. The only saving grace was that they weren't all *bad* kids.

"You'd better give them a call," Colton said loudly, breaking her concentration. "We're gonna be late."

Putting down her coffee, Molly bit back a sigh, then started to scroll through her phone; she knew she had the number somewhere. Probably hidden in her emails along with the permission forms and risk assessment she'd had to organize.

She found it, and was about to dial the number, when she stopped and strained her ears. Through the dull chatter toward the back of the bus, she could hear the unmistakable flick of a lighter. She bit her lower lip. What if she pretended she hadn't heard it? What if she just hunkered down at the front of the bus, stared out of the window at the slow-moving landscape, and imagined the scrawny trees at the side of the highway were actually a vast and glorious forest that she could escape to? A place where she could hide herself away and not have to deal with any of this anymore.

Flick. Flick. Flick.

Molly placed her palm on the armrest and steadied herself as she stood up. Slipping her phone into her jeans pocket, she cast her eyes over each seat in turn until she came to the obvious culprit: Lucky.

"Hand it over."

Lucky had been so busy staring at his phone that he didn't notice Molly standing over him until she spoke. "The phone?" he said, slipping his phone-free hand down into the space between his hip and the side of the bus.

"The lighter." Molly held out her hand and wriggled her fingers. "Now, please, Lucky."

For a moment, she thought that Lucky might protest. But he was only fourteen, younger than the others, and essentially a decent kid. So, after looking around to see whether the others were watching, he did as he was told. "I wasn't going to do anything," he said. "And I don't think you've got a right to take my personal property from me."

Trying not to smile at the fake bravado, Molly folded her arms. "Well, you haven't exactly got a good track record, have you?" she said, even though she knew that she shouldn't really be getting into it with him.

Rolling his eyes, Lucky leaned a gangly arm on the rim of the window and waved his hand at her. "It was an accident," he said. "How come no one believes me?"

From the back of the bus, Jenna, who had been in more fist fights than Molly cared to count, shouted, "Because you're a pyro freak, that's why!"

Ignoring her, Molly put the lighter into her pocket and said, "Whether it was an accident or not, you set fire to your uncle's barn. You're on this trip for a reason. Plus, you and I both know that if you're caught in possession of a lighter, you'll be in a whole world of trouble—*especially* if you're caught trying to take a lighter into a prison. So, consider me confiscating this a little taste of what it's like in jail. No luxuries. No control. Someone else deciding what you can and can't do—"

"All right," Lucky whined. "Can we wait till we get there before starting the lectures?"

Molly opened her mouth to reply but thought better of it; she'd been teaching long enough to know that the worst possible thing you could do was allow yourself to be sucked into an argument. Especially if you were trapped in an airless bus on the longest school trip in history.

"If you want it back, you can collect it from the principal's office at the end of the day." Ignoring Lucky's grumbles, she continued her walk down the bus; now that she was up, she might as well check on the others.

At the back, the Banks twins, Erik and Scarlett, were leaning into the aisle and bickering with Jenna. *Seriously?* Molly muttered, *There's only five of them—how can they be this much hard work?*

"Right," she said, positioning herself between the twins and Jenna. "What's going on with you three?"

"Nothing," Scarlett replied, narrowing her eyes at Jenna, and sinking back into her seat to look at her phone.

"Yeah," Erik agreed. "Nothing."

Molly looked from Jenna to the twins, then shook her head. "Okay, well, keep it down. Mr. King is trying to concentrate up there." She had turned and started to head back to her seat, when she unmistakably heard Erik mutter loudly to his sister, "No wonder she gets in so many fights—she's got arms like a freakin' dude."

Scarlett sniggered loudly. There was a millisecond of silence before Jenna yelled, "Yeah, so what if I have!"

Molly spun around, waving her hands calmly in front of her, ready to de-escalate the situation, but Jenna had clearly had enough of Erik's jibes and, ignoring Molly completely, she lunged for him. Erik had already started to scrabble backwards, almost right into his sister's lap, but Molly dashed forward and positioned herself in front of him. Placing her hands on Jenna's shoulders, she met her eyes. Jenna was breathing quickly, her eyes were wide and furious, and her cheeks were flushed.

"It's not worth it," Molly said, willing Jenna to listen to her. "Really, it's not."

Jenna was trembling, but she'd been in too many fights. One more, and she'd be kicked out of school and sent straight to Juvie.

4

"Jenna—it's not worth it," Molly repeated. Slowly, she saw Jenna's shoulders drop. "Good. Right. Now why don't you go sit up front?"

Jenna nodded. Molly let out a long slow breath as she watched her release her clenched fists, pick up her backpack and move several seats away from Scarlett and Erik. Jenna could easily have taken Erik; he was mouthy when he was with his sister, but he was skinny too, and had never so much as thrown a punch as far as Molly knew. Thank God she'd managed to calm Jenna down and hadn't had to return the kids to their parents with black eyes and bloodied noses. Although, at least if she had, it might have assured she was never selected to chaperone a trip like this again in the future.

Sitting down opposite the twins, in the seat Jenna had just vacated, Molly leaned forward and put her hands on her knees. "Come on, you two. You need to behave and not instigate anything. Out of everyone, I thought the two of you were the ones who probably didn't deserve to be here. Maybe I was wrong."

Scarlett wasn't looking at her; she was buried in her phone. But Erik looked sheepish and almost apologetic as he said, "Yeah. Whatever."

"Well, not 'whatever', Erik—"

Ahead, Colton swore under his breath and it caused Molly to look up. Standing up and stepping away from the twins, she saw that he was shaking his head and gesticulating at something out of the window.

"What the hell is this?" he said loudly.

Molly dipped her head and narrowed her eyes. Ahead, a couple of yards away, the road sign which had—a few seconds ago—announced a detour due to a traffic accident, was flickering. It continued to flicker. The orange lights flashed on and off and on again. Then they disappeared completely. Molly frowned.

At the front of the bus, Lucky let out a clap of laughter. Jenna was sniggering too.

"What the…" Colton turned to look at Molly and she felt her cheeks begin to flush, because the sign now read: SHEEPLE MAKE GOOD VENISON. It was accompanied by a crude drawing of what she could only assume was supposed to depict cannibalism. And Molly knew exactly who was responsible.

"Scarlett…." She whirled around and snatched the girl's phone from her hands.

"Hey!" Scarlett and Erik yelled at the same time.

Molly didn't give in. She put her hands on her hips and shook her head. "You're on this trip because of exactly this kind of behavior."

Scarlett opened her mouth to speak but Molly interrupted her.

"And don't even bother trying to tell me it wasn't you. Change it back." She handed Scarlett her phone. "Now."

With the road sign back to normal, Jenna sitting in the middle section of the bus with her headphones on, and the others seemingly done with causing trouble, Molly returned to her seat. Without meaning to, she exhaled loudly as she sat down, and Colton turned to her.

"Don't know how you do it," he said, looking past her at the unruly concoction of students she'd been put in charge of. "This lot. Every day."

Molly attempted to smile. Her temples were aching with tiredness, and what she wanted to say was, *I don't know either. And I don't know how long I can keep doing it for.* But she didn't. "You don't have it too easy yourself," she said. "Driving busloads of rowdy kids around every day."

Colton shrugged at her. "Nah," he said, smiling with the corner of his mouth. "I'm just the driver. I don't have to keep them in line."

"Well, you might have more luck at it." Molly looked briefly at the tattoos on Colton's forearms, and his short, sharp, military haircut.

"I'd say you do all right," he said, turning back to the road. "Listen, we're almost at the detour. Should be at the prison in half an hour."

Molly nodded. "I'll call them."

After speaking to the warden's assistant, Molly hung up, put her cell phone in her bag, and took out a battered copy of *The Call of the Wild* —an adventure novel she picked up at a flea market a few years ago and had devoured several times since. In the seats opposite her, Zack, the only student yet to cause her any problems, was also reading.

Smiling a little, Molly peered around his book to look at the cover. She knew Zack—he was in one of her English classes—and she was pleasantly surprised to see him reading. In class, he was pretty much always silent. Clever, but silent. The kind of kid who gave off a serious 'leave me alone' vibe and who no one ever wanted to get that close to.

"Good book?" she asked, angling herself toward him.

Slowly, Zack looked up at her from beneath his dark greasy hair. He wore glasses, was extremely pale, and had piercingly blue eyes that were more than a little unnerving. Molly had known kids like him before; kids who leaned into the 'I'm a loner' thing as a form of self-preservation. Closing the cover, he placed both hands on top of it.

"I've read it a couple of times myself," Molly said, gesturing to the book. In fact, it was one of her favorites. "I love dystopian stuff."

With a withering look, Zack pursed his lips.

"Psychopath." A couple of seats behind, Lucky was rolling his eyes. "I don't even feel safe being on the same bus as him, Miss O'Neil."

Molly ignored Lucky, but Zack was already opening the book back up and adjusting his glasses on the bridge of his nose. Sighing a little, Molly turned away. As she did, Zack said, in a gruff teenage voice, and without looking at her, "You know, the dystopian worlds in these books might be more interesting if we didn't see the exact same

7

behavior in other people every single day." Facing away from her, he gestured to the window. "Every time we step outside."

Molly swallowed hard. She hated to even think it, but she saw where the other kids were coming from—whether he meant to be or not, Zack was a little creepy. Although he did have a point; a lot of the time, for a lot of people, life wasn't all that kind. For years now, Molly had felt an increasing need, deep down in the pit of her stomach, to escape. To run away to a little piece of land somewhere and to live totally and utterly by herself. Off grid. No papers to grade. No kids to try and drag through high school, so that they could have half a chance in the big bad world.

She contemplated saying this to Zack. Sometimes, she thought that if she could get a student to see that she was on their side, that she was human, and that she got where they were coming from—that it would make a difference. With Zack, a lot of people had already tried that. And all of them had failed.

"What was that about?" Colton asked, turning and lowering his voice. "The psycho thing?"

Molly sighed and leaned in a little closer. "Zack's got a bit of a... reputation. His older brother Tommy killed someone. He's in prison. Last year, Zack was kicked out of military school for beating another kid unconscious."

"Shit." Colton sucked his cheeks in and shook his head. Turning back to the steering wheel, as the traffic finally began to move again, he looked into the rearview mirror. But he wasn't looking at Molly; his eyes were fixed on Zack, and something flashed across his face that Molly hadn't seen before. Was it understanding? Or pity?

8

2

LAURA

Laura's arms burned fiercely as she lifted them above her head. She'd chosen the twenty-pound weights. She wasn't ready for them, but she was sick of not making any progress. At her feet, Argent looked up at her through large chocolate brown eyes—an expression that said, *You're pushing yourself too hard, you know.*

"Oh, don't you start," she said, counting to ten and speaking through quick shallow breaths as she brought her arms back to her sides. "You know what it's like to feel as if you've been put out to pasture."

At that, Argent simply closed his eyes and put his head on his paws; he knew better than to argue with her. He'd been by her side for so long now that, these days, Laura was fairly sure he was more in tune with her than her own family was.

After forcing herself to complete five more reps, Laura finally stopped. She'd been sitting on the specially designed bench that Alex had installed for her, but now used her tired, shaky arms to lift herself back into her wheelchair.

Releasing a long, slow breath, she reached for her water bottle. Sweat glistened across her shoulders and, despite it being five whole years since the accident, she still hated the way it felt when she leaned against the wheelchair's nylon backrest. As Argent stood up and yawned, aware they'd soon be leaving, she removed the small white earbuds from her ears and asked Siri to stop the music.

Looking at herself in the wall-length mirrors opposite, Laura gritted her teeth and forced her eyes away from her flushed and tired-looking face. Her home gym was at the side of the house, with large glass doors that looked out into their neat but not particularly impressive garden; neither she nor Alex was the green-thumb type. When they first got married, and she was starting out in her career as a personal trainer, Alex had suggested they convert the garage into a studio for her. Even now, despite the big mirrors, it was her favorite room in the house.

It was *her* place. A place where she could pretend things were as they used to be. A place where she could work out, drown herself in loud music, and ignore the rest of the world.

Without the soothing drum beat of the music she'd been listening to, however, quiet filled her ears. As always, the lack of noise seemed to amplify the dull ache in her lower back, and she winced as she moved. Closing her eyes, she tried one of the breathing exercises her PT had recommended. She was visualizing herself, pain free, beneath a giant oak tree in a field full of sunflowers—something she'd always felt was kind of ridiculous, but which she tried anyway—when her husband's voice broke her concentration.

"Goddamn it!" Alex's cry was followed by the sound of something being tossed across the room.

Laura glanced at Argent. "What's he up to?"

Grabbing the towel that was slung over the arm of her chair, she patted her face, then slung it around her shoulders and wheeled out of the gym. "Alex?"

"In here." His voice came from their daughter Scarlett's room and as Laura approached, she shook her head; he was doing DIY? They had a day to themselves. The kids were out of the way and Alex, for once, wasn't working. And he'd decided to do DIY?

"What are you—" Laura stopped in the doorway of Scarlett's room. She'd always been a little disappointed by her daughter's bedroom; when Laura was a teenager, she'd put up fairy lights, hung posters of boy bands, and pinned photos of her girlfriends to a large cork board. But Scarlett's room was ... grungy. Gray walls, not a photograph in sight, and dominated by a huge computer desk with three screens and two keyboards. Erik's was similar, although not quite so dark, but it was Scarlett's that bothered Laura the most.

Alex looked up at her. He was on the floor, kneeling, with his shirt sleeves rolled up, and was surrounded by what looked like the innards of Scarlett's computer. Blinking at her, he rubbed the back of his neck, and Laura instantly knew that he was doing something he felt bad about.

"Alex, what is this?"

"I'm taking it apart."

"Why? Is it broken? You know nothing about computers...."

"I'm not fixing it, Laura. I'm dismantling the damn thing." Alex's features sharpened as he spoke, and beneath his beard she could see his cheeks flushing.

Laura felt her mouth drop open. Her heart fluttered uncomfortably in her chest. "Dismantling it? Why?" Already, she was picturing their daughter's face when she came home and realized what he had done.

Alex waved his hand at her and picked up a screwdriver. "Erik's too. I've had enough."

"So, this is a punishment?" Before the accident, Laura would have stormed into Scarlett's room and snatched the screwdriver from her husband's fingers. Now, that kind of outburst wasn't an option.

"Yes. A punishment. They can't get away with what they did, Laura."

Trying to soften her voice, because if they both started yelling, they'd get nowhere, Laura tilted her head at him and said, "The Scared Straight trip is their punishment, isn't it?"

Alex looked up at her and sat back on his heels. "No," he said bluntly, weighing the screwdriver up and down. "The prison trip is to show them where they'll end up if they keep on like this. They might get some street cred from being teenage cyber criminals, but if the twins keep on like this... with the hacking... they'll end up in jail, Laura."

"Alex...." Laura took the towel from around her neck and placed it in her lap so that she could fiddle with its corners. "Betraying their trust like this—what will that teach them?" She held his gaze and, for a moment, thought he might give in and see where she was coming from. But Alex had always been stubborn and as usual, he simply shook his head at her.

"No, I'm sorry. I've made up my mind. They can't get away with what they did to that TV station. There has to be a consequence."

"The Scared Straight trip *is* the consequence." Finally, Laura's voice had gone up both in pitch and volume. She was exasperated and she *hated* it when Alex was like this—obstinate, inflexible, and with absolutely no regard for how his actions might make other people feel. Yes, the twins had been getting a little out of control lately, but they'd seemed genuinely remorseful after their last stunt, and something like this would not help matters.

"It's a *trip*, Laura, a school trip. Right now, they're probably smoking with their buddies at the back of the bus." Waving his hands at Scarlett's dead computer, he said, "*This* is a real punishment. *This* is a consequence."

Before she could stop it, anger bubbled in Laura's chest. "It's not a consequence, Alex, it's a betrayal of their trust. Can't you see that doing this when they're not even here, without even talking to them, will make things worse?"

Alex looked away. His jaw twitched. "Can they get much worse?"

Studying her husband's face, Laura knew she wasn't going to change his mind. Beckoning for Argent, who'd settled on Scarlett's bed to watch the two of them, she turned back to the hallway. She was about to leave when she stopped, palms resting heavily on the wheels of her chair. "You know," she said, her shoulders drooping, "everything they've been getting into lately? It's just their way of coping."

Laura could feel Alex watching her. The events of the past few years hung in the air between them. As always, neither of them said what they were feeling out loud.

Finally, as she was leaving, she heard Alex mutter, "I'm sorry." Not for the first time, Laura had no idea what he was sorry for.

"Put it back together, Alex," she said quietly. "Please."

3

DOUGIE

"So, what's the plan?" Santi, the old guy with the Jesus tattoo on his forearm, was looking at Dougie—as if he gave a crap what the plan was.

"Why are you asking me?" Dougie leaned back in his chair so that the two front legs hovered above the floor.

"Didn't you do one of these once? As a kid?" Frank said, wide-eyed.

"Yeah. And how d'you think it turned out?" Dougie shot Frank a look that made the younger guy shudder. Rolling his eyes, and remembering the camera that was trained on them, recording every bit of what was about to happen for the warden to look at later, Dougie took the gum he'd been chewing out of his mouth and stuck it behind his ear. "We go in hard," he said. "Scare the shit out of them. Then get a bit softer... make the kids see that ending up here is the last thing they want to do. Make them—and the guards—think we've seen the error of our ways."

"We have. Haven't we?" Frank looked confused. Santi was nodding, but wasn't half as stupid as Frank. He knew that, out of the three of them, the only reason Dougie was here was for the perks. Extra yard time. Another tick in the good behavior column.

"Sure. Course we have." Dougie slapped his chair back down and dragged it back into line beside the other two. In front of them, a line of five chairs had been set up about ten feet away. Ignoring Santi and Frank, Dougie stood up and moved the chairs closer.

"Should you be doing that?"

Dougie gritted his teeth. Frank was getting on his last nerve. Spinning around and widening his eyes, he grinned manically at him. "I want to smell their fear," he said. As Frank folded his arms in front of his chest and swallowed hard, Dougie laughed loudly at him. Stupid fucking moron. Putting someone like him in the Scared Straight program was a joke. Frank's crime was so minor it might as well have been an unpaid parking ticket. Plus, he'd be out next month.

"Dougie," Santi warned. "Leave him be."

If they'd been back in F-block, or in the yard, Dougie wouldn't have left him be. He'd have taunted Frank just enough to get some pleasure from it, but not enough to cause a problem that the guards would notice and penalize him for. Here, he was supposed to be on his best behavior.

Deciding his best tactic was to ignore Frank completely, Dougie fixed his eyes on the metal door at the opposite end of the room. After a few long moments, he heard the buzz and click of one of the internal doors. Then another. And then the door to the visitor room swung open.

Immediately, Dougie grinned; he couldn't help it. Behind his two least favorite guards were five teenage kids. They were flanked by two chaperones. And one of the chaperones was hot. Not his type, but undoubtedly hot. Late thirties, early forties, she definitely looked like a schoolteacher; smart blue jeans, black boots, long white shirt, hair scraped up into a bun. Behind that prim and proper exterior was a pair of sparkling green eyes that made his mouth go dry.

"Gentlemen..." Fox, the bigger and fatter of the two guards, waved his hand at the prisoners. "Meet the students of Gilbert High. You know the drill. You've got two hours...."

The female teacher raised her eyebrows as if she were waiting for something more formal, but Fox and Grayson had already retreated to the corner near the door, put their hands behind their backs, and fixed their eyes on the distance as if they'd rather be pretty much anywhere else.

"Okay," she said brightly. "Shall we all introduce ourselves?" She was talking to Dougie, Santi, and Frank as if they were pupils instead of criminals, and it made Dougie narrow his eyes. Most people, he got the measure of pretty quickly. But her? She was hard to read.

"I'm Molly O'Neil, this is Colton King, and here we have Scarlett, Erik, Lucky, Jenna, and Zack."

As she pointed at each kid in turn, they offered a stiff wave. All except Zack. *That's the one*, Dougie thought instantly. *There's always one. And that kid there. That's him.* Beside him, Santi was introducing himself. "Come and sit," he said, gesturing to the chairs in front of them. "Please."

Molly O'Neil nodded, but before the kids could move, the guy beside her—Colton—stepped forward. "You left all devices on the bus, didn't you? Phones? Tablets?"

Dougie tilted his head and looked Colton up and down. He walked with a slight limp, which was intriguing, and spoke as if he was some kind of drill sergeant. He was big, too. The all-muscle kind of big.

"Don't worry, they wouldn't have got anything past security," Frank piped up.

Looking at one of the girls, the one with long dark hair and black lipstick, Colton's nostrils flared. "With this lot, I wouldn't be so sure."

As the kids moved toward their seats, Dougie watched them. And he continued to watch them as Santi and Frank used every trick in their arsenal to give them a good scare. Santi was pretty good at it; he was an old-school criminal. He'd been around. He'd seen things, and although he was straight as an arrow now, the scar above his right eyebrow and the look in his eyes as he yelled in their faces should have been enough to send a shiver down the spine of most kids.

Despite his best efforts, only one of them looked scared; the younger one, Lucky, who reminded Dougie a little of Frank. The others barely blinked. In fact, one of them, Jenna, the butch-looking girl with thick-set arms and a rounded stomach, simply clenched her fists as if she were fighting the urge to punch Santi in the face.

Dougie chewed his lower lip thoughtfully. Time to get down to business.

Without warning, he stood up. After kicking his chair so it flew back-wards and hit the rear wall, Dougie strode forward and pointed his finger. "You. What's your name?"

The kid he'd picked out when they very first entered the room, Zack, smirked at him, but Dougie knew his type. He'd seen it all before. In fact, *he* used to be Zack's type.

"Zack, weren't you listening?" Zack had folded his arms in front of his chest and now blew a long strand of thick black hair back from his face. Dougie *hated* guys with long hair.

"Oh, I see," Dougie said loudly, laughing at the ceiling. "You're that kid, are you?"

Dougie waited for an answer. No one moved. Zack was staring at him, but the longer Dougie waited the more uncomfortable he seemed to become. Finally, he said, sharply, "What kid?"

"You think the world can't touch you. Your life's so crappy, you think there's no point in being a decent person. You think you've got nothing to lose. Well, guess what?" Dougie raised his voice. "EH EHHHH. You're wrong, kid. It can get a lot worse, trust me."

Zack swallowed hard but was holding his nerve.

"Well, I was like you once. I thought I knew it all. I thought I was untouchable. Guess what?" Dougie waved his arms at their surroundings. "It did. It got a lot worse."

"What did you do?" the girl with the black lipstick asked, narrowing her eyes at him.

"Nothing serious. They'd never put real criminals in a room with kids," Zack retorted, sitting up straighter in his chair and tipping his chin at Dougie.

"You know," Dougie said, "you're right, Zack. I'm not a real criminal. I got life for killing a cop, but you were probably hoping for something a bit grislier than that, right?"

Zack pressed his lips together and swallowed hard. He made a scoffing sound in the back of his throat, but his bravado was starting to waver.

"Let me guess...." Dougie folded his arms and stood back, scratching his chin with a short stubby-nailed finger and scrutinizing the kid from head to toe. "Home is pretty shit for you, right? Single mom. Probably with a nasty habit she can't kick." Dougie made a snorting gesture by pressing his finger to his nose, and Zack looked away. Crouching down in front of him, so the kid couldn't ignore him, Dougie continued. "Older brother got himself in trouble, abandoned you, left you all alone to deal with Mommy's problems. And Dad? Well, he's a fucking waste of space, right?"

Zack's cheeks had turned a violent shade of pink. The other four kids were staring at him.

"Zack...." The female teacher had stepped forward. She knew her students, could read the situation even from across the room. Knew he would blow if he was pushed too far.

"Oh, you're embarrassed, huh?" Dougie leaned in closer, pressing his palms on his knees and fixing his eyes on Zack's. "Well, here's the thing. Letting people think you're big and bad to get them to respect you? That might work for a while." His eyes darted to Frank and he tensed his jaw. "With the stupid ones. But it won't last forever. Someone always calls your bluff, sooner or later."

From the corner of his eye, Dougie could see Zack's fingers clench into a fist. Any minute now....

"You know how I know? Because I *was* you, and the smartest thing that people like us can do is stay far away from people like judges and prison wardens and, yes, even teachers." Dougie paused to allow his words to sink in and noticed Zack glance at his chaperone. "Because those people?" Dougie said, purposefully *not* looking at the teacher, "they punish us not for what we've done, but for who we are—or at least who they think we are."

"Oh yeah? And what do they *think* we are?" Zack's voice was low, barely a whisper. His fist was clenched so tightly that his knuckles were beginning to whiten.

Before Dougie could answer, Fox looked over at them and stepped forward. "Dougie...." His face had tightened into a warning frown and he was puffing heavy breaths through his nostrils as if he were preparing for a confrontation. "That's enough."

"We're just talking, boss."

"I said *enough*." Fox gestured to Zack. "Leave the kid alone now."

As a smile crinkled the corner of his mouth, Dougie nodded solemnly, but when he turned back to Zack, he whispered, "They think we're trash. Pure and simple. Trash."

Zack blinked. Unclenched his fist. Looked away. Then he bit his lower lip, clenched his fist again, and looked at Dougie with pure hatred in his eyes.

Dougie smirked. *Here we go... let the fun and games begin....*

But then the lights went out.

4

ALEX

With a coffee in one hand and his phone in the other, Alex scrolled mindlessly down his social media feed. As pictures of people's food, children, and latest DIY projects filled his screen, he realized that he was grinding his teeth. Setting the phone down on the arm of the couch, he drummed his fingers on it and sighed.

Outside, it was warm. The kind of day that would have been perfect for a run or a walk down to the river. Laura loved it there. He could have packed a picnic, surprised her. Since the accident, running made him feel guilty. And surprising Laura never seemed to end well. If he was honest, he was too tired. Tired of working so hard, tired of fighting with Scarlett and Erik every single day, and tired of all the things he and Laura didn't say to each other that floated from room to room and never went away.

Sending the kids to the Scared Straight program was supposed to be a positive thing. It was supposed to be a step forward—to make them see where their behavior would lead if they didn't make a change.

When the school suggested it, he jumped at it. Probably because, before that, he'd been at a total loss over how to handle them. Seventeen years of being a parent, and he still didn't have a clue what he was doing.

Of course, Laura hadn't been keen, but he'd persuaded her it would be a good thing. Scarlett and Erik weren't bad kids. They had just gotten knocked off course by everything that happened and needed some nudging to get them back on track. This morning, though, when he deposited them at the bus stop and looked at the other kids who'd be joining them—a heavy-set girl with a frowning face, a gangly young boy holding a lighter, and a surly, long-haired one who looked like he might be packing a knife—Alex had almost changed his mind. Surely, his kids didn't fit in with these others?

However, as he'd said he would, he left them there. He told them to *behave* and frowned at them as he said it. He told them he hoped they'd come back with a whole new perspective, and then he waved goodbye.

It was on the way home that he'd decided to dismantle their computers. He'd been waiting for the light to turn, when it had hit him—if there were no computers in the house, no devices of any kind, they wouldn't be able to cause havoc by hacking into local TV networks and broadcasting obscene images, or by getting into the school's computer system and changing their grades, or by exposing private emails and texts belonging to the school principal.

It had seemed like an utterly inspired idea. For the entire journey back to the house, Alex had felt more energized than he had in a long time. A solution. He finally had a solution. Until Laura found him. Glistening with sweat after her workout, in a pink tank top and yoga pants, she'd looked at him the way she always did lately—slightly disappointed, slightly perplexed, as if she wasn't quite sure how she'd ended up married to someone like him. He knew she was right; taking apart Scarlett's and Erik's computers would achieve nothing except to start a fight and make the twins even more determined to kick back against him.

So he'd put Scarlett's PC back together. Thankfully, he hadn't gotten very far in the dismantling process. After unscrewing the back of it, he'd realized that it would actually have been a lot simpler to lock the thing away where they couldn't find it. But he hadn't told Laura that.

Looking toward the hallway, he leaned back into the couch and brushed his fingers through his hair. Sometimes he envied Laura for having Argent at her side all day. He was such a soothing presence; a big, fluffy German Shepherd who helped his wife do things that he should probably have been helping her with, like putting on her socks or passing her the TV remote. Like most of the other alterations they'd made to their life since Laura became unable to walk, Argent had been expensive. Despite what Laura thought, Alex never resented spending the money. Not once. Sure, he was tired. Sure, he wished he didn't have to work so hard, but he'd do anything for her. If only he could find a way to make her see that.

Alex picked up his phone and began to scroll through his photo album. Almost five years ago exactly, he and Laura had been at a dinner party —a fancy event held every year by his company that involved too much champagne, too much music, and suits that were too expensive. Gently, he pressed his thumb on the only photograph he had of them from that evening. Laura's dark, shoulder-length hair was thick and glossy, her face was bright, and her dress looked incredible. Beside her, he didn't think he looked too bad himself. A hint of gray in his beard, good jaw, nice tux.

Then his eyes went to the glass he was holding, and he swallowed hard. Even now, he couldn't remember how many drinks he'd had. He knew that they left, arm in arm, giggling and looking forward to being home alone because the kids were with their grandparents. He knew that afterwards, as he paced up and down beneath the harsh light of the hospital corridor, waiting for news, totally unaware of the cut on his own head that was bleeding, the police had found him and confirmed that he wasn't over the limit. Even so, night after night, he had tried to remember. Was it one or two? Had he eaten beforehand? Why didn't they take a cab in the first place?

His eyes were becoming moist. He shouldn't be looking at it. If Laura found him, she'd think he was longing for the days when she was normal. She'd think he was unhappy with the way things were now because of the way *she* was. That he was thinking of those dreadful months before she finally admitted she needed help and went to rehab to get off the eye-watering number of painkillers she was taking. But that wasn't it....

Blinking at the screen, Alex narrowed his eyes at it. A message had popped up and, although his first thought was that it was a hoax, as he began to read it, his blood ran cold.

THIS IS AN EMERGENCY BROADCAST...

Zip.

The screen went black before he could read any further. Alex stood up and shook the phone. Straining his ears, he realized that the usual hum of household electronics was missing. A few moments ago, someone had been mowing their lawn. Now, the sound of the engine was gone.

"Alex?" From the kitchen, Laura was calling him. Seconds later, she wheeled in and waved her phone at him. Argent trotted in beside her. "My phone just died. And the coffee machine stopped working."

"Mine did too." Alex slipped his phone into his pocket and went to the electrical panel near the front door. He flicked the switches. Right, left. Nothing.

When he returned to the living room, Argent was passing Laura the TV remote. "Thanks, boy," she said, taking it gently from his mouth. When she pointed it at the screen... "Everything's off," she said, frowning.

"Laptops too?" Alex strode over to their desk and tried to start up both their shared laptop and their tablet. "Jesus," he said, looking up at her and trying not to let her see the knot of panic that had wedged itself in his throat.

"What's going on?" Laura laughed nervously, but Alex was looking out the window. Up and down the street, people were stepping outside and asking one another what was happening. The neighbor who'd been mowing his lawn was talking to his wife, both gesturing as if they thought the other had somehow caused the power to go out.

"Is it the whole street?" Laura wheeled up beside him and strained to see out of their large bay window.

"Looks like it."

Without hesitating, Laura took off. Telling Argent to stay, she opened the front door and headed down the ramp they'd fitted out front. "Jerry?" she called, approaching their next-door neighbor. "Is your power out?"

Jerry Macintyre crossed his arms in front of his chest and nodded at Alex. Then to Laura he said, gravely, "There was some kind of emergency broadcast on the TV. Barb saw it. You didn't?"

"I got a message on my phone," Alex said, "but I didn't get chance to read it."

"Sounds like it could be out a while," Jerry said, shaking his head. "I don't know much about it myself but—"

Alex was listening to the old man speak but stopped when Laura gripped his arm. "Alex… the children."

"The kids?" Alex muttered, his mouth becoming dry as he looked at his wife's pale, worried face.

"They're at the prison…" Laura whispered, "and the power's gone out."

Back inside the house, Alex knew that if Laura was able to, she'd be pacing up and down the living room. From the floor by the couch, Argent was watching them with one ear pricked, his eyes darting from

Laura to Alex and back again, as if he were trying to decipher why his humans were suddenly so agitated.

"They're at a freakin' prison, Alex!" Laura's face was ghostly white, and she was wringing her hands in her lap. "A prison. With violent criminals."

"Hey," Alex said, crouching down in front of her. "They'll be fine. Most likely, the power will come back on soon and they'll be brought home safe and sound. Besides…" He smiled at her and took her hands between his. "They won't be anywhere near the real bad guys. The school wouldn't do that."

Laura bit her lower lip, and then shook her head. "Alex," she said, "if this is an EMP, the power won't be back on in a few hours. It won't be back on *ever*."

Alex almost laughed. "An EMP? Honey, this isn't—"

"They don't send out emergency broadcasts for nothing. And what kind of power outage would stop our phones and laptops from working?" Laura widened her eyes at him. "Alex," she said forcefully, "we need to get the kids back here. Now."

Alex studied her face. A painful tug in his gut told him she was right; if this was an EMP, or something like it, then he'd sent their kids off to pretty much the worst place on earth they could be. "Okay, but just me," he said, standing up.

"No way. I'm coming."

"Laura, no. Stay here and start packing provisions. If things are as bad as you think they are, then we may not be able to stay here for long. We'll need to be ready to leave quickly. If we have to."

Laura nodded slowly and reached for Argent, placing her palm flat on his head.

"I'll take the bike. The prison isn't far. I'll be back soon with the kids, and then we'll either hunker down here or head somewhere safer."

"Safer?"

Alex nodded grimly, then strode over to the gun cabinet, unlocked it, and took out one of his hunting rifles.

"Alex…." She was watching him, blinking quickly as if she was trying to fight back tears.

"I'll leave the keys here. If you're afraid, you grab a gun. And if you have to use it—you use it. Okay?"

Laura nodded as Alex kissed her forehead.

"I'll be back soon," he said, already at the door. "I promise."

5

MOLLY

B esides the lights flickering, the first thing Molly noticed as the power went out was the sound of the door's automatic lock engaging. In an instant, they were plunged into utter darkness. A darkness so thick that it made her skin crawl.

The room didn't descend into darkness; it became dark. Pitch dark. One second it was so bright it was almost giving her a headache, the next it was like they'd fallen into a black hole. Instantly, Molly felt panic begin to scratch at her chest.

For as long as she could remember, she'd hated the dark. Even now, in her small but bright apartment, she slept with a nightlight plugged in next to her bed. Her ex-boyfriend Carl had hated it. At first, he'd teased her about it, as if the teasing would make her change her mind and get rid of it. He'd mocked her at her friend's birthday party, in front of people, and in front of his folks when they went to their house for lunch one Sunday. When that didn't work, he made a show of going to sleep on the couch whenever he stayed over—because he simply couldn't be expected to get a good night's rest with a light "blaring." Eventually, they broke up, and Molly bought a sunset lamp to go with her nightlight.

These days, she fell asleep while the fake sunlight was fading and woke to it gradually brightening. Never, ever, was she immersed in darkness.

Except now, that was exactly what was happening.

"Okay guys, don't panic...." Her voice was shaky, and she hoped no one had noticed.

"What the hell?" one of the kids, it sounded like Jenna, shouted.

"Erik? Where are you?" Scarlett's voice was panicked.

Molly breathed deeply. This was not good. Beside her, she could feel Colton's presence. Moving closer to her, he whispered, "Stay calm. They'll have a generator."

"Prisoners, back against the wall!" The male guard was shouting, and Molly heard him curse as he realized his flashlight wasn't working. "Back!"

"Oh, we're back. Don't worry." It was Dougie. The one who'd been goading Zack. In the darkness, his voice made her shudder.

Then, with a loud hum, as suddenly as they went off, the lights came back on. Molly blinked hard against the fluorescent lights and shook her arms to release the tension in her shoulders. *They're back. Thank God.*

"Back-up generator," Colton muttered, looking around the room.

"Of course," Molly said. "Kids. Come over here, please."

Willingly, for once, all five students obeyed, and Molly breathed a sigh of relief as she realized that the prisoners had followed orders and were now lined up, hands clasped in front of them, by the back wall.

As one guard, the female one, walked forward and told Santi, Frank, and Dougie to remain still, the other tried their radio. "Fox to base. Hello? Anyone there?" Looking at his colleague, he shook his head. "Nothing," he said.

"I'm sorry…" Molly interrupted tentatively. "What's going on?"

"Power outage. Happens occasionally around here. Nothing to worry about." Fox looked past her and waved at the other guard. "Grayson, I'm going to step outside real quick, see what the problem is, go fetch a radio that works. You okay here?"

Grayson nodded. "We're okay."

As Fox closed the door, Molly chewed the inside of her cheek. Dougie was watching her. She could feel his eyes on her, and now that there was one less guard in the room, she was decidedly more nervous.

"Don't they know that a power outage wouldn't stop a *battery* radio from working?" Erik Banks muttered to his sister.

Molly glanced at Colton; clearly, he'd heard him too. Without speaking, he sucked in his cheeks and slotted his hands behind his back. In that moment, he looked exactly like a Marine waiting for orders and, momentarily, Molly felt a tiny bit better. Surely, no one would mess with them with Colton around.

"Erik," she whispered, taking his arm. "What you said about the radios? What did you mean?"

Erik glanced at Scarlett and bit his lower lip. "Nothing, Miss O'Neil. Sorry, I shouldn't have—"

"No, if there's something… tell me." Molly met his eyes and nodded. "Tell me, Erik. You think this is more than a power outage?"

"He thinks it's an EMP," Scarlett said quickly, keeping her voice low as if she was worried Grayson might hear.

"An EMP?" Molly knew that word. "Isn't that when…?"

"When an electromagnetic pulse destroys pretty much every electrical device on the planet? Yeah," Erik said gravely. "It is."

"And when that happens, it's not temporary, is it?" Molly knew the answer before she'd even asked the question.

Erik shook his head. "If it's an EMP, it's bad news, Miss O'Neil." He looked at his sister, whose face was whiter than it had been a few minutes ago. "Really bad."

Molly inhaled sharply and had to resist the urge to reach out and steady herself on the wall. Across the room, Dougie was watching them intently. Frank looked bored, Santi had closed his eyes and was muttering what Molly assumed was a prayer, but Dougie—who had been staring at her strangely ever since he walked in—was focused solely on them. When he caught her eye, a slow smile spread across his lips, as if he could sense the fact she was shaken. Had he heard what Erik said?

Molly turned away, angled herself so that all he could see was her back, and shook her head. "I'm sure it's like the guards said. A power outage, that's all."

Erik nodded and raised his eyes as if to say, *If that's what you want to believe, go ahead.* Next to him, Scarlett was twisting a strand of hair between her thumb and index finger. "Erik's not usually wrong about this kind of stuff," she said matter-of-factly.

Molly was about to launch into some very good reasons why she was certain Erik *was* wrong when Jenna said loudly, "Isn't this the kind of thing that usually causes riots?" She was staring at Dougie and the other two.

"No," Grayson shouted over. "It is not. Maybe don't go putting ideas in these guys' heads. Okay?"

"Oh yeah, because we're so stupid, we wouldn't have thought of it ourselves already," Frank said, laughing loudly at his own joke and snorting. "Right, Dougie?"

"Shut it, Frank." Dougie took his eyes away from Molly and glanced up at the security camera in the corner of the room. Molly looked at it too and, as she realized that the blinking red light was now absent, a knot of nervousness settled in the pit of her stomach.

"Doors in these places lock automatically, right?" Colton took a step toward Grayson as he spoke.

Grayson nodded. "Sure do. Which is why there won't be a riot. Any loss of power causes the doors to lock, so the only way for prisoners to move about is if they have a set of keys." Looking at Dougie, Santi, and Frank, she said, "Do you guys have keys?" Then she scoffed. "No, of course you don't. Because you're *prisoners*."

Molly felt herself wince at the guard's tone of voice. Colton, too, was watching her closely.

"And if the generator fails before the power's back on, do you have contingency plans?"

Grayson pursed her lips. She was about the same age as Colton, maybe a little older, with frizzy blonde hair that was scraped into a tight bun at the base of her neck. As she scowled at him, wrinkles formed on the ridge of her upper lip and at the corners of her eyes. "Of course we do," she said patronizingly. "But I'm hardly going to share them with civilians and inmates, am I?"

The way Colton looked at Molly told her that he didn't believe for one second there was a contingency plan, and the fact he was concerned about it worried her.

"Besides," Grayson added, "the generator won't fail. Why would it? That's what they're for."

"I wouldn't be so sure," Erik piped up, ignoring the look Scarlett gave him, which implied he should keep quiet. With everyone staring at him, Erik continued, "I mean, I'm guessing it's pretty old. Which is why it's still working when your radios aren't. And if it's that old...."

Grayson tutted at him and turned away, lacing her hands together behind her back and focusing on the prisoners.

Turning back to the kids, Molly said, "It's going to be fine. When Mr. Fox gets back, we'll ask him to escort us back to the bus. After all, I think we've all had quite enough excitement for one day."

To her surprise, the kids nodded. Clearly, they'd had quite enough of their prison experience already. As had Colton, who'd begun to pace up and down beside them.

Trying to ignore the trembling in her belly as she thought about the lights going out again, Molly leaned back against the wall. She'd have to fill in an incident report about this when she got back. Tell the kids' parents. Probably even fill in a second report to note that she'd failed to list 'potential power outage' on the risk assessment forms. Which meant that, even if they were back at the high school by mid-afternoon, she'd end up—as always—staying at her desk way past the end of the school day.

When she first trained as a teacher, she didn't mind it. She remembered the years after she qualified, when she'd frequently worked until midnight planning lessons, and when she'd loved every second of it because she felt like she was *making a difference*.

Looking back, she couldn't quite figure out when it had changed, but she knew that for at least the last couple of years, she'd stopped loving it and starting feeling... tired. Really tired.

"I'm forty-two years old. I have no husband, no kids, no social life, and no hobbies," she'd complained to Rebecca Knowles, an older and more pragmatic English teacher who inhabited the classroom opposite Molly's. "I can't even commit to getting a cat because I'd never be home to feed it. Surely, there's more to life than this?"

Rebecca had nodded sympathetically and given her a soft, heart-felt smile. Looking at Molly over the rim of her coffee cup, she had replied, "Well, if there is, make sure you let me know when you figure out how to find it."

Molly bit back a sigh and looked at her students. Had today changed anything for them? Or was it just an outing, a bit of fun, something to keep their parents quiet and the school off their backs? Was there really any *point* in them being here?

She had just begun to tap her foot impatiently on the floor, irritated by her own skepticism, when Fox returned. His cheeks were flushed, and he was a little out of breath.

"Find a radio?" Grayson asked.

Fox shook his head. "Listen," he said quickly. "We have an emergency situation going on right now. It's nothing to worry about, but what I need to do is to escort the prisoners back to their cells. Grayson, you're with me. Everyone else—teacher, kids—stay here and we will come back for you."

Molly released a shaky breath and flexed her fingers. "See," she said, smiling at the kids. "Everything's under control."

With the prisoners out of the room, the five students filtered away from her and back to their seats. Huddling in a sort of semi-circle, they began to talk in hushed tones and Molly found herself thinking that at least for a few minutes, they seemed to be getting along okay.

"Colton?" She had folded her arms in front of her stomach and was watching the door. "Do you think maybe we should go with the guards? Ask them to let us wait somewhere outside? I mean, I don't like the idea of us being trapped in here if something—"

In the middle of the room, Scarlett screamed.

Once again, they had been plunged into darkness.

6

DOUGIE

Frank was almost high with excitement. As Fat Fox and Grim Grayson led the three of them out of the visitor room, he let out a loud whoop. "It's all going *down* around here, mother—"

"Shut it, Frank." Santi shot him a withering look, and Frank's smiled dropped; the old man was a pussy cat, but not one you wanted to make so mad it decided to scratch your eyes out.

Quickly, Fox locked the door, sealing the teacher and kids inside. Dougie exchanged a look with Santi; why lock them in? Something was happening. Perhaps Frank was right....

"This way," Fox said, starting to hustle them down the hallway, through door after door, and then instead of the usual way—past C-block and the yard—they took a right.

"Taking us on the scenic route today, are you, Mr. Fox?" Santi asked in a deep calm voice.

"Just do as you're told, Santi," Fox snapped back, looking briefly at Grayson before quickening their pace.

As they walked, Dougie watched. He watched Fox fiddling with the keys on his belt. He watched the dart of his eyes as they headed down the dimly lit corridor. He was nervous. Too nervous. Grayson had noticed too; she wasn't as stupid as she looked but was holding back from asking what was going on.

"Fox, if there's something you feel you should tell us..." Dougie said, smiling.

Fox turned to him and had opened his mouth to speak when an unmistakable cry rang through the corridor. "RIOT!"

Instantly, Grayson's face became drained of all its color. She reached for her pepper spray. Fox did too, although Dougie was pretty sure from the looks on their faces that they were wishing they had something a bit more hardcore at their disposal than a can of spray.

"A riot? No way!" Frank was jumping up and down. "I told you. I freakin' told you!"

Dougie looked at Santi and raised his eyebrows at him. The old man nodded, almost imperceptibly. He was reformed, yes, but he was ready for a fight, too.

"This way!" Fox was hurrying them as quickly as he could toward their cells. "Now!"

As they walked, almost ran, the sound of whoops, hollers, and shit being broken followed them like a tidal wave. Then they were back in their block, in their cells, doors shut, locked, and Dougie was peering through the cell bars, desperately trying to catch a glimpse of what was about to happen.

In the middle of the gray concrete floor of the day room, Fox and Grayson stood quivering, holding their pepper spray out in front of them even though they both knew they'd be utterly useless in preventing what was about to happen.

It was every guard's worst nightmare.

Breaking up fights, they had the upper hand. Dishing out punishments, they had the upper hand. But if they became outnumbered? If the tide turned? Well, that was scary as hell.

Dougie had been in only one riot in his prison career, before he was transferred to Fairfield, and as a young prisoner, it had both terrified him and enthralled him. The smell and the sounds and the way it felt to do whatever the hell you wanted to do with no regard for consequences.

He'd tried many times to figure out how it had ended, but the details were hazy. By that point, he'd been high on adrenaline and crack sticks and had given very few shits about what was going on around him. He knew how it started, though—the guards. They'd been beating on an inmate. A popular inmate. Three of them had pinned him to the ground. Other inmates had started shouting. They'd been out of their cells for rec time, and it was like they knew in an instant that this was their moment. The stars aligned and in a split second the mood changed.

A small female officer, who Dougie had actually liked, had started to shepherd them all back into their cells, but a big guy with sleeves of tattoos had grabbed hold of her. He'd pulled a shiv, put it to her throat.

The prison was short-staffed. No one to come and help. No weapons. So they crumbled. Like scared animals, they retreated, promising to leave as long as no one harmed the female guard.

They got slaughtered for it in the press afterwards, of course, but instead of fighting back, they ran. The big guy let the girl go, and the lot of them headed for the door, locked it behind them, and watched the chaos take hold from behind a reinforced glass window.

For hours, the block had raged. Everything not fastened down was smashed up. Things that were fastened down were pulled free. Cells were trashed. Old grievances between inmates had a chance to be finally aired. Four guys wound up dead, although Dougie couldn't remember their names or their faces. Through the whole thing, though, Dougie had found himself thinking very clearly that if someone had taken charge—if someone had come up with a plan, done things *properly*—they could have achieved much, much more.

Dougie rolled his tongue over his teeth and concentrated on watching Fox and Grayson. He liked watching. He liked thinking. Everyone saw him as a mindless criminal, but he wasn't completely stupid. Somehow, there had to be a way he could spin this to his advantage. Sure, kicking a few guards' teeth in would be fun, but it wouldn't achieve anything in the long run. He'd been working hard to secure an appeal. Maybe, just maybe, somewhere in amid this mess, there was an opportunity....

"Stop!" Fox was yelling. "Stop this now and get back to your cells. No one has to get hurt."

At least ten prisoners had raced into the room and were crowded together, staring at the guards with wide, hungry eyes. One he recognized—Luther—strode forward and without hesitating smacked Fox in the face before knocking the pepper spray from his hand. Grayson closed her eyes and cowered. Fox was bleeding and he was staring at Luther like he wanted to punch him. At his sides, his hands were bunched into tight fists, but he knew better than to fight back.

"Yo!" Dougie started to bang on his cell door. "Luther. Let me out of here, man...."

"Me too!" he could hear Frank shouting nearby. "And Santi. The old guy's here too! Let us out, man."

Luther looked up, spat on the floor in front of Fox and gestured for him to hand over the keys. With shaking hands, Fox obeyed.

"Dougie." Luther looked him up and down. "Good to see you. How'd you end up in there?"

Dougie looked at Fox and Grayson, and Luther grinned. "In that case, they're all yours."

Tilting his head, Dougie reeled quickly through his options. He was a cop killer. Everyone would be expecting him to lose his cool and beat Fox to within an inch of his life. Probably spare Grayson, as she was a woman, but definitely not Fox. He had to play this carefully.

"Nah, man. I've got bigger fish to fry. I'm getting out of here." He raised his eyebrows and grinned at Luther.

Luther looked at him and then at the others, who seemed ready to lunge forward and dismember Fox as soon as Luther gave them the go-ahead. When he turned back to Dougie, his lips parted into an enormous gap-toothed grin. "Ha!" he said, whacking him on the shoulder. "Good luck to you."

"So, if I could just have these...." Dougie reached over and plucked the keys from Grayson's belt. Wiggling them at Luther, he said, "I'll let you do your thing, and I'll go do mine."

Luther nodded at him, already moving on to his next plan of action. Grabbing Fox by the arm, he told someone else to get Grayson, took one last look at Dougie, and dragged them away.

For a moment, Frank lingered between Luther and Dougie. Then he clapped his hands, yelled, "See ya!" and hurtled after Luther.

Dougie pressed his lips together and tilted his head from side to side. His neck clicked loudly, and the sensation made him smile. He had handled the situation well. Luther had no interest in a bid for escape; there had been riots here before, and they were almost always shut down before anyone got close to the outside.

"Santi?" he said, turning to the old man. "Want to join me?"

Santi raised his palms at Dougie. "I'd stick up for myself if I had to, Dougie. But all this...." He waved his hand at their surroundings. "It's not my thing. I'll go back to my cell to pray, and I will see you when I see you."

Dougie nodded. *Now,* he thought, *where's that teacher?*

7

MOLLY

The lights flickered several times before finally staying on. But they weren't as bright as before, and Molly was fighting the rising sense of panic in her chest.

In the middle of the room, Erik was talking loudly, waving his arms and ranting about the market for second-hand industrial generators, and how the prison should have sprung for a newer system if they wanted it to actually work right. "Some of the super-new stuff even has EMP protection," Erik said pointedly.

As if he was looking for an escape hatch, Colton was pacing the perimeter of the room. His limp seemed more pronounced, and Molly wondered whether the stress of the situation was making it worse. He'd completed three laps when the lights dimmed again, faltered, and failed. This time, they didn't come back on.

"Not again," Jenna said with panic in her voice.

"Not really surprising," Erik muttered. "If it's dipping in and out like that, it probably hasn't been serviced in a while."

"Like, a *long* while," Scarlett added.

"Since when do you know so much about generators, Erik?" In the darkness, Zack's tone was even more sinister than usual, as if he hated Erik merely because he knew things that Zack didn't.

"Since he spent an entire semester studying EMPs for a science project, that's when." Scarlett jumped to her brother's defense, and Molly felt sure that if it wasn't so dark the boys couldn't see one another, they'd be squaring up preparing to throw punches.

"If my lighter hadn't been confiscated, we wouldn't be standing here in the pitch black unable to see our own fingers," Lucky said bitterly.

"That's enough, you lot." Molly stepped in what she thought was the direction of the wall and searched for it with outstretched palms. It was cold and smooth, and she leaned against it to steady herself. With every second the lights remained out, her chest was becoming tighter, and she was struggling to even hear what the kids were saying, let alone keep the peace between them.

"If the power's out for good, that lighter will be worth a fortune. You better watch Miss O'Neil doesn't try to keep it permanently." Erik was making a joke but, while Lucky, Jenna, and Scarlett laughed, Zack remained unimpressed.

"The power's not out for good though, is it? How can it be? If an EMP destroys all electronics, then the lights wouldn't be able to come back on—with or without a generator."

Zack sounded pleased with himself, but Erik quickly bit back at him, "*Wrong.* If the circuit breakers get fused or burned, then yeah. But I'll bet at least half of the prison's system hasn't been updated since the seventies."

"Okay, guys, seriously, that's enough." Molly's head was spinning, and she felt as if the floor beneath her feet was moving.

"Zack, seriously, why are you such a jerk all the time?" Scarlett sounded pouty and annoyed.

"Because he's a *psycho*," laughed Jenna. "And that's kind of the go-to behavior of a psycho."

"I said enough!" Molly yelled so loudly that her voice echoed around the room. "Do you think this is helpful?" She was close to hyperventilating when she felt a firm hand on her shoulder.

"Molly? Are you okay?" Colton's voice brought her back into her own body, and she inhaled deeply.

"I'm sorry," she whispered as he moved her away from the kids' voices.

"It's going to be fine. The power will come back."

"I...." Molly closed her eyes, even though it was so dark she didn't need to. "This sounds ridiculous." She shook her head at herself, then added in a whisper, "I'm afraid of the dark. Not just afraid. *Terrified.* Have been since I was a kid. It makes me feel like the walls are closing in, like I can't breathe." She was shaking and could feel her forehead becoming slick with beads of sweat.

"So, close your eyes, and imagine you're somewhere bright. Somewhere so bright you can hardly see."

"Somewhere bright?"

"The beach. Florida. The sun's shining and it's bouncing off the sand, and it's so bright you can hardly see. Right?"

Molly nodded. "The beach."

She'd only just started to breathe normally again when, without warning, the lights sprang back to life.

Squinting, Colton smiled at her. "See, so bright you can barely see," he said, looking up at the caged lighting on the ceiling above them. "Although not quite as luxurious as the beach."

Molly laughed and straightened herself up. "Sorry, kids, I shouldn't have shouted." She was about to tell them she was certain that, any minute now, the guards would return, when the door handle began to move. The lock was turning.

Colton breathed a sigh of relief. "Here we go," he said, stepping forward. But when it swung open, it wasn't a guard who stepped into the room. It was Dougie.

"Hey there, folks," he said, grinning. "I heard you could use some help."

"From you?" Jenna's voice was loud and scathing. "I don't think so."

Molly shot her a look, but moved backwards as Dougie walked in. Still smiling, exposing a set of crooked, grimy teeth, he shut the door behind him and leaned casually against it.

He wasn't a big guy—not as big as Colton—and Molly suspected he wasn't as old as he looked, but something simmered beneath the surface of his tattoos and his shaved head. Something that made her skin crawl. She'd been around enough troubled teens to recognize repressed anger when she saw it, but Dougie wasn't just angry inside —he was furious. She could see it in his dark sunken eyes and in the way he constantly wrung his fingers together as if he were fighting the urge to punch someone. Beneath his less-than-white prison tee and baggy gray sweatpants, and beneath the smile he'd been offering them since they arrived, he was not someone to be messed with. And now they were stuck in a room with him.

Molly exhaled slowly through her nose, wondering how quickly she could make it to the door if she needed to, and glanced at Colton. He had moved toward the kids and looked as if he was ready to jump to their defense at any moment. But Dougie wasn't paying any attention to the kids; he was looking only at Molly.

Battling the instinct to cross her arms in front of her stomach, Molly left them at her sides and said, "What's going on? Where are the guards?"

Dougie moved further into the room and tipped his head back at the door. "Looks like Bruiser Barbie was right." He widened his eyes at Jenna, whose face became instantly gray.

"A riot?" Jenna shifted closer to Scarlett and, surprisingly, Scarlett didn't seem to mind.

"Afraid so." Dougie's gaze lingered on the students, but then he snapped his eyes back toward Molly and looked her up and down. "Which is why I figured I should come help you out."

A scratchy panicked sensation was rising in Molly's chest, but she ignored it. Tuning out the voice in her head that was yelling, *You're stuck in a prison, with a bunch of school kids, in the middle of a freakin' riot,* she nodded slowly at Dougie. Still watching her, he was weighing a set of keys up and down in the palm of his hand.

"So," he said. "If you follow me—"

"How did you get the keys?" Molly pointed at his hand and watched as a flicker of irritation flashed across his face.

"Officer Fox gave them to me. He and Officer Grayson were... detained." Dougie's tone of voice was sickeningly polite. "He wanted to make sure you all got out safely. Back to your bus. So he asked me to come fetch you."

It was a lie. Molly knew it was a lie, and Dougie knew that she knew. He also knew she wouldn't challenge him on it in front of the kids. Molly pressed her lips together as she willed her brain to think more quickly.

"You know what?" Dougie said. "I can see why you'd be a little concerned. So... here you go, big guy." He walked over to Colton and handed him the keys. They clinked loudly as Colton wrapped his fingers around them. "They're all yours." Dougie shrugged. "Better for me anyway if I have nothing to do with them. When all this settles down, I don't want to be accused of anything."

"Where's the warden?" Scarlett suddenly piped up. "Wouldn't *he* come and fetch us if there was really a riot going on?" She looked at her brother to see if he agreed with her. "Surely he wouldn't leave us here if we were in danger? And I'm not sure a guard would trust a *felon* with a set of keys."

"She's right, Miss O'Neil. You can't trust this guy," Erik added, looking from Molly to Colton.

"The warden?" Dougie let out a loud snort. "Princess, you clearly don't have much experience with people in authority. When shit goes down, the guys in suits hot-foot it to somewhere safe. They don't get their hands dirty."

"There was a riot in my brother's prison. Last year." Zack had been standing toward the back of the group and was speaking quietly, but the other kids immediately turned to look at him. An hour ago, they'd mocked him for being a psycho. Currently, he was the closest thing they had to real experience at a prison. Now he was a voice of authority. Zack tucked a long strand of hair behind his ear. He was looking at Dougie. "Tommy said it went on for days. A couple of guards were taken hostage. In the end, the cops went in with tear gas."

Dougie nodded solemnly. "Kid's right. It's gonna get ugly out there real quick. Right now, me, Frank, and Santi are the only ones who know where you are. Santi's a good guy, but Frank's an idiot. So it won't stay that way for long." He looked back at the door. "If we're going to do this, it needs to be now."

Molly's stomach was in knots. What she really wanted to do was tell Dougie to leave them alone, lock the door behind him, and wait for help. But if the riot really did go on for days....

Colton's fingers on her wrist made her look at him. "We should stay here," he said through thin lips. "We can't trust this guy."

"He didn't have to come back for us," Molly whispered. "He could have taken the keys and escaped."

"We were told to stay put, so we should follow orders."

Molly could feel Dougie watching them and angled herself away from him slightly. "I feel the same," she said quietly. "What if the riot goes on for days? What if the prison loses power again? We've got no food, no water, no cell phones to call for help." She swallowed hard and tried to stop her voice from trembling. "I don't believe for a second that Fox or Grayson told him to come fetch us. But if Dougie can get ahold of a set of keys, I'm sure the other prisoners can too."

"I wouldn't let anything happen to you or the kids." Colton's eyes were searching her face, as if by wanting to leave she was questioning his ability to protect them all.

"I know that." Molly finally gave in and folded her arms. "There's only one of you, Colton, and a whole prison full of them. We wouldn't stand a chance."

"Okay," she said firmly, side-stepping in front of the kids so that she was standing between them and Dougie. "What's the plan?"

"Right now, all the action is in D-block. They were on yard time when the power went out. If they've got keys, which I'm pretty sure they have, it won't be long before they move through the other blocks too."

"We're not far from the main entrance, right?" Molly asked, as Colton stood beside her quietly simmering.

"Just a few doors between you and freedom," Dougie agreed. "Like I said, if we're going, it needs to be now."

As Dougie told Colton which doors to open once they were out of the visitor room, Molly instructed the kids to walk single file between the two of them.

"Don't worry, Miss O'Neil," Dougie said as they lined up near the door, "I'll stay close—make sure no one takes you by surprise."

Molly shuddered but was glad Colton hadn't overheard; she sensed that he was looking for an excuse to take Dougie out. As much as she detested the man, right now, they needed him.

"Just one question," she said, narrowing her eyes at him. "What do you get out of this?"

"Me?" Dougie's lips twitched into a smile. "Why, I'm just trying to be a good citizen, ma'am."

Molly opened her mouth to speak, but the sound of Colton opening the door stopped her in her tracks. As a whoosh of cooler, less stale air crept through the gap, so did a sound that she hadn't noticed before—a mixture of voices, whoops, and incoherent shouting. Distant. But petrifying.

8

DOUGIE

Positioning himself behind the teacher, Dougie followed her as the bus driver led them toward the front exit of the prison. Like Dougie had told him, he opened the doors swiftly and ushered them all through before locking them again. Dougie could see from the determined look on the guy's face—his jaw set tightly, his eyes darting around as if he were watching for snipers—that he was loving it. Judging by his limp and the stench of dejection that followed him, it was a good few years since he experienced any kind of adrenaline rush. He'd dine out on this story for months—tell it to his fancy friends because, at last, he could claim to have done something interesting with his day. *Let him have it*, Dougie thought. *I've got bigger fish to fry than this guy.*

Dougie had hoped to avoid giving over the keys, but he knew as soon as he walked into the visitor room that the teacher wouldn't have trusted him if he hadn't. Of course, she still didn't trust him, but at least this way she could convince herself that he was helping them because he was a reformed character—a good egg in a rotten batch, who wanted to guide some helpless civilians out of danger. It was irritating losing possession of them, but not the end of the world. He'd still get what he wanted; he just needed to think a little more carefully about how.

"Hey, Dougie, which way?" The bus driver had stopped and was looking at two doors. One to the left. One to the right. Momentarily, Dougie was tempted to direct him toward the bowels of the prison. Toward Luther and whoever else was baying for blood. No matter how much fun it would be to watch the bus driver get torn apart, that wasn't Dougie's end game.

"Left," he called back. "Nearly there."

Colton reached for the door. The key was in the lock, about to turn, when the lights flickered. As they dipped in and out, a loud clamor of shouts broke through the quiet. Something that sounded like glass shattered and then… the unmistakable sound of a gun.

The youngest kid, the one who couldn't have been more than fourteen, slapped his hands over his mouth to stifle a scream. The others pressed themselves against the wall. But Dougie was listening carefully. Had the guards taken back control? Or had the prisoners overpowered one and taken their weapon? After no further shots followed, he guessed it was the latter.

"Was that a gun?" The teacher was looking at him. Her face was pale, but her fists were clenched at her sides as if she were ready to protect her kids at all costs.

Dougie nodded.

"It sounds like they're coming this way…." The girl with black lipstick had looped her arm through the arm of the boy beside her. Dougie was still trying to work out if he was her brother or her boyfriend—they looked similar, but it was hard to tell beneath all her makeup. "Are they coming this way?" She was looking at Dougie. He tried not to smirk.

"Maybe."

"Mr. King, hurry up," the girl whined. The tone in her voice set Dougie's teeth on edge.

The bus driver was fumbling with the keys. A small bead of sweat had broken out on his forehead. It was hot in here, but not *that* hot—Mr. King was getting nervous.

"Any time," Dougie called, at which the teacher spun around to look at him, her green eyes flashing him a look of contempt that he figured she usually reserved for her most troublesome pupils.

"Can you help him?"

Dougie waved his hand at her. "Of course, ma'am. I'd be happy to." Before he could step toward the front of the line, Colton shouted, "Got it," and pushed the door open. The kids had filed through and Colton had stopped next to Dougie to lock the door again when the shouting behind them seemed to change direction.

"There's someone up ahead." The teacher had taken hold of the bus driver's arm and was pointing down the corridor. They were tantalizingly close now. Just a few yards and they'd be staring at the front entrance to the prison.

"It's fine," Dougie said hastily. "Let's go."

"No, wait." The teacher was still holding on to the bus driver's arm. "Colton, I'm not sure about this. Something doesn't feel right."

Dougie closed his eyes. Beyond the big steel door at the end of the corridor was an area he hadn't set foot in since the day he arrived at Fairfield Prison fifteen years ago—a large, low-ceilinged space with gray metal chairs, no natural light, and a sealed box containing a reception desk. A purgatory between prison and *not* prison.

He could almost taste the outside on his tongue. Sure, prisoners were allowed to exercise in the yard, but he couldn't remember the last time he'd stood next to a tree or looked up at a view unencumbered by wire fences and CCTV cameras. He licked his lower lip and whacked Colton on the shoulder. "Let's go, big guy."

"No," the teacher said firmly. "We should check it out first." Nodding at the kids, she told them to wait by the door and began to inch forward. Colton moved to accompany her, but she shook her head at him. "Stay with the kids." She turned to Dougie and tipped her head toward freedom. "Dougie? Will you…?"

Nodding, Dougie slowly followed the teacher to the end of the corridor. Several times, he had to stop himself from watching her walk. It had been too long since he'd been close to a woman, and this one in particular was intriguing him.

Side by side, they stepped up to the door and looked through the pane in its upper half. At first, they saw nothing. The room was empty. Two big doors at the far end led out into the front parking lot. There was no one in the glass reception box. Dougie was about to call back and tell the bus driver to get a move on when the teacher raised her finger and pointed at something. "The door," she said, "that one there, it's opening."

Flick. Flick. Flick.

The lights dipped on and off. This time, they stayed off longer than they stayed on. Dougie realized he was holding his breath, and when the lights sprang back to life, the door they'd been looking at was wide open. Dougie swore out loud as at least fifteen inmates burst into the room. The teacher had reached out to steady herself against the wall, perhaps suddenly realizing that Dougie and a steel door were pretty much the only things that stood between her and a group of convicts who were high on adrenaline, and who knew what else, and looking for a good time.

In the visitor room, with guards and cameras watching over them, men like Dougie might not seem all that intimidating. As a group, they were fucking terrifying. As some rushed to the exit doors, a couple of others picked up chairs and began to hammer them against the glass of the reception desk. It was reinforced, so nothing much happened, but the sound was enough to make the walls vibrate.

The teacher was wide-eyed, frozen to the spot. "What do we do?" she whispered.

"We wait." Dougie was biting his lip, trying to think. "They might leave."

As they watched, it became obvious the prisoners had no intention of leaving. Luther might be happy with causing a little chaos, messing up the guards, and looting the place. These guys wanted out. The emergency locks were doing their job, not budging even with the bulkiest of the prisoners slamming their bodies into the steel-reinforced doors hoping to break them open.

"We can't get past them," Dougie said, almost to himself. "If they see us with the keys, that'll be it. They might let us go if we offer to open the doors for them." He looked at the teacher and smiled with the corner of his mouth. "Then again, they might decide it'd be more fun to stay and play."

The teacher blinked at him, but her expression didn't change. "There must be another way."

Dougie folded his arms in front of his chest. The shouts and hollers in the room behind the door were growing louder. He nodded slowly. "We can try the laundry exit. It's not far."

The teacher pursed her lips tightly. "Okay. Let's go. This time, you go up ahead with Colton."

As they reached the stairwell that would take them down to the basement of the prison, the teacher hurried the kids through and stopped to look at one of them. The goth girl was hyperventilating. Breathing heavily and clutching at her chest as if she were about to have a full-blown panic attack. Dougie rolled his eyes as the teacher put both hands on the girl's shoulders and tried to calm her down.

"We don't have time for this," he said impatiently.

Next to him, the bus driver was watching him. He could feel it. His eyes burned into the side of Dougie's face, so Dougie purposefully did not look at the guy.

"I know what you're doing." Colton's voice was a low whisper. Stepping in front of Dougie, he added, "It's not going to work. You can't slip away unnoticed. As soon as this is over, they'll realize you're gone and they'll catch you."

Dougie didn't reply, just narrowed his eyes and scrutinized the other guy's face.

"You think by acting alone you've got more of a chance of getting away." Colton tipped his head in the direction from which they'd come. "Those guys, one big group, they've got no hope. You? Even if you are caught, you can claim you were simply helping some civilians and got carried away."

Dougie swallowed back bile that had risen in his throat. Every muscle in his body had begun to quiver. This guy thought he was so fucking smart. Smarter than Dougie. Well, maybe he wouldn't be so smart when he was writhing around on the floor with half his teeth missing.

"Listen." Colton met Dougie's eyes. "Do the right thing and I'll put in a good word for you with your parole board."

"Why the hell would the parole board care what you've got to say?"

Colton straightened his shoulders and suddenly seemed much larger than he had a few moments ago. "I'm a Marine," he said tightly.

"*Ex*-Marine," Dougie quipped. "Real Marines don't drive school buses."

A flash of fury crossed the bus driver's face. It gave Dougie a satisfying warmth in the pit of his stomach, but he squashed it down and forced himself to look contrite.

"Okay," he said, holding up his palms in a gesture of defeat. "You're right." After a pause, he added, "You'll do that? If I help you guys out of here, you'll put in a good word for me?"

"I will," Colton said, without missing a beat.

Dougie nodded. "All right, then." Looking at the teacher and raising his voice, he said loudly, "Let's go, people. We can't stay here all day."

9

MOLLY

Watching Scarlett struggle to catch her breath, Molly began to feel a little panicked herself. If they were in school, she'd be able to sit Scarlett down, make her a sweet cup of tea, and call her parents to come fetch her. Here, all she could do was tell her to stick her head down between her knees and count to ten as she breathed in and out. Here, she had no resources. No backup. And she was beginning to wonder whether the kids sensed that she, too, was deeply worried about their situation.

Scarlett was still breathing too quickly when Dougie shouted for them to get moving.

"The longer we stand here, the greater the chances of someone else beating us to it."

Molly raised her index finger at him, indicating *just a minute*. "Scarlett, honey, we've got to get going now. Okay?"

When Scarlett didn't reply, Erik Banks tentatively put his hand on his twin sister's back and said, "Scarlett? We need to move now, okay?"

"I can't, Erik."

"Sure you can. Take my hand?" Erik held out his hand and smiled at her.

Eventually, Scarlett looked up at him and nodded. "Okay," she whispered.

"Right." Molly put her hands on her hips and looked at Dougie. "What now?"

He and Colton had been whispering. She'd been too distracted by Scarlett to pay attention to it, but now it was worrying her. Dougie clearly wanted to be the hero in all this—the one who got them to safety and claimed a nice big tick in the good behavior book, but Colton couldn't stand him. Dougie, and people like him, were the opposite of everything Colton stood for, and Molly was worried that his dislike for the man might jeopardize their chance of escape if he got too carried away with it.

She didn't know Colton well, but what she did know—from the few school trips they'd chaperoned together—was that he was a man who followed the rules. Everyone knew he'd been a Marine and he didn't hide the fact that he liked order and discipline. His bus was run like a tight ship, and everyone knew that bullying and misbehavior were simply not tolerated when Colton was in charge.

Molly remembered him saying to her once—in a brief but honest exchange on the way back from a local theatre production—that his father had been 'no good'.

"Probably not your kind of thing," Molly had said, referencing the play they'd watched about a young man from the wrong side of the tracks trying to turn his life around.

"Rang a lot of bells, actually," Colton had replied gruffly. "As a kid, I was the same. Wanted something better, something more than what was on offer."

"And that's why you joined the Marines?"

Colton had nodded and pursed his lips. "No excuse for taking the wrong path. Everyone has choices. Everyone has a way out if they choose to take it."

Looking over at Colton and Dougie, Molly tried to interpret the expressions on their faces. She expected Colton to look annoyed because, frankly, Dougie epitomized everything he had fought against when he was a young man. Instead, he looked... sympathetic.

"Dougie says we need to go this way." Colton pointed to the stairs.

Molly's gut tensed as she looked at them, looping down into darkness. "Down there? Are you sure?" She looked at Dougie.

As he nodded, the corner of his mouth twitched into a smile that made Molly feel even more uneasy. At this point, they were dependent on Dougie to get them out of there; she had no choice but to follow.

Walking quickly, then taking two steps at a time, Dougie gestured for them to follow him. At the bottom of the stairs, they exited through an unlocked door into another corridor.

"Why wasn't that door locked?" Molly asked Colton in a low voice.

"I don't know," he replied. "I don't like it."

Up front, Dougie was striding ahead of them, clearly eager to get to where they were headed. Offering Molly the smallest shake of his head, Colton gestured for her and the kids to stay behind him, and he slowed his pace behind Dougie.

Now that they were beneath the prison, in the basement, the muffled sounds of the chaos above reminded Molly of the grumble a thunderstorm makes—right before the clouds split open and rain covers the earth. It was dark. Darker than it had been upstairs, with some sections of lights completely out. Suddenly, she wished she'd worn sneakers instead of boots—something less loud, less *obvious*.

Up ahead, Dougie stopped at a pair of large double doors. "Laundry gets taken through here. It used to be done on site, but now some cheap foreign firm picks it up every Monday."

"We can get back to the parking lot this way?" Colton was examining Dougie closely, as if he suspected him of lying.

Dougie rapped his knuckles on the door. "Just need to head through the old laundry and past the storage rooms to the service entrance."

"And the service entrance will get us out?"

"As long as you have a set of those...." He pointed to the keys Colton was still holding, then grinned and waved his hand at the lock. "So, after you...."

As Colton led them through an old disused laundry room, Molly felt her skin begin to prickle. It was cooler down here, almost too cool after the closeness of the main prison. At least they were heading away from the danger. Ahead, a light was flickering through an open door-way. They moved quickly toward it but as they rounded the corner, before her ears had a chance to alert her to the sound of people within, it became apparent that they weren't the only ones planning to escape this way.

In front of them, huddled in front of the door that Molly guessed led outside, was a group of three men dressed in the same gray sweatpants and white tees that Dougie and the other Scared Straight inmates had worn. Unlike the prisoners who'd been trying to simply bash down the doors at the front entrance, these three seemed to be talking about a logical way around their lack of keys.

"There's a security office back there," one of them was saying. "They'll have keys."

"Probably took them when they ran away," said another.

"Worth a look. I'm not breaking my arm trying to bash down the door if we don't have to."

Molly's heart was beating so fast she was almost certain the men would hear it. She didn't know what to do. Colton and Dougie were standing stock still, as if by playing dead they'd avoid being spotted.

Behind her, she could feel the kids starting to inch back toward the laundry room. Before she could follow suit, one of them tripped. It was Lucky. With his gangly arms reaching out to try and stop himself falling, he clattered into an abandoned mop and bucket. The metal bucket bashed against the wall. The mop toppled to the floor. All five kids froze, wide-eyed. When Molly turned back around, she was met by three more pairs of eyes. Except these were glistening with curiosity.

For a long, quivering moment, no one spoke. The three prisoners in front of them had turned away from the door. One had a cut on his forehead. Blood was trickling down the side of his face and as it pooled at the corner of his mouth, he made a hacking sound in the back of his throat and spat a globule of red saliva onto the floor. The one in the center, who'd suggested they look in the guard's office, was rubbing his knuckles into his palm. When he saw Dougie, his forehead wrinkled, but he didn't speak.

Molly was holding her breath. She glanced at Colton and saw his fingers twitch. He was moving his hand slowly, very slowly, to his pocket, trying to slip the keys out of sight, but it was too late.

"What have we here?" The one with blood on his face stepped forward. The others moved with him, like a pack of hyenas who'd stumbled upon prey they weren't expecting to find.

Next to Molly, Dougie began to slowly shrink backwards. She was about to grab hold of his arm, tell him to help them, say something, speak up. Before she had the chance, and before she could do anything to stop him, Colton broke ranks and charged forward.

"Colton, don't!" Molly yelled. Behind her, the kids gasped. For a second, the prisoners looked pleased. They began to whoop and holler, laughing at Colton's limp. Then their faces changed. The one with blood on his face raised his fists and stepped forward, bouncing on the balls of his feet as if he were about to start a fight in a boxing ring. Colton didn't bother raising his fists. In one swift movement, he used his good leg to knock the prisoner's knees out from under him and as the prisoner writhed on the floor, Colton kicked him hard in the ribs.

Molly held her arms out to her sides. Standing in front of the kids, she started to usher them backwards. A second prisoner moved forward, and Molly saw the glint of a blade as he took something sharp from the waistband of his sweatpants.

"Colton, he's got a knife!"

Quick as a flash, Colton turned, caught the prisoner's knife-holding fist in mid-air and used the guy's body weight to push him back to the wall. While they battled for the knife, the third prisoner, who looked scrawnier than the other two, bent to help the one on the floor. His friend whispered something in his ear and he looked up. Straight at Molly. A grin spread across his lips.

Colton was still tackling the prisoner he'd pinned to the wall. The knife had fallen to the floor and the third guy swooped to pick it up. Then he sped past the other two, straight toward Molly and the kids.

"Dougie! Get the kids out of here!" Molly yelled and turned around, but Dougie was gone. He left them. The son of a bitch left them. Turning around, as pure instinct took over, Molly did the only thing she could think of—she slammed her body, shoulder first, into the prisoner's stomach. He had been holding the knife out in front of him but didn't let go of it even as the force of Molly's body against his sent them tumbling to the floor.

For a second, Molly was on top of him, but then he flipped her over, onto her back. His thighs were on her chest. The knife was at her throat. She grabbed his wrists and held onto them with every ounce of strength she had. A guttural scream escaped her lips.

"Kids! Run!"

They didn't run. Erik and Scarlett ran forward and took hold of the man's upper arms. He pushed them off, but they came back. The pressure on Molly's chest was making her vision blur. From nowhere, a fist slammed into the side of the prisoner's face. His fingers loosened on the knife. It fell to the floor and he wobbled. Another fist, then a shove, and he was on the floor.

Molly scrabbled away from him, grabbing the knife and holding it out in front of her. She was panting, thinking of the self-defense classes she took in college and the fact that, when it came down to it, she hadn't remembered anything she was taught. Thank God instinct had taken over.

When she looked up, Jenna was rubbing her knuckles and Erik was looking at her in awe. "I take back everything I ever said.... Thank God you've been in so many fist fights."

As Scarlett patted Jenna's shoulder, and Lucky gave her a short round of applause, Jenna grinned and nodded as if to say, *Heck, yeah.*

"I couldn't agree more," Molly added.

10

ALEX

A t the end of the street, Alex stopped pedaling and looked back at his house. Leaving Laura home alone didn't feel right. He knew he had to. He knew that her priority, the same as his, was to get the kids back home. It didn't make it any easier. His only comfort was that Argent was with her. That dog wouldn't let anyone hurt her. Never.

Forcing himself to turn away, Alex jammed his hands onto the handlebars and began to ride. It was spring and sunny. Any other day, he'd have enjoyed the ride. He'd have taken his time, breathed long and deep as he moved slowly through the neighborhood. Today he didn't have that luxury. He needed to move *fast*.

As he started to pedal harder, he thanked his lucky stars that he'd stayed in shape. Plenty of guys started to let themselves go as they reached middle age. Especially if they had jobs like his—jobs that required them to spend an inordinate number of hours in an office, behind a desk or frequently attending executive lunches and dinners.

When they first met, he and Laura had worked out together all the time. As a personal trainer, she was in far better shape than he was and even after the kids were born, they managed to find time to go running or cycling on the weekends. When Scarlett and Erik were young, Alex had pictured the four of them going on family hikes once the children got older, renting a cabin somewhere for school breaks, and cycling through the forests. It turned out that Scarlett and Erik weren't the outdoor type, and before Alex had managed to persuade them otherwise, the accident happened.

Alex clenched his jaw and puffed loudly as he pushed himself to go faster. If the power really was gone, vacations were the last thing they'd be worrying about.

Usually, at this speed, he'd have made it to the outskirts of the neighborhood in record time but—despite it being the middle of the day—he found that every shadow, hedge and tree made his muscles tense. It was eerily quiet. Even the birds and the crickets seemed to have noticed something was going on.

Turning right, Alex headed in the direction of the train tracks that ran behind their house. Usually it would take him a few minutes to navigate the busy intersection, but now he fed easily into the empty road. Except, it wasn't empty.

On his street, most of the neighbors' cars had been parked in driveways. It was a quiet block and, on weekdays once everyone had headed off to work, he'd always liked that it remained relatively car-free. It was part of why they chose the house in the first place, because it was a *quiet* neighborhood.

Here, though, there were cars everywhere. Some, which had obviously been driving at speed when their engines cut out, had swerved and ended up at the side of the road. Others looked like bumper cars at the fair that had bumped into one another before the ride stopped. Thankfully, none of them reminded him of the way their own car looked on the night of their car accident.

Alex cycled through the cars, weaving in and out and wondering where all the drivers had gone. Presumably, on realizing that something awful had happened, they'd left on foot to get back to their homes and families.

He was on the bridge above the train tracks when he heard a baby crying. At first he thought he was imagining it. That his mind was playing tricks on him, making him remember the twins when they were young as some kind of clever way to get him to speed the hell up. Then his front wheel caught on something. He stopped and looked down. A child's doll. Well-loved and gray around the edges.

Alex leaned his bike against a nearby car and picked the doll up. When he raised his head, he saw that the car opposite had a broken windshield and that its rear passenger door was open. A child, a girl of no more than three, was strapped into a bright pink car seat in the back, wailing.

Immediately, Alex hurried over to her. She continued to wail even when he passed her the doll, but quieted a little as he lifted her out and bounced her lightly up and down in his arms.

"Shhhh," he whispered. "It's okay, sweetheart. My name's Alex. Where's your mommy?"

The girl looked at him with watery eyes. Snot was running from her nose onto her top lip.

For a moment he thought she might answer him, but when she opened her mouth, all that came out was another ear-splitting scream.

Alex peered into the front of the car. A woman's purse was on the front seat, but there was no sign of the driver. "Shit," he muttered.

Looking back toward his house, he considered taking her back to Laura. With the child balanced on one hip, he patted his pockets. If he'd had a pen and paper, he could have left a note in case the child's mother returned, although why she'd left in the first place he couldn't fathom.

Briefly, he looked toward the train tracks. The neighborhood on the other side of them was known as Southside. Every time Alex drove through it, which wasn't often, he thanked a god he didn't really believe in that he hadn't, through bad luck or bad judgment, ended up somewhere like that. Thanked God that Erik and Scarlett hadn't grown up around the kind of people his mother would have called 'down and outs' and his father would have called 'scum'.

"Right, well I don't have a pen. Maybe Mommy does. Huh?" Alex tried to smile at the girl, but it only made her bunch up her fists and try to whack him on the shoulder. "It's okay, sweetie, just a minute." He tried using the voice he'd heard Laura use with their own kids a million times, but it didn't sound nearly as soothing coming from him.

Pulling at the front passenger door, Alex tugged it open and stuck his body awkwardly inside, still trying to keep hold of the little girl. He was opening the purse, hoping to find even some lipstick he could use to scribble a note with, when the girl sank her teeth into his shoulder.

"Ahhhh!" Alex bellowed and whacked his head on the roof of the car.

The girl was pulling away from him, screaming at the top of her lungs now, "I want my mommy! Leave me alone!"

"It's all right." Alex set her down on the ground but kept hold of her arms, crouching down in front of her and speaking as softly and calmly as he could manage. "Sweetheart, I'm trying to help you find your mommy. Can you tell me where you live? Over there?" Alex pointed toward the tracks. "Or that way?" He pointed toward his own neighborhood.

"I suggest you leave the child alone."

A deep, growling voice met his ears at the same moment something cool and hard met the back of his head. *Shit. A gun.*

Alex let go of the girl's arms. "Daddy!" she screamed, hurtling forward.

"Get back in the car, Petal, while Daddy deals with the bad man."

Alex watched from the corner of his eye as the girl ran back to the car, scooping up her doll and clambering back into her seat. Still crouching, he raised his hands and said, "I was just trying to help her find her mom, that's all. I didn't realize her folks were nearby."

"Stand up and turn around. *Slowly*," the voice said.

Alex did as he was told.

In front of him, a large forty-something-year-old with a bulging belly and a beer-stained t-shirt stood holding what looked like an old hunting rifle. "Where's my wife?" he spat.

"I have no idea where your wife is. I was cycling through, I heard your daughter crying and I was trying to help, that's all."

"Trying to help by robbing my wife's purse?" The man pointed the gun at the passenger seat, where his wife's purse lay open and emptied.

"I was looking for something I could use to leave a note, that's all. I was going to take your daughter home to my wife." Alex winced as he spoke, then tried to rectify it. "To look after her. There was no sign of the driver and she was out here all alone."

The man bit his lower lip. He had a small wiry beard that barely covered a bulbous frog-like chin. It wobbled when he spoke. "I don't know as I believe you." He looked at his daughter and she smiled at him. "Luna. Was this man trying to steal Mommy's things? Was he trying to hurt you?"

Luna thought for a moment, then shook her head.

The man blinked at her. "You sure?"

She nodded.

"Okay, so where's Mom?"

Luna shrugged. "She got out. There was a man."

"This man?"

Alex took a step back as the gun was waved at him.

"No. Another man. He said he had something. Mommy went with him. She said she'd come back." Luna sniffed loudly and started to cry again.

"All right, baby girl." The man walked over to lift her out of the car and, at the same time, swing the rifle onto his shoulder. "My wife is a useless, good-for-nothing junkie," the man said loudly. "Probably saw an opportunity to score. Wouldn't be the first time she left Luna all alone."

Alex swallowed hard, trying not to let even the smallest hint of an expression show on his face. As he was concentrating on looking contrite, the man thrust out his hand and grabbed hold of Alex's, shaking it forcefully up and down.

"I got you wrong. I thought you were trying to hurt my Luna."

"Never," Alex said solemnly.

"Good thing I didn't shoot you, huh?" The man whacked Alex *hard* on the shoulder and let out a guffaw of laughter.

Alex tried to laugh back. "I'll say," he muttered.

"My name is Dean. Where you headed?" the man asked, narrowing his eyes as he stopped laughing.

"Alex. My kids are at Fairfield Prison. I need to get to them."

The man raised his eyebrows, looking Alex up and down as if he were surprised that his kids were locked up. Alex didn't bother to tell him they were only there for a visit. "Darn. Well, that's not somewhere I'd want to be when hell breaks loose," the man said grimly. Then, looking at Alex's rifle, he added. "You know how to shoot that thing, buddy?"

Alex nodded firmly. "I do," he said.

"Well, you keep it close. Especially round here, there's plenty who'd try and rob you for it." The man glanced at Alex's wrist. "And for that fancy watch of yours too."

Alex looked down at his watch. A fancy sports tracker that Laura had bought him last Christmas. "It doesn't even work anymore," he said quietly.

"Doesn't matter. They'll have it if it looks valuable." The man looked behind him in the direction of the tracks. "You headed this way, then?"

"I am."

"Us too."

Alex smiled thinly. "Actually, I need to get going." He gestured to his bike.

"Ah, come on now. Don't be unsociable." Dean wrapped his thick fingers around the handlebar. "We'll walk together. Okay?"

11

MOLLY

As Molly sat with her back against the wall, trying to stop her hands from shaking, Colton dragged the three prisoners into a nearby room. When he came out, he wasn't alone.

"Look who I found." He shoved Dougie into the corridor before turning to lock the prisoners inside. Following close behind Dougie, Zack looked at the others from behind his curtain of long black hair. Lucky shook his head at him.

"Seriously? You ran away? Miss O'Neil jumped in front of a dude with a knife, and you *ran away*?"

"Guess he's not as hard as he makes out," Jenna said scathingly.

"Oh yeah, what the hell did you lot do?" Zack's cheeks had begun to flush.

"What did *we* do?" Jenna lunged forward as if she were about to grab Zack around the throat, but before she could, Dougie pushed past and positioned himself in the middle of the corridor, blocking Zack from view. "You all might have a death wish but I sure as hell don't, and I'm not going to apologize for being smart. Besides…" He looked at Colton and raised his eyebrows. "Looks like Rambo took care of it."

"We can discuss this later," Colton said gruffly. He was rubbing his leg and breathing heavily. "When we're outside." He offered Molly his hand but winced as he helped pull her to her feet. "Here," he said, giving her the keys. "I'll catch up."

Molly wanted to ask him if he was okay, but she also wanted to be as far away from Dougie and the prison as possible, so she took them and sprinted to the end of the corridor. The gray metal door had a small window of reinforced glass that looked out at a fenced-in parking lot. At the far end of the lot were two enormous gates. Molly bit her bottom lip. A niggle of uncertainty had lodged itself in the pit of her stomach and even as she put the keys in the door, somehow, she knew it wouldn't open.

"What is it?" Scarlett was standing next to her, looking as though she might begin to hyperventilate again.

"The door won't open," Molly muttered.

"What?" Dougie pushed forward and began to rattle the door handle.

Fighting the sense of rising panic in her chest, Molly looked up. "There's another lock. There. At the top. We need a second set of keys."

"No." Dougie shook his head and began to kick the door. "That's not right. These keys should work. *These* ones."

Slowly, Molly reached past Dougie's stomach and took the keys back out of the lock. As Colton approached, she passed them back to him and shook her head. "It's no good," she said. "We'll have to go back to the front."

Kicking the door one more time, Dougie let out a throaty groan and braced his hands behind his head, then stalked back to the opposite end of the corridor. As Zack followed close behind him, Molly closed her eyes; perhaps if she didn't see the way that Zack was looking at Dougie—with adulation instead of fear or contempt like the others—she wouldn't have to decide what to do about it. Because there wasn't time for that. Not now.

Think, Molly, think. She kept her eyes shut and counted to ten. When she opened them, Colton was leaning against the wall, his hands braced on his thighs, and the kids were staring at her.

"Okay," she said. "Before we do anything else, we need a timeout."

"A timeout?" Scarlett looked at Erik, then back at Molly as if she'd lost her mind. "Now? Here?"

"One of the prisoners said there's a security office down here somewhere. They might have a first aid kit, and if there's a floor plan of the building, we can find another way out."

Without waiting for the kids to agree, Molly started toward the door that sat mid-way down the corridor, on the opposite side from the room in which Colton had sealed their attackers.

Limping, much worse than before, Colton followed her and, this time, the keys worked. Once they were all inside, Colton locked it again and then fell into the nearest chair—a high-backed swivel chair positioned behind a large, curved desk.

On the desk were four blank screens, which looked like they were connected to a computer that probably switched itself off when the power went out. "This must be where they man the service exit," Scarlett said. "And access the security cameras." She paused and began to chew the inside of her cheek. "If we could get into the system, we could see where the other prisoners are...." Motioning for Colton to move his chair out of the way, she stood behind the desk, her eyes suddenly brighter. "And we can email someone for help."

Usually, Molly wouldn't encourage a teenage hacker to use their superpowers, but under the circumstances, she was suddenly extremely relieved that Scarlett and Erik Banks were on the Scared Straight trip that day. "Hang on a minute, Scarlett," she said, raising her index finger. "I want to talk to you and Erik. Jenna, Lucky, look in the cupboards and see if there's a first aid kit to patch up Colton's knuckles."

Colton opened his mouth to protest but Molly shot him a look that she hoped imparted, *Just play along, I need them preoccupied for a minute.*

"Dougie, Zack, search for another set of keys."

In the corner of the room, Zack and Dougie were leaning against the wall, watching her, but reluctantly did as they were told. As Molly turned her back to them, she perched on the edge of the desk. "Scarlett," she said, quietly, "Erik... I think our best bet is to find another set of keys. Even if we do..." She rubbed the back of her neck and noticed it was aching. "When I was trying to open the door, I looked outside. There's a ten-foot-high gate out there that I'm guessing operates on the main power system. It looked like there was a keypad on it."

"It'll need a code," Erik said thoughtfully.

"A code we don't have," Molly agreed.

The Banks twins exchanged a knowing look. "Got it," Scarlett said, already turning to the computer. "No problem."

Molly watched carefully as Scarlett's entire body instantly became lighter, buoyed by purpose and hope. She wanted to believe that the twins could find a solution. She wanted to believe that in a few hours they'd all be safe, heading for town and their families. But she didn't. Deep down, she didn't believe it one bit.

Looking around the room, she saw her own feelings reflected in the defeated faces of the others. Colton was obviously in pain, his jaw set tight, a scowl on his face that told her he was concentrating hard on not giving in to it. Jenna and Lucky had found a first-aid kit and given it to him, but Colton was simply holding it.

Although she'd told Dougie and Zack to search for more keys, they were muttering to each other and moving far too slowly for her liking. The way Zack looked at Dougie made her nervous. It was as if he found him... impressive. Perhaps Dougie reminded Zack of his brother. Perhaps it was because Dougie was showing an interest in him. Whatever the reason, Molly knew she needed to keep a close eye on them.

Just as she thought this, she saw Dougie mutter something to Zack. She couldn't hear what it was, but she didn't like that he was trying so hard to buddy up with one of her students. Dougie was planning something, she was sure of it, and it was up to her to make sure it didn't involve Zack.

Molly was helping to bandage Colton's hands when, behind her, Scarlett swore loudly. As Molly turned around, she saw Erik whisper something to her, his eyes wide. Seconds later, Scarlett picked up the keyboard and threw it across the room.

Jenna and Lucky looked up from where they were sitting, huddled together, talking in low whispers. On the other side of the room, Zack was slouched in a chair and, beside him, Dougie was spinning round and round in an old, battered desk chair. Looking at him made Molly feel a little dizzy.

At Scarlett's outburst, Dougie stopping spinning and tilted his head, clearly intrigued.

"Scarlett?" Molly walked over to her, but Scarlett was violently unplugging the computer screens. Waving her arms, she began to swipe things off the desk. The mouse. A second keyboard. She was about to push the screens off the back of the desk when Erik grabbed her arms and pulled her backwards.

"Scarlett, what is it?" Molly ducked to meet Scarlett's eyes, putting her hands lightly on the girl's thin shoulders.

Scarlett was crying, so hard she couldn't speak.

Turning to Erik, Molly repeated her question, "What is it? What's going on?"

Through tight lips, Erik replied solemnly, "We can't turn them on."

Molly frowned. "Oh. Okay." She rubbed Scarlett's shoulder again. "Well, that's okay. Thank you for trying, you two. We'll find another solution."

"You... don't... understand," Scarlett said through stilted sobs. "Everything is fried." Another sob, and then, as Molly continued to look at her with a confused expression, she shook her head. "Don't you get it, Miss O'Neil? It's not just a power outage. It's an *EMP*. Like we said from the start."

Molly almost laughed. She wasn't sure why; it was just a feeling that bubbled up inside her chest. "An EMP?" She looked from Scarlett to Erik. "Come on, you two. That's science fiction stuff. You're getting a little carried away with yourselves, which is understandable. It's a scary situation. But there'll be a logical explanation."

"An EMP *is* the logical explanation," Erik said, clearly calmer than his sister.

Molly began to reel through her bank of teacher tricks, trying to think of a way to defuse the situation without making the twins feel as if she didn't respect their opinions or sympathize with the fact they were clearly very, very worried. Before she'd settled on one, Colton got up and walked gingerly over to her.

"EMPs aren't science fiction," he said solemnly. "We ran drills in the military for this kind of scenario. EMPs are a very real possibility."

Molly frowned at him. Back in the Scared Straight room, Colton had seemed dismissive of the twins' suggestions. She, too, had assumed they were trying to wind the others up. Or at least, that was what she'd told herself. "So you agree with them?"

Colton shrugged his broad shoulders. "That depends," he said, turning to the twins. "What makes you think this is an EMP?"

Scarlett had stopped crying and was attempting to slow her breathing, but Erik spoke for her. "We thought it was odd that the guards' radios stopped working." Gesturing to the mess his sister made, "The computers won't turn on either."

"Surely that could be something to do with the way the generator works?" Molly asked. She didn't have a clue what she was talking about, but she sure as hell wanted there to be an explanation—*any* explanation—apart from this one.

Erik tilted his head from side to side. "Maybe, but there are three laptops here too. They're plugged in, which suggests they were charging or charged when the power went out. If that's the case, they'd still be working." Before Molly could counter what he'd said, he added, "There's a cell phone too, probably one of the guards'. It won't turn on."

From behind them, Jenna's voice piped up, "Would that explain why none of the flashlights in the cupboard turn on?"

Erik nodded at her. "Yep. Although you might want to check them all just in case." Looking up at the ceiling, he said, "We're in the basement, which means there are plenty of layers of cement or cinderblock between us and outside."

"Why would a flashlight work if a computer doesn't?" Lucky asked, frowning deeply as his brain tried to process what Erik was suggesting.

Quietly, as if she had almost no energy left to speak, Scarlett answered, "The flashlights are small. They don't have much wiring. Plus, they were in a metal cupboard, which might have protected them. Like Erik said, it's worth checking...."

"But the generator... wouldn't an EMP destroy that too?" Molly looked at the extinguished lights, the computers, and the dead cell phones on the desk. As she thought about none of them ever turning back on, her mouth turned dry.

Erik frowned at her, in a way that she might if she was having to repeat herself in class. "Like I said back in the Scared Straight room, Miss O'Neil... with an EMP, anything with an electromagnet can be destroyed. Cars. Phones. Computers. *But* the prison generator is ancient and protected, so it's probably not affected. Everything else, though...." He splayed his fingers out and mouthed the word *boom*.

Molly felt her legs waver and steadied herself on the edge of the desk. Looking at Colton now, so the kids didn't see the color draining from her face, she whispered, "So, even when we get out of here...."

Colton nodded slowly.

Again, Scarlett began to cry. "Everything I worked for," she muttered. "It's gone." Turning to her brother, she grabbed his hand. "It's all pointless now. Yesterday, we were geniuses. Today, we're useless."

Despite a hot, creeping sense of fear taking hold of her, Molly took a deep breath, stood up and clapped her hands. "Okay," she said firmly. "Erik, Scarlett, you might be right. But we don't know for certain what's going on beyond the walls of this prison and until we do, I'm not allowing anyone to panic or talk about being useless. Our focus is on getting out of here. Once we're out, we'll figure out what to do next."

Scarlett sniffed loudly but eventually nodded. As Molly turned back to the others, she heard Zack mutter something that made Dougie loudly swear and say, "Ain't that irony for you?!"

"What is?" Molly put her hands on her hips. She was beginning to wish that Dougie would leave them alone because, clearly, if things got rough, he wasn't going to put himself in danger for her or the kids.

Zack looked up at her and shrugged his oversized hoodie back onto his shoulder. "If this really is an EMP, and this place has a working generator, well...." His eyes sparkled and he laughed a deep disturbing laugh. "Fairfield Prison just became a castle."

Pouncing on the obvious ripple of fear in the room, Dougie grinned. "Kid's right. If there's no power out there, this place just became a freakin' palace." He stood up and pointed at the shuttered window, where small slats of dull sunlight were only just managing to filter into the room. "In here, we've got everything we need. Out there, the world is ending."

12

TOMMY

Tommy was riding in the back of the wagon, watching the world go by with a slight sense of disbelief. It was as if he'd gone to sleep and woken up in a zombie movie. Abandoned cars everywhere. People wandering the streets looking confused. Quiet. So much quiet.

He'd only been out of jail for ten days, having been released just a few days after his long-time cell mate Luke. At first, he'd hoped Ma might have come to meet him; he'd written to tell her the date and the time. Unsurprisingly, she didn't.

At seven-thirty in the evening, Tommy had ended up outside the prison with nowhere to go and nothing but a small plastic bag containing the things he'd had with him the day he went down—a wallet, a watch, and some candy. He thought about calling home. Maybe Ma forgot. Except, if she had, it meant she was in a bad place, and he didn't know if he was ready to deal with that right now.

So, instead, he called the telephone number Luke gave him before he left.

Luke's mother was the one who answered. She had a soft, welcoming voice, and seemed genuinely pleased that Tommy had called them.

"Say no more," she'd replied quickly when Tommy muttered something about perhaps crashing on their couch for a night or two. "Beck will come get you."

An hour later, Luke's dad Beck Robinson had pulled up in a large battered-looking truck and driven Tommy home to the family farm.

When the power went out, Tommy and the Robinsons had been in the middle of a late breakfast out on the porch. Pancakes, waffles, juice, coffee.

Tommy had felt like he was in heaven.

Now, sitting in the back of the wagon, he wondered how long it would take for the Robinsons' coffee supplies to run out.

Next to him, Luke's little brother Chris was holding a large metal case. Hugging it to his chest as if it was his most prized possession.

"What's in it?" Tommy asked, leaning back against the side of the wagon, and trying not to think of his own younger brother.

"It's a Faraday cage." The boy's eyes lit up as he spoke.

When Tommy frowned, Chris laughed loudly and called up to the front where his brother Luke—the guy Tommy had shared a cell with for three years—was holding a pair of reins and geeing on their slightly skittish horse.

In front, a second wagon driven by Luke and Chris's parents, and containing three goats, two pigs, and a cage full of chickens, was slowing down as they rounded a corner.

"Hey, Luke," Chris yelled. "Where'd you find this guy? He doesn't even know what a Faraday cage is!"

Luke smiled wryly and shook his head. "So, teach him then."

"Okayyy, so it's basically a metal box that can shield stuff from the effects of the EMP. We've got a computer. Batteries. Spare parts for the truck."

"Truck?" Tommy laughed and looked at the horse that was pulling the wagon. "What truck?"

From the front, Luke answered, "Mom and Dad bought an old diesel truck a couple years back. It's in the woods. Waiting for us."

Tommy raised his eyebrows; when he first arrived at the farm, the Robinsons had seemed like a completely normal family. As soon as the power went out, Tommy had quickly realized they were anything *but* normal.

Almost instantly, their eyes had darkened. For a moment, as Luke tried all the switches in the kitchen and Beck examined the electrical box, no one spoke. Then, standing solemnly in the center of the room, Beck had put his arms around his wife and children and said, "We knew this day would come."

The others had nodded and looked down at their feet.

"Sorry, guys, am I missing something?" Tommy had almost laughed.

"It's an EMP, Tommy," Luke had replied through thin lips. "The power's gone."

"And it ain't coming back," Beck had finished.

After that, everything had kicked up a notch. As if they were following some well-rehearsed plan, the Robinsons had begun to flit around the house, gathering things, emptying cupboards, packing.

For a few minutes, Tommy had simply watched, but then Beck had thumped him on the shoulder and said, "Come on, Tommy, make yourself useful and start loading this stuff into the wagon while I go down to the basement for the rest."

"Wagon?"

"We can't stay here," Luke's mother Felicia had said quietly, while pulling bottled water from the cupboard beneath the kitchen sink. "But it's okay. We acquired some land a few years ago and we've been preparing for this."

"Preparing?"

"It's always been a very real possibility. Not one that most people want to confront, but..." she had smiled at her husband. "We're not like most people. We have enough supplies to keep us safe and fed for many years. But we have to leave. Now."

Doing as he was told, Tommy had helped Luke heave box after box of supplies into the wagon that Beck had pulled around to the front of the farmhouse. When they'd finished, he had stood back and rubbed his neck.

"Well, I guess I'll be seeing you then," he'd said solemnly.

"What are you talking about? You're coming with us, man. We're not leaving you."

At that, Tommy's heart had soared. Since the moment he'd set foot in the Robinsons' household, he'd thought to himself that *this* was what family was supposed to be like. A mother who smiled a genuinely loving smile when she saw her boys. A father whose voice filled with pride whenever he spoke to them. A home. A real home.

Now, though, as he watched the back of Luke's head swaying from side to side with the motion of the wagon, a queasy sensation settled in his stomach.

His own family was not like Luke's. His own family was almost the opposite. A deadbeat mom. An absent dad.

And Zack.

"Luke," he said, shuffling up the bench and tapping his friend on the shoulder. "I don't think I can go with you."

"Huh?" Luke looked round. "What do you mean?"

"I need to go home. Check on my family."

"Your mom? Come on, Tommy. She abandoned you. She didn't even come get you when you were released. You said yourself she's probably on another bender."

"She probably is. Which means Zack will be all alone."

"Zack? The brother who hasn't spoken to you since you got locked up?"

Tommy hung his head and wiped his hands over his face. When he looked up, he gestured to Chris. "He's just a kid. Only a bit older than Chris. If the friggin' world is ending, I can't leave him."

Finally, shaking his head, Luke shouted for his parents to stop.

As the wagons slowed, Beck jumped down and ran over to them. "What's wrong, boys?"

"Tommy's leaving." Luke was pissed, or sad, or both.

"Leaving?" Beck gripped hold of the wagon with his large work-worn hands. "Son? You don't want to come with us?"

"I do," Tommy said, a little weakly. "I really do. But I need to fetch my brother Zack."

Beck looked from Luke to Chris, then back to Tommy. "I wish we could help you, Tommy, but we need to get to the woods and secure the cabin."

Tommy nodded. "I understand."

Beck reached out and helped Tommy down from the wagon, then clicked his fingers at Chris. "Chris, pass me one of the loaded packs."

"The packs? But Pa, there's only four. One each."

"Well, Tommy's going to borrow this one," Beck said, taking hold of the small green backpack that Chris was passing to him. "And he's going to return it when he comes to find us." Beck patted Tommy's shoulder. "Right, son?"

Tommy swallowed hard. He felt suddenly tearful and coughed to try and distract himself from it.

"Now, you take this." Beck thrust a piece of paper into Tommy's hand and forced him to close his fingers around it. "This is a map that'll bring you to the cabin, but you don't show it to a single living soul. You don't *tell* a soul. Even your brother. Understand? What's going to keep us safe, is people having no idea we exist."

"I won't tell anyone." Tommy tried to smile as he slid the map into his pocket. "I'll eat the map if I have to."

Beck laughed. "Good boy." Then he headed back to his wagon.

"See you soon, I hope," Luke said, waving as the horses started moving.

"See you." Tommy waved too. As soon as they were out of sight, he took a deep breath, turned around, and headed in the direction of his old neighborhood.

13

MOLLY

"No matter what's going on *out there,* our goal hasn't changed." Molly turned her back to Dougie and Zack and spoke only to the others. "You all need to get back to your families, and we need to be as far away from the prison as possible. Agreed?"

Lucky, Jenna, Scarlett and Erik nodded fervently. Although Zack might think it was a good idea to stay put, at least these four wanted to stick to the plan.

"Dougie," Molly said firmly, "you can do whatever the hell you want but, for now, you promised to help me get the kids to safety. Can you still do that? Or should we part ways?"

Zack was watching Dougie, who looked as if he was seriously considering how to answer her question. Eventually, looking straight into Molly's eyes, he said, "I'm many things, but I'm also a man of my word."

"Right. Good." Molly was about to turn, but then looked back. "Did you find any spare keys, by the way?"

As Molly fixed her eyes on Dougie's, his mouth twitched into a smile. "Sorry. No."

"Did you look? You two seemed to be deep in conversation. I wasn't sure if you'd had the chance…."

Without breaking eye contact, Dougie frowned earnestly at her. "We looked, Miss O'Neil. We didn't find them."

Molly's hands were on her hips. She wasn't sure she believed him, in fact it was probably stupid of her to entrust Dougie with the task of looking for keys in the first place, but she could hardly insist that they empty their pockets. Turning away, she focused on Colton. If he'd trained for this kind of situation, surely, he must have some kind of idea how to get them out of Fairfield. "So," she said, "what do you think? What should be our plan of action?"

Colton immediately straightened himself up. Without hesitating, as if he'd been rehearsing this very speech in his head, he said, "If we're stuck in here, then the guards must be too. I think we have to assume they haven't abandoned their posts yet. They're probably sitting tight waiting for the cavalry to arrive."

"Except it won't," Dougie cut in, a note of excitement in his voice. "Not if the whole city is without power. The cops will have bigger problems."

Colton ignored him and continued. "I say we head for the main Guard's Station. They'll have guns, riot gear. If we explain what's going on—tell them it's unlikely help will arrive any time soon—they can help us get out."

"And if they *have* abandoned their posts?" Dougie looked Colton up and down. "The big guy might have taken out three losers, but he can't take out an entire prison."

Molly fixed a steely gaze on Dougie's face. Calmly, she said, "If the guards have already left, then *you* are going to have to persuade your friends up front to let us out. I'm fairly sure that if we offer to open the doors for them, they'll agree."

"And free a bunch of convicts?" Scarlett looked utterly disgusted by the idea. As did Colton.

"If that's the price we pay for getting out, then that's the price we pay," Molly said firmly, trying not to think about a gang of convicts ripping through the neighborhood in the middle of a power outage. "Let's hope we don't have to go down that road." She was already moving toward the door, but then she stopped. Turning back, she pointed to the cupboards around the room. "We should see if there's anything useful in here." She strode over to the nearest one and began to rifle through it. On a shelf at the top, she found a black gym bag and emptied out the oversized clothes inside it so they could use it to carry anything they found.

As she did, a book fell to the floor and Zack quickly bobbed down to pick it up. While the others began scouring the room, Molly noticed that Zack was turning the book over in his hands, reading the blurb on the back.

"I've been meaning to read this," he muttered to no one in particular. Jenna strode over to him, grabbed it, and tossed it across the room. "Miss O'Neil said to look for things that could be useful. I don't think books are going to be high on the list."

"Sure they will," Lucky said. He was smiling and reaching for his pocket. When he lifted his hand, he was holding a lighter. It glinted as it caught a slim ray of sun from the shuttered windows. "We can burn them for fuel."

Molly was about to take it from him. The same instinct she'd had when they were on the bus—to stop Lucky from getting himself in more trouble—still rumbled in her belly. But if the twins were right, then a kid with a talent for lighting fires might come in handy. So she simply looked away and let him keep it.

"Right, what have we got?" she asked the others as they walked over and started laying out their spoils on the desk.

"Candy," Scarlett said, smiling. "From the desk drawers."

"Water and cereal bars too," Erik added.

"And I checked the flashlights." Jenna had shoved four together in a bunch but was holding one in her hand. "Those ones don't work," she said, pointing to the group. "But this one…." She waggled the one she was holding and raised her eyebrows. When she flicked it on, an *oooh* sound rumbled through the other kids.

"Oh my God," Scarlett breathed. "It works?"

Jenna nodded solemnly, holding onto the flashlight as if it was made of solid gold.

"Well, that's going to be valuable, little girl. You should hold on to it." From across the room, Dougie stood up and nodded at the flashlight.

"Put it in your back pocket, Jenna, in case the lights go out again." Molly ignored Dougie and gestured to the four nonworking ones. "Zack, Scarlett, Erik and Lucky, grab one of these dead ones and keep it with you."

"In case they miraculously start working?" Zack picked one up and turned it over in his hands.

"No. In case we need weapons." Molly stared at him with her hands on her hips and watched as his eyes flickered with concern. Hiding it well, he made a snorting noise and shoved the flashlight into his back jeans pocket.

"Okay. Anything else before we go?"

"We should take the first aid kit," Colton said, massaging his knuckles. "And that would have been useful." He pointed to the wall, where a picture frame labeled 'Emergency Exits' hung empty.

"Someone must have gotten here before us," Molly muttered.

"Well, then, we better get moving." Dougie was striding toward the door. "In case they come back."

"Okay, Dougie, which way?" Molly looked at him expectantly. They were back at the top of the stairwell, preparing themselves to push the door open and reenter the main body of the prison.

He narrowed his eyes as though he was trying to picture an imaginary map of the prison, and then he pointed right. "That way."

"Are you sure?" Colton asked abruptly. "That's the total opposite of the way we came."

"I'm sure," Dougie replied. "You want to reach the Guard's Station; we go that way."

Before they had a chance to start arguing, Molly took a deep breath. Holding it in her chest, she opened the door. The corridor was empty and felt darker than it had before. There was no one there. "Okay...." She beckoned for the others to come out and, this time, went up front with Dougie while Colton walked behind the kids.

The dryness in her mouth was beginning to ease, just a little, because it seemed as if all the prisoners were somewhere else causing havoc, when she stopped dead in her tracks. Up ahead, right in front of the door they needed to open next, was a body. A guard.

"Is he... dead?" Molly was staring at the guard's head. It was surrounded by an ugly red halo of blood and his eyes were swollen.

Dougie walked over and nudged the guard's side with the toe of his shoe. "Sure as hell looks like it."

Molly swallowed forcefully. Her tongue felt too big for her mouth and there was a knot in her throat that was threatening to turn into vomit. She let out a long shaky breath. Then stepped forward. "Dougie," she said, loudly, "help me move him."

A rumble of appalled sounds swept through the kids, but she didn't look at them; she'd already taken hold of the guard's wrists and was waiting for Dougie to grab his feet. Without protesting, he did as she'd asked, and Molly looked away as they heaved the dead man's body to the side of the corridor.

With a shudder, Molly reached down. Her fingers trembled as she gently tugged the can of pepper spray from the guard's belt. When she stood up, she closed her eyes for a moment, then she turned and offered it to Scarlett. Blinking at her, without saying a word, Scarlett took it. Molly nodded, but when she asked Colton for the keys so she could open the door, she realized that her hands were covered in blood.

"Take a minute," Colton said, catching her wrist as he passed the keys to her.

Molly shook her head. "We don't have a minute."

After stumbling upon the dead guard, Molly found herself expecting to find dead people around every corner. For what felt like forever, Dougie led them silently down one corridor, and another, and another. Deeper into the prison, probably toward the front exit, they could hear shouting. The occasional gunshot. Things breaking. *People breaking....* Molly pushed the thought from her mind and focused on putting one foot in front of the other.

The further they moved, the darker it seemed to become. The hallways got narrower, the ceilings got lower, and there were occasionally entire stretches where the lights were out, and she had to force herself to stay focused instead of allowing the scratchy panic in the pit of her stomach to take over.

Watching the kids helped. Keeping her eyes on them and making sure they were still together, still doing okay, kept her from giving in to the gnawing anxiety that was threatening to come out. She tried not to think about the kids' parents and how they must be feeling right now.

The Banks twins especially—everyone knew they'd been through a lot in the last few years. Now this…. She bit her lower lip and straightened her shoulders; she *had* to get these kids to safety.

Finally, Dougie stopped and pointed to a large metal door up ahead. "That's it," he said. "The Guard's Station is through there."

"You're sure?"

Dougie rolled his eyes. "I've been here fifteen years. I'm sure."

Molly nodded and let herself breathe out. "Okay, then." She strode forward, still holding the keys. They turned easily in the lock and she felt the tiniest ounce of tension leave her muscles. But when she pushed, nothing happened. Colton was now standing next to her and leaned his shoulder into the door as she tried the handle. This time it budged, but only an inch.

"There's something on the other side," Colton said, pushing again. This time, it opened a fraction wider. Colton turned round to look at the kids. As if he was sizing them up, he examined them each in turn then said, "Zack, come here."

Zack hesitated, so Jenna shoved him in the middle of his back. Stumbling forward, Zack shot her a look of contempt, then shoved his hands into his pockets. "What?" he said gruffly.

"You've got thin wrists. Can you fit your hand through the gap? See if you can feel what's blocking the door."

Zack's cheeks flushed a vivid shade of pink. He was undoubtedly skinnier than the other two boys, but to be publicly called out on it was clearly a bit too much. "Fuck off," he said, surprisingly loud. "I'm not putting my hand through there. What if there's some psycho on the other side who decides to chop off my fingers?"

"If there's some psycho on the other side," Lucky piped up, "then he'll probably sense your psycho vibes and ask you to be his best buddy."

Despite the situation, Jenna and the Banks twins sniggered.

Rapping his knuckles on the door, Colton glowered at Zack. "Kid, I'm not asking. I'm telling. We need to know what's stopping us getting through."

Zack was still hesitating when Dougie nudged his elbow. "Go on, kid. Get it over and done with and they'll stop their moaning."

Zack nodded. Seconds later, his hand wedged through the gap and his shoulder pressed up against the door as Colton held it as far open as possible, Zack grunted and said, "I... I think I can feel... yeah. It's a padlock. The door's been padlocked." He pulled his arm free and started rubbing it.

Colton let the door close and rested his back against it.

"It's padlocked? Why...?" Even as she asked the question, Molly knew the answer.

14

DOUGIE

"Because they're cowards, that's why. All guards are cowards." Dougie clenched his fists at his sides and fought the urge to kick something.

"They padlocked it to keep the prisoners in. They've retreated." Rambo looked like he wanted to punch something too. Although, with his messed-up knuckles, he wouldn't stand much of a chance.

"But they knew we were in here..." Lucky said in a whiny voice to no one in particular.

Dougie let out a loud sharp laugh. Lucky's stupid floppy hair fell in front of his face as he looked desperately from his teacher to the bus driver. Dougie rolled his eyes. "Yeah, they knew you were here. And they didn't care."

"Oh, come on. Of course, they *care*—we're kids." The kid—Erik— who knew way too much about EMPs was fronting up to Dougie, and from the look on his face Dougie knew instantly that *this* kid was one of his least favorite kind of criminal; *this* kid thought he was clever. Thought he was above people like Dougie. Thought he was too smart to get caught. Dougie knew plenty of guys like that. Guys who'd committed easy crimes like fraud. Cybercrimes. Victimless crimes. Except, in the end, they all ended up in places like Fairfield, didn't they?

"Really? What makes you think you matter more than we do?" Dougie tapped his chest as he said 'we'.

Erik scoffed. "Because we're *kids*."

"Delinquent kids," Dougie bit back. "What makes you think they'd give a damn whether you were okay or not? You're on the same road most of the guys in here started out on. You're no different. It's only a matter of time before you end up in here as an inmate, so you might as well get used to it." Dougie adjusted the tone of his voice, so it wasn't quite as antagonistic as he felt. "Get used to being treated like your life doesn't matter. Because that's what it's like in here. No one gives a damn."

As the teacher opened her mouth to reprimand him, Dougie stalked away from the group. He'd barely moved a couple of feet when his sneaker scratched against something on the ground. Looking down, he smiled. Someone, an inmate, had dropped a shiv. A razor blade taped to an old toothbrush handle, its tip was covered in blood, but this didn't stop Dougie from pretending to adjust his shoelaces and slipping it into his sock. When he stood up, he braced his hands behind his head and tried to think. Those damn guards had made his life hell for years. If the world outside had crumbled, then there wasn't going to be a parole hearing and there'd be no one to care about, or even notice, his heroic behavior helping the kids to escape. In which case, he might as well have stuck with Luther and had some fun.

Glancing back at the teacher and the bus driver, who were tapping politely on the door as if someone would open it for them, he bit the inside of his cheek and considered his options. He could leave them behind, go join Luther. Use his new-found weapon to take revenge on every single guard who'd never given him a shot or looked at him like dirt. But that seemed a little short-sighted. What if Zack was right? What did he say? That the prison was like a castle now. A castle. A castle....

Dougie knew nothing about EMPs, but he'd had a cell mate a few years ago who was big into the whole prepper scene. The guy had spent hours drilling Dougie on what to do if the power went out and now, Dougie was beginning to wish he'd listened. The only thing he could remember was what the guy had said about resources—there'll be a fight for resources. Those with food, water, and shelter will thrive. Those without will be toast. So perhaps the kid was right. Perhaps fate was, for once, giving Dougie a sign; a sign to stay put.

Behind him, the teacher was speaking in a not very discreet whisper to the bus driver. *What do we do now? Where do we go? It'll be getting dark soon... blah, blah, blah.* Then Dougie heard a loud crash. He turned around to see Erik running at the door—still trying to show off. In an almost comical fashion, he slammed his weedy goth body into it. It barely moved. "Come on, guys." He turned to his friends. "If we all do it together...."

"It's *padlocked*, you idiot, it wouldn't budge even if there were twenty of us trying to bash it down." Zack had folded his arms and was watching his classmates. Dougie didn't *like* this kid. But he was warming to him.

"I don't take advice from psychos," Erik bit back.

In that second, something in Zack's expression changed. Dougie saw it. Clear as day. He was done taking their shit. "What did you say?" Zack's arms were straight as arrows at his sides, his forearms twitching.

"Boys...." The teacher had looked up from her conversation with the bus driver.

"You heard me." The goth boy—Erik? Was that his name?—folded his arms and tipped his chin at Zack. "You're just like your brother. You

93

shouldn't be visiting this place; you should be locked up here. In fact, we might as well do the world a favor and leave you here."

Dougie's eyes flitted from one boy to the next. They were squaring up to each other—a miniature version of the kind of fight Dougie had seen a million times before. Erik was bigger than Zack. He was tall and fit, but Zack was scrawny. The kind of guy who looked like he might snap in half if he was caught by a strong breeze. Dougie had a sneaking suspicion he could prove to be more of a whip than a wimp.

For a moment, Dougie thought Zack might back down. His muscles relaxed, and he looked like he was going to turn away. Then suddenly, he charged at the other boy, ran toward him and lowered his head like a battering ram so that it slammed into Erik's chest.

Dougie was impressed. Zack had pinned Erik up against the padlocked door and was pummeling him with clumsy but vicious fists. Erik began to smack him back but couldn't get free enough to throw a good punch.

"Boys! Stop!" The teacher had run forward and was pulling at Zack's arms, but it wasn't until the bus driver came to her aid that she managed to pry him away. Fussing over him as if he were a wounded soldier, the two girls ran up to Erik and tugged him away from the door. His nose was bleeding, and his eye was already swelling up. Zack, other than a small wound on his temple, looked relatively unscathed.

"That's it!" The teacher was yelling, and it was making her cheeks flush a delicious shade of pink, bringing out the freckles on the bridge of her nose. "Enough. Don't you realize how serious this is?" She put her hands on her hips and stared angrily at her five students. "We should be focusing on getting out of here, not making catty comments or *fighting* amongst ourselves. It stops. Now. Do. You. Understand me?"

Erik and Zack both hung their heads, but when Zack looked up, Dougie was certain he saw a glint of pride in his face that wasn't there a few minutes ago.

15

MOLLY

As she paced away from the group and tried to stop herself from punching one of the kids for being so flipping stupid, Molly tried to work out what time it was. They'd arrived at eleven-thirty. Which meant it would probably be getting dark soon, and she very much didn't want to still be stuck inside the prison at night. If the generator went again, for good this time, that would be it; they'd be in the pitch dark surrounded by murderers and rapists. Which wasn't an option.

"Isn't there usually a rec room or something that the Guard's Station looks out onto? I mean, it's not a sealed box, is it?" Molly was looking at Dougie and feeling irritated that—although he seemed to do what-ever she asked of him—he wasn't exactly forthright in coming up with ideas.

Slowly, as if he were thinking about it very hard, Dougie nodded. "Yeah," he said. "Come to think of it, you're right. It's got a window into the cafeteria. But it's reinforced glass."

"That doesn't matter," Molly said briskly. "If they see us, they'll undo the padlock. They won't just leave us in here."

Dougie smirked, clearly unsure of the idea, but Molly didn't have time to stop and argue with him about it. Gesturing for the others to follow, she asked him to show them the way.

The cafeteria wasn't far, and the door wasn't locked. As Colton pushed it open, motioning for the others to stay back until he'd verified the coast was clear, Molly held her breath. A voice in her head was telling her that somewhere with food would, surely, be the kind of place prisoners would congregate, but when they entered, it was empty.

The smell of the room reminded her of hospitals—the memory of stale, microwaved food and harsh cleaning products hung in the air. Not dissimilar to the school lunchroom, long empty trestle tables with benches on either side lined the room, and, at the far end, there was an empty serving station and a door, which Molly assumed led to the kitchen.

At the end closest to them, a window—just as Dougie had promised—took up almost half of the entire wall. Molly ran to it. Her boot heels clopped loudly on the slick concrete floor.

"Dougie, guard the door," she yelled.

"Yes Ma'am," he replied sarcastically.

Beyond the glass, the Guard's Station was in darkness. Molly looked up. Two small skylights that exposed dusky pink flashes of sky told her it was approaching sunset. Maybe the guards really had left. Made a run for it and abandoned them to their fate. She was starting to feel tearful but bit back the lump in her throat and began to knock on the glass.

"It's reinforced," Colton said quietly.

"Yes, but if we can get someone to hear us..."

He gave her a look full of something that resembled pity. She was desperate, and it was beginning to show. With a nod, he joined her, knocking his bandaged fists against the glass and telling the kids to do the same.

At first, the kids' attempts were pretty weak. But as they got into it, trying to bang louder and harder than the person next to them, they began to laugh. The sound of their giggles eased the ache in Molly's chest; despite everything, they were laughing. That had to be a good sign.

Zack, however, wasn't laughing. As Molly and the others finally gave up and stepped back, a little breathless, she noticed that Zack had stayed over by the door and that Dougie was mumbling something in Zack's ear. It made Zack grin, and almost instantly the notion Molly had felt a moment ago—that everything was going to be okay—disappeared; the sooner she got the kids out of here, and Zack away from Dougie, the better.

She had turned and was about to start banging again when Jenna tugged at her arm. "Miss O'Neil, I'm sorry but I *really* need to use the bathroom."

Molly was about to ask her whether she couldn't hold her bladder until they were out of imminent danger, but the look on Jenna's face told her she really couldn't.

"Okay, guys. Stop." A little louder, she added, "Stop!"

The boys paused, fists in the air, and looked at her. Scarlett, who was standing next to Jenna, tugged her sleeve and asked if she was okay.

"I am. I just…."

"We need to find a bathroom," Molly said, hands on hips.

Colton looked at her quizzically.

"Seriously?" Erik said, exasperated. "You need a bathroom break right this second?"

By this point, Jenna was bobbing up and down on the balls of her feet. "I'm sorry, I've needed to pee pretty much since we got here, and I don't think I can hold it anymore."

"There's a trash can over there, help yourself," Dougie said loudly, pointing to a half-full trash can down near the serving hatch as he peeked through the crack in the door to confirm no one was approaching.

Molly looked at Jenna. The poor girl seemed like she might pass out at the thought of having to pee in a trash can in front of her friends. "Isn't there a washroom nearby?" Molly was looking at Dougie, willing him to—just once—be a little more helpful.

"Toilet block's opposite. Down the hall."

"Not a good idea," Colton said firmly.

Molly nodded. He was right. It was *not* a good idea for them to go wandering off on their own. "Okay, guys, you keep trying to get the guards' attention. Jenna, come with me. Anyone else need to go? Scarlett?" Scarlett shook her head fervently.

As Molly marched Jenna in the direction of the trash can, the girl looked at her with wide worried eyes. "Miss O'Neil, I don't think I can go if they're right there." She glanced over her shoulder at the others, who'd resumed their banging and shouting.

"Of course not," she said. "We'll go back there."

Walking straight past the trash can and heading for the serving hatch, Molly took hold of Jenna's hand and squeezed it.

At the hatch, Molly tried the door next to it, but it was locked, so she gave Jenna a leg up and the two of them scrambled over the empty serving trays into the large empty kitchen.

A rack of shelves in front of them held pots and pans of various shapes and sizes, although looking at the wall Molly realized that anything sharp was locked in a reinforced glass case.

"Okay," she said, "pick a pot."

Jenna grabbed a large saucepan and looked around. In the corner of the room, a plastic curtain separated the pantry from the rest of the kitchen.

"Let me check it first," Molly said, taking her broken flashlight from her pocket and holding it above her head in case she needed to hit someone with it.

Gingerly, she pulled aside the plastic. Apart from bags of pasta, canned food, and a tub of what looked like out-of-date coleslaw, the pantry was empty. "Okay, go for it," Molly said, stepping back to let Jenna through.

"Thanks, Miss O'Neil." Jenna disappeared into the pantry and Molly stood guard. A few seconds later, Jenna called, "I don't suppose you could sing or something? I can't go when people are listening."

Molly hid a smile and rolled her eyes; she had a terrible singing voice. Breaking into a loud rendition of "Sweet Home Alabama", she scanned the rest of the kitchen. If those knives had been accessible, they could have armed themselves properly. She squinted at the lock, but it looked different from anything that was on Colton's set of keys.

Finally, Jenna emerged.

"Better?" Molly asked.

Jenna breathed a sigh of relief. "Much. Do you need to...?" she glanced back at the pantry.

Molly was about to say no, but then she realized that actually, yes, she did need to.

"It's okay, I'll keep watch."

"All right, I'll be quick." Molly ducked behind the curtain and unbuttoned her jeans.

"Do you need me to sing?" Jenna asked.

"Sure, why not."

"Oh, for a land where I can be freeeee," Jenna belted out a loud, surprisingly in-tune verse from a song Molly had never heard before.

When she stopped abruptly, Molly laughed. "What happened? You forget the words?" She stood up, refastened her jeans, and ducked back out of the curtain.

"Jenna?" Her heart flipped over in her chest. Jenna had vanished. "Jenna, this isn't funny. Where are you?" Dashing around the tall shelves in the middle of the kitchen, before she had chance to call for the others, Molly stopped dead in her tracks.

In front of her, a skinny sunken-eyed inmate had his arms clasped around Jenna and was holding a makeshift knife to her throat.

Molly held up her hands, palms out, and waved them. "Okay, it's okay, Jenna."

"Where in the world did you come from?" the inmate spat as he talked.

"Let her go," Molly said firmly. "She's just a kid."

"I can see that." The inmate made a show of sniffing Jenna's hair, and Molly watched as a tear rolled down her cheek.

Molly looked at her hand. The flashlight was useless against a knife. "What do you want?" she asked.

The inmate licked his lips. "Ain't decided yet." He cocked his head and pushed the blade a little closer to Jenna's throat.

"Let her go. Deal with me instead." Molly had no idea what she was offering, but she knew she'd do pretty much anything to keep Jenna safe.

"Interesting offer," the inmate said, lowering the knife ever so slightly. "But how do I know you won't run as soon as I let her go?"

"I won't," Molly said firmly. "I swear." She glanced at her hands. "And here, take these." She slipped the expensive looking costume jewelry from her fingers, hoping it looked like real gold, then unclasped the locket she always wore around her neck. "This too." Shrugging, she added, "It's not as if I'll need it now that the power's gone for good. Money won't really mean anything anymore, will it?"

As Molly spoke, she saw Jenna's eyes widen.

"What did you say?" Okay, good. She'd caught his attention.

"The power. An EMP has taken it out and, from the little I know about it, it won't be coming back any time soon."

"EMP? What the hell are you talking about?"

Molly held out her hand, offering him the flashlight. "See. Even the flashlights don't work."

Molly braced herself, but the inmate didn't hesitate. As soon as she held it out, he reached for it, lowering the hand at Jenna's throat so he could lean forward and take it.

And in the split second that the blade was away from her, Jenna seized her chance. With all the force she could muster, she thrust her elbow into the inmate's ribs, then ducked out of his grip and kicked his legs from beneath him.

"Run!" Molly yelled as she heaved a shelf-load of metal pans down on top of the inmate.

Trying to push them off, he struggled to stand up and lunged for Molly, but she hurled herself toward the serving hatch and scrambled through after Jenna.

Behind her, the inmate screamed, calling for help, and Molly heard more men pound into the kitchen.

At the opposite end of the cafeteria the others had stopped banging and were staring in her direction. As they saw Molly and Jenna, their faces changed.

"What happened?" Colton started to jog over to them, but Molly yelled, "We need to get out of here!"

As Jenna reached Colton, and he put his arm around her, ushering her back to the group, a sharp clattering noise made Molly's insides plummet. She stopped, looking at Dougie, who was still standing by the door. "Shit," he muttered.

Molly followed his gaze and, as she did, her blood ran cold.

On the other side of the serving station, four prisoners were staring at them. The one Jenna had escaped from licked his lips. He was waving his knife. Staring at Molly, he pressed his index finger on its tip and let out a bone chilling laugh.

"Run..." Dougie whispered at first, but then shouted. "Run! Now!"

As Molly and the kids flew toward the door, the weapon-wielding prisoners scrambled through the serving hatch, sending metal trays clattering across the room. Dougie reached the door first, yanked it open and let it start to swing backwards as he ran through. Colton was next and held it while Molly and the kids escaped.

"This way!" Dougie started to turn left, but another group of prisoners had appeared at the end of the hallway. Seeing Dougie, they started to yell. At first, they sounded friendly. When they saw Molly and the kids, it changed. One of them was holding something. It looked like metal piping, and he banged it hard on the wall. "Come here, pretty lady!" he shouted at Molly.

"Hey, Dougie, aren't you going to share your toys?" another voice yelled.

As Dougie wavered, looking as if he wasn't sure whether to stick with her and the kids or switch sides and turn them over, Colton grabbed Molly's arm and pulled her back toward the padlocked door outside the Guard's Station. Molly's legs felt like they might fall out from under her. The kids were silent and running hard, but she knew that when they got to the door they'd be stuck. They were steaming toward a dead end and no matter how strong Colton was, he couldn't protect them against fifty angry men.

"The door's open!" Colton yelled. She must have misheard. Open? Molly looked up; he was right.

"They heard us! The guards heard us!" Scarlett was clutching the pepper spray Molly had given her and upped her pace, hurtling toward the now open door.

"Hey!" Colton yelled again. "Help us!" Ahead, a figure was emerging from the doorway. And another. Dressed in riot gear and holding shotguns, they strode into the corridor. Molly's heart almost clean flipped over in her chest, but before she could speak, she saw one of the figures raise their arm and throw something. A canister flew over their heads and clattered as it hit the ground.

"Cover your eyes...." Colton had grabbed hold of her, but it was too late. Gas filled the hallway. Molly began to cough. Her eyes burned. Scarlett was screaming. Then someone else was at her elbow, dragging her forward through the door, and telling her to sit down with her back up against the wall.

A few excruciating moments later, through eyes streaming with tears, Molly looked up. The kids were huddled together. Colton was wiping his face with his bandaged hands, and the door was locked again. Except, this time, they were on the right side of it.

16

LAURA

L aura had changed out of her workout clothes into jeans and a pale blue sweater and was now in the living room staring out of the window. Argent was next to her, sitting at attention so that her palm could rest on the flat of his head. She'd spent the last few hours going room-by-room through the house, collecting and cataloging anything that could be useful for a world in which electricity had ceased to exist.

At first, a strange sense of purpose had settled over her. Usually, there was no *real* point to her day. She no longer worked, and the kids were old enough to get themselves out of the house in the mornings. Most of the time, she got up late, worked out, did some housework, took Argent for a run to burn off some energy, then worked out some more. That was it. Suddenly, though, she had a task; something that needed to be done. Quickly.

She had started in the kitchen. As she'd emptied the cupboards and begun to list the contents on a notepad she'd found in one of the drawers—four packets of pasta, six cans of chopped tomatoes, rice, more rice—she'd thanked God that she stayed up late one night and sat through one of those awful 'end of the world' documentaries on Netflix. At the time, she'd rolled her eyes at the stupidity of it. Now, she was reeling through her brain desperately trying to remember what the presenter had said: canned goods, dried goods, bottled water....

After the kitchen, Laura had headed to the garage. Stacked at the back next to Alex's meager selection of tools were several crates of bottled water with added electrolytes. When she was a PT, she'd bought them in bulk, and had never quite gotten out of the habit. There were also a few old cartons of protein powder, which eased the knot in Laura's chest a little—even if they had to live on protein shakes and water for a few weeks, they'd survive.

Now, as she watched the sky outside grow rapidly darker and listened to the unnatural lack of sound that hung in the air, she began to pick nervously at the hem of her sweater. What if it was longer than a few weeks? If the power was out for good, what would they do when the bottled water ran out?

Her mind was running away from her. Suddenly, she was thinking about the water supply, the sewage system, *food*. Where would it all come from?

Laura slammed her eyes shut. Her back was starting to ache—a dull, familiar throb that would soon become a shooting pain that took her breath away if she moved so much as an inch.

Before rehab, before the painkillers she was taking became a problem, she'd have reached for her prescription bottle and swallowed a couple of pills without even thinking about it. Now, she couldn't. A couple of pills would lead to a couple more. Before long, she'd run out. She'd ask her doctor and they'd say, *But, Laura, you should have plenty left.* They'd look at her with such deep concern that she'd laugh, shake her head, say, *Oh, gosh. Really? I must have misplaced a bottle.* Then she'd drive to a new doctor, shame burning in her stomach. She'd get a new prescription. Then the cycle would start all over again.

Laura nestled her fingers into Argent's fur and sighed at the warmth of it. She didn't need pills. Stress was making her pain worse. As soon as Alex returned with the kids, she'd feel better.

Without thinking, Laura wheeled over to the coffee table and picked up her cell phone to check for a message from Alex. Staring at the dead, unnaturally black screen, she bit her lip. Her fingers tightened around it. Of course, he couldn't text her. She would have to wait.

Next to her, Argent nuzzled the palm of her hand. His nose was cold and wet. "Oh," she said, glancing at the clock before remembering that it wasn't ticking, "I'm sorry, boy. Is it dinner time?"

Understanding her immediately, Argent got up and walked toward the kitchen. Glad of something to do, Laura followed him. She'd just finished scraping dog food into a bowl, and wishing she'd picked up a few more bags of kibble when she was last at the grocery store, when she heard a knock at the door.

Dropping the empty container, she headed for the door as quickly as she could and was about to fling it open when she stopped, her hand reaching for the doorknob. She flexed her fingers. From the chair, she couldn't see through the peephole in the door and, of course, the video doorbell Alex had installed wasn't working.

"Who is it?" she called. As she spoke, Argent left his food and came to stand beside her, head cocked, staring at the door.

"Laura? It's Dave. Are you okay?"

Laura released the breath she'd been holding in her chest and, for a moment, rested her forehead on the door. It was Dave. Only Dave. They'd been in rehab together, had sat in group sessions baring their souls to the world, and had been friends ever since. Thank God, she wouldn't be alone anymore.

Opening the door, Laura smiled. "What are you doing here?" she asked, glancing furtively up and down the street.

"I was on the outskirts of town, driving. My car just stopped." Dave's face was a little gray around the edges. "Just like that… stopped. I wasn't going fast, but this other car crashed into me and pushed me off the road." He rubbed the back of his neck and shook his head. "I started walking and when I ended up here, I thought…." He trailed off and breathed out slowly.

Laura shuddered. "Of course. Come in." She opened the door wider and moved aside for Dave to enter. As she closed it again, she noticed Dave inch backwards.

"Is he friendly?" He was looking at Argent.

"Oh, sure." Laura patted Argent's head. "He's my service dog. He'd be a hopeless guard dog." Almost as soon as she spoke, Argent began to growl. Laura frowned at him. His hackles were up, his head was lowered, and he was staring at Dave. Laura laughed and ruffled the dog's ears. "Silly boy, don't show me up now that I've said you're friendly." But Argent's top lip had curled upwards to reveal a row of extremely sharp teeth and his growl suddenly turned into a bark.

Dave was now pressed against the wall looking absolutely terrified.

"I'm so sorry…." Laura tugged Argent's collar and moved so that she was blocking Dave from view. "Argent, no," she said firmly. "Dave is a friend." When Argent didn't seem to be listening to her, Laura reached for his leash, which was on a hook by the door, clipped it on, and said, "Come on, boy, come have some time out in your crate." In the kitchen, she secured him in the crate he'd slept in since he was a puppy and slipped a few treats through the bars.

Dave, who had followed her from the hallway, was now standing in the living room looking nervously at the crate in the kitchen. "Dogs usually like me," he said with a shrug.

"I'm sorry, I think he's picking up on my stress. And with Alex not home…" she trailed off. Something inside her head told her that perhaps she shouldn't have admitted she was alone. But she shook it loose; Dave was a friend. She was being paranoid.

"Where is Alex?" Dave was looking around as if he expected Laura's husband to pop out from behind the curtains at any moment.

"Fetching the kids home. Do you know what's happened?" Laura offered Dave a bottle of water from the kitchen counter and he accepted it, swallowing down at least half before coming up for air. When he looked at her vacantly, she began to explain. "It seems like the power's out everywhere. Everywhere in Maine, at least. Anything that runs on electricity or has a circuit board is dead."

Dave swept his fingers across his forehead, wiping away invisible sweat, and let out a low whistle. "Shit. That's—"

"Hard to take in?" Laura said. "Tell me about it."

"So, when will Alex be back?" Dave had perched on the corner of the sofa and was looking at his feet as he spoke.

"Soon," Laura said. "Any minute now."

"How's your back?" Dave was still finding it hard to look at her. "How's the pain these days? It's been a while since we saw each other."

Laura nodded. For a while, they'd met at weekly outpatient sessions, but for at least a month, Dave hadn't been there. "It's okay," she said softly.

"Are they going to do any more surgeries?" Dave was looking around the room, taking in the family photos, and was rubbing his thighs with the palms of his hands. He was sweating, even though it wasn't warm, and Laura wondered if he'd been running before he got to the house.

Laura shifted in her chair; she didn't really want to get into all this. Not now. "No," she said, hoping that if she answered the question they could move on and talk about something else. "The last three didn't work, they only made the pain worse. So, I said no more. If I'm going to stay clean, I can't risk it."

Dave nodded slowly. "So, you're still clean?" His eyes darted across her face.

"Yes." Laura laced her fingers together in her lap. "I am."

For a long moment, Dave didn't move. Then his lips spread into a grin and he made a loud *pffft* sound with his lips. "Laura, come on. It's me. You don't have to lie. There's no one else here. No nurses, no therapists, no husband."

Laura inched her chair backwards, a tiny amount. Something wasn't right. Then it hit her; Dave wasn't here by chance. He was here looking for drugs.

"I'm clean, Dave. There are no painkillers in the house. Not even aspirin."

Slowly, Dave stood up. "Come on, Laura." He was walking toward her. "Tell me the truth. You're an addict. I'm an addict. And we addicts *always* have an emergency supply. So, where is it? In your underwear drawer? Behind the toilet tank?" He was speaking through clenched teeth, and then leaned down, grabbing hold of the arms of Laura's chair, his face inches from hers. "I'll ask again, one more time... where is your stash?"

Laura started to back away. Trying to sound calm and authoritative, she pointed to the door. "Dave, I think it's best for everyone if you leave now. If Alex finds you here—"

Before she could finish, Dave had grabbed the back of her chair and begun to push.

"Dave! Stop!" Laura tried to stop the wheels turning but he wouldn't let go and the rubber grated angrily against her palms. Argent began to bark. A staccato, on-off bark to start with, and then almost a howl.

Dave was pushing her down the hall, shoving doors open. When he came to Laura and Alex's bedroom, he wheeled her inside. Panic gripped Laura's chest. She was helpless. Utterly helpless. She should have grabbed a gun before opening the door. She should have been smarter. Dave stopped in front of her walk-in closet, flung the doors open, then grabbed Laura's chair and tipped it up, spilling her onto the floor.

Instantly, a lightning rod of pain shot up Laura's back. She cried out, but Dave kicked her so that she rolled inside, and then he slammed the doors closed.

17

DOUGIE

Dougie's eyes were still streaming. Fucking tear gas. Still, he supposed he should be grateful the guards had taken him with them. Or should he? Dougie stood up from where he'd been crouched on the floor and wiped his red watery eyes with the back of his hand. To the prisoners on the other side of the padlocked door, Dougie now looked like a snitch. Pure and simple. Which meant he had only one option... find a way to come out on top.

"Dougie was helping us." The teacher was talking to one of the guards not wearing riot gear. The bus driver nodded, although a little reluctantly.

"It's true," he said. "Dougie came back to fetch us from the Scared Straight room and guided us through the prison."

The guard, a big black guy who Dougie didn't recognize, nodded. "Okay then, follow me." He gestured for the group to follow him down the corridor.

They were in the only section of the prison that Dougie had never entered; the section that housed the Warden's office, the staff break room, the main Guard's Station, and a bunch of supply closets. As they moved down the corridor, Dougie noticed that most of the guards they passed were not wearing riot gear. That seemed to be reserved for the ones manning the door.

The Guard's Station, which looked onto the cafeteria, was empty—presumably because they didn't want the prisoners to know they were in here—but none of the other doors appeared to be locked. As they walked, the kids whispered between themselves, but the teacher and the bus driver remained silent.

"Here…." The guard ushered them into the staff break room and the kids immediately sat down on a large brown leather sofa, clearly pleased to see something that resembled home.

The room was bigger than Dougie had expected. He bit the inside of his cheek; all this time, the guards had been living it up between shifts, playing pool and eating microwave pizzas, while the prisoners barely got an hour of natural daylight, let alone decent food or something comfortable to sit on.

The teacher had spotted a pot of coffee and gestured to it. "May I?" she asked.

The guard nodded. "Sure. But it's cold."

While the teacher poured herself a mug, the kids reached for bottles of water that were stacked on the coffee table in front of them.

"Do you have anything the kids could eat?" the teacher asked.

Dougie fought the urge to roll his eyes. Eat? Was she serious?

The guard seemed similarly unimpressed but tossed a multipack of potato chips at the students, then leaned against the large table in the middle of the room. A couple of other guards were milling around. One, at the far end, was standing next to a door, which was intriguing.

What's behind there, I wonder? Dougie took a bag of chips for himself and began to eat them as slowly as he could manage.

Behind him, the bus driver was asking the guard to fill him in.

"We're still running off the generator. Power seems to be out just about everywhere and..." the guard paused, and when Dougie glanced at him, he was shaking his head, "we can't get ahold of the police. Radios are dead. Nothing."

"Scarlett and Erik think it's an EMP," the teacher said softly. "They're computer whizzes. Apparently—"

"I know what an EMP is," the guard cut her off, then stood up. "Listen, our priority right now is to sit tight, and keep this section of the prison secure. That's all we can do. Wait."

"What about the warden?" Colton asked the question, and Dougie wondered whether he was thinking of what Dougie had told them back in the visitor room.

"The warden left before the power went out, which means he's sure to be back soon with reinforcements." The guard was doing his best to sound as if he believed what he was saying, but Dougie wasn't falling for it; if the world was ending, the last thing on the warden's mind would be returning to the prison.

"So, you folks wait in here. We've got guards manning all the doors into this section of the prison. You'll be safe here."

As the guard left, two others entered and positioned themselves near the door. They were staring at Dougie, and he knew exactly what they'd been told to do—watch him, make sure he doesn't do anything he isn't supposed to.

Crushing his empty chip bag, he stood up and sauntered over to the trash can near the now defunct fridge. He tossed the bag inside, then leaned against the wall. On the couch, Zack was sitting with his arms folded, ignoring his classmates.

"Hey, Zack?" Dougie raised his voice and pretended not to notice when everyone stared at him. "Bring me a bottle of water, dude?"

Zack hesitated, looked at the guards, then nodded.

"Good man." Dougie grabbed the bottle and took a drawn-out sip. Then he lowered his voice, purposefully resting his hand on Zack's shoulder. "So," he said, "how's the head?"

Zack reached up and touched his temple with his index finger. "Fine. It doesn't hurt."

Dougie took his hand away and folded his arms. "Good," he said quietly. "Now, listen. What you were saying about this EMP...."

"Yeah?"

"About this place being safe...?" Dougie was studying the kid's face, but trying to keep his expression lighthearted, as if they were having a mentor-to-mentee conversation.

Zack shrugged. "Well, yes. If the world outside is falling apart, then the prison is exactly where you want to be. You have light, heat...." Zack met Dougie's eyes. His lips twitched at the corner. "It's the kind of place that could be a castle... if the right person was in charge of it."

Dougie's lips twitched too. The kid was smart. He could see things, which meant he could be very, very useful.

Still looking into Dougie's eyes, Zack tilted his head. "What are you planning to do with the shiv?"

Dougie's eyes narrowed almost imperceptibly.

"The one you slipped into your sock?"

"So, you saw that, huh?" Dougie thought he'd been quick, discreet. The second he saw it lying on the floor, he'd put his foot on it, bent down to adjust his shoe, tucked it into the palm of his hand, then into his pants. He'd done it before. And he'd never been caught.

Zack nodded.

"Well, kid. That's for emergencies." He chuckled, more amused than annoyed that he'd been caught out by a lanky teenager. Tipping his head toward the other end of the room, indicating Zack should follow him, Dougie began to walk. He could feel the guards watching him, but focused on Zack. Just mentor and mentee. Taking a walk.

They were by the pool table when Dougie said, abruptly, "Who's Tommy?"

Zack stopped, pressed his lips together, then kept walking. "You know who he is."

They were passing the door, which had a guard standing next to it. Dougie wanted to look through the glass, but there was no way to stop without making it obvious, so he kept walking. "Your older brother?" Dougie looked at Zack, who nodded.

"He's in jail."

Sore spot, Dougie thought, watching Zack's face grow pale. *Big bro's gone and abandoned you. I get that.*

"Everyone used to be afraid of him," Zack said, as if this were something Dougie should be impressed by. "He was big. Didn't take shit from anyone."

They were on their second loop of the room, so Dougie stopped a little way up from the door he had his eye on. That guard would move eventually. He had to. "Really?" he said to Zack, prodding him to talk more. Mentor and mentee. Talking. Bonding.

"Yeah."

"What did he do to get himself put away?"

Zack tipped his chin up. Was he proud? Or pretending to be proud? "Stole a car. Crashed it. Killed a guy."

Dougie nodded.

"It was years ago, but people still talk shit about him. They're always whispering about it when I walk past—"

"At school?"

Zack gave a quick nod. "They say he killed more than one guy. Maybe a cop. Maybe even our dad."

"Your dad?" Dougie couldn't help frowning.

Zack shrugged. "We don't know where he is. So…."

"So, people filled in the blanks?"

"Pretty much. And just 'cos he's a murderer, they think I am too. Or that I could be."

Dougie was nodding sympathetically, but out of the corner of his eye he saw the guards near the door that led into the hallway beckon over the other guard—the one standing near *his* door. Trying not to move too quickly, Dougie upped his pace a little. When they reached the door, he slowed down again. Zack was still talking. He was on Dougie's left, so when Dougie turned to him, he was able to look right past him, at the door.

"They never even gave me a chance. As soon as Tommy went to jail, that was it." Zack sniffed loudly. Was he about to cry?

Dougie stopped, turned his back to the room and put his hands firmly on Zack's shoulders. Zack was facing away from the unguarded door. Dougie dipped his head and looked at him. "Listen," he said. *Mentor and mentee.* "I get it. It must suck to live in the shadow of someone like that."

Zack blinked quickly, and Dougie instantly knew that he'd said the right thing. "Yeah," he said. "It does."

Dougie straightened up and was about to muster up some more wisdom that he could impart when the teacher appeared beside them.

"Zack," she said, "is everything okay?"

"Sure it is," Dougie answered for him. "We were talking about Zack's brother."

The teacher nodded, then folded her arms in front of her chest. "I see. Well, Zack, you know the best way to deal with the Tommy situation is to prove to everyone that you're different. That you're not the same as your brother."

Dougie bit back a smile; she thought she knew kids like Zack, but she didn't. She didn't have a clue.

"I am *nothing* like him," Zack spat, stalking away from the pair of them. "I never have been. It's only people like *you* who assume that I am."

Watching him walk away, Dougie looked at the teacher. She sighed and glared at Dougie before trailing after Zack. After a few short moments, Dougie walked away from the door and followed her back to the brown leather couch.

A few minutes later, the guard once again took up his post, but it didn't matter, because while Zack had been whining on about his brother, Dougie had gotten a good look through the window. He knew what was in there now and, to be frank, he couldn't believe they had only one guard watching over it. Behind that door was a cage. And in that cage were weapons. Guns. More guns.

Dougie sucked in his cheeks, biting them between his back teeth as his mind began to whirr.

There were ten times more prisoners than guards, and the only reason they hadn't taken over the place yet was that they didn't have what the guards had—weapons. Except, now, Dougie knew exactly where the weapons were. He just needed to figure out how to get his hands on them without getting himself killed in the process.

18

TOMMY

It took just under an hour for Tommy to reach the train tracks on the outskirts of the neighborhood. The bridge above was littered with abandoned cars, but very few people. Adjusting his bag on his shoulder, Tommy shuddered. He'd been away for six years. *Six* years. Zack was a little kid when he left, and that had been the worst thing about it.

In fact, compared to home, prison wasn't bad. He'd been lucky. Given his age and that it was his first offense, the judge had taken pity on him and had sent him to the minimum-security prison, which he didn't deserve but was thankful for. Not Fairfield. Not where the *real* bad guys were sent.

At home, there were times when they barely had electricity or running water or food on the table. In prison, those things were provided free of charge. Sure, it was no holiday camp, but it beat waking up every day and wondering whether he'd find his mom dead on the couch from a meth overdose.

Leaving Zack was a different matter, though. Leaving Zack was hard.

Their whole lives, Tommy had tried to protect his little brother from their deadbeat mom and her even worse deadbeat boyfriends. Tommy had made sure he was the one to clear up after her, to get her into bed when she was too strung out to even walk, to make sure she was propped on her side, so she didn't choke on her own vomit. He remembered the number of times he'd willingly pawned his crap when she ran out of money because watching her in withdrawal was worse than watching her high.

He knew, when he got locked away, what that meant for Zack; it meant whatever sliver of childhood he'd had was over. It was his turn to be the grownup.

Talking it over with Luke one day, he'd decided—after Zack failed to show for three visitor sessions in a row—to call social services. Somehow, the Hargrove family had slipped under their radar. Somehow, they'd never been allocated a social worker. No one had ever checked on them at home or told Mom to get clean if she wanted to keep her boys.

So Tommy had called them. When they asked for his name, though, he'd found himself unable to say it. As much as he hated himself for it, he couldn't report his own mother.

Now, as he walked in the shadow of the run-down apartment buildings near the tracks, he prayed that he hadn't made an enormous mistake.

Usually, the perpetual sound of sirens punctured the air in Southside. Today, it was eerily quiet. He was approaching the liquor store around the block from his house when he heard shouting. Glass smashing. Whoops and hollers, but no alarms.

Tommy stopped and peered around the corner of the laundromat. He could see the window of the liquor store, splintered into a million pieces and now scattered across the sidewalk. There was no one in sight. He was about to make a move, dart in front of the liquor store and around the corner, when a large group of teenagers hurtled into view. Seeing the smashed window, they stopped.

"Someone got here first!" one of them yelled, throwing down the baseball bat he'd been holding.

"Doesn't mean there's nothing left. I say we go in." Another picked up the bat and handed it back.

Tommy looked behind him. He could circle back and go around the block, but it would take longer. His house was only a minute's walk from where he was standing, and while he wasn't *afraid* of the angry-looking kids, he didn't want a confrontation. Not now. Not when all he was trying to do was reach his brother.

Narrowing his eyes at the group of teenagers, he scanned their faces for one that was familiar. Was Zack among them? No. No, Zack wasn't there.

They looked like they were about to charge into the store when the group who'd broken in appeared from inside, clambering back through the broken window.

The two groups stared at each other.

Tommy swallowed hard. *Shit.*

And then it happened… the one with the baseball bat squared up to a member of the opposite group. They did the same. For a long, shaky moment, no one made a move. They just stared and shouted and waved whatever makeshift weapons they were holding.

Then one broke ranks. There was a holler, and the sound of metal meeting someone's skull.

Tommy's stomach lurched as he saw a boy who couldn't have been much older than Zack fall to the ground.

Finally, he made his move. Darting across the street and staying in the shadow of the hedges opposite, he ran as fast as he could past the liquor store. When he rounded the corner, he stopped.

There it was. Home.

Despite it being his house, Tommy knocked on the door. There was no sign of life or movement from within, but the power was out, so perhaps that was normal.

When no one answered, he gave the door a push. It didn't open, so he went around back. The kitchen window was always half open because of mold and damp and the stench of unwashed dishes. Thankfully, that hadn't changed, and he was able to stick his hand in, fumble for the latch, open the window all the way, and climb inside.

Scrambling over a sink full of dirty plates, Tommy called out, "Zack? Mom? Are you here?"

As soon as his feet touched the ground, he began to feel nauseated; it smelled the same. The exact same. Body odor, and illness, and filth humming in the air.

Coughing and raising his t-shirt to shield his nostrils, Tommy stepped farther into the kitchen. The curtains were drawn, letting in so little light that the whole place felt a little like it was underground. Humid. Closed in.

Tommy kicked a discarded plastic tray, from a microwave meal, out of the way and called out again. "Zack? Buddy? You here? It's me, Tommy."

Finally Tommy heard a noise. It had come from the living room.

As quickly as he could, stepping over and through the trash that had been ditched on the floor, he headed for the door at the end of the hall. When he pushed it open, his heart sank; it wasn't Zack who'd shouted. It was his mom.

Lying on the couch with her arm flopped across her eyes, as if even the muted light of the living room was causing her discomfort, she muttered, "Zack? Honey? Is that you?"

Tommy lingered in the doorway. He could leave. Right now. He could leave and be back with the Robinsons by this time tomorrow.

But not without his brother.

Striding over to the couch, Tommy tugged his mother's arm away from her face and tried not to notice how pale and sickly she looked. "Mom. It's Tommy. I came to find Zack. Where is he?"

His mother groaned and tried to roll away from him. Making a shooing gesture with her hand, she said, "Tommy, go to the store and get me some beer."

Tommy felt his jaw twitch. "Mom, where is Zack?"

"School."

"It's Saturday, Mom. Where is he?"

His mother groaned again and grappled for a blanket that was barely big enough to cover her legs. "I don't know."

"If you tell me where he is, I'll go to the store." Through clenched teeth, Tommy used the voice he'd used a million times before; a coaxing, gentle, *easy does it* kind of voice that parents used with their children all the time, but children should never be forced to use with their parents.

At that, his mom became still. Finally, she muttered, "Fairfield. He's at Fairfield."

"The prison?" Tommy shook his mother's shoulder. "Mom? You're telling me Zack's at Fairfield Prison?"

"That's what I said, ain't it?" she yelled, looking at him with her hollow eyes. "Now go." She flicked her hand at the door. "Go to the store."

Tommy turned away from her and strode back out of the room. In the hallway, he braced his hands on the sides of his head and tried to slow his breathing. What the hell had Zack done to get himself put away? Why hadn't Tommy heard about it?

Marching back to the kitchen, he started to sift through the piles of unopened envelopes and paperwork on the kitchen table. Finding nothing of use, he went back through the house, up the stairs, and barged into Zack's room.

As always, it was immaculate. Everything was clean, neatly organized, and *normal*. Ever since his brother was little, he'd always kept his room that way, which ran contrary to the general disarray of anything their mother touched.

Tommy headed for the desk and started to open the drawers. He'd almost given up, but when he looked up his eyes caught something pinned to the noticeboard near the door. Ripping it from its pin, he held it to the light of the window and began to read.

Dear Mrs. Hargrove,
I would like to request your permission for Zack to attend our annual Scared Straight trip to Fairfield Prison. As you're aware, his behavior has been troubling of late, and we believe such an experience would be of huge benefit.
Please see the attached form for details and return the enclosed permission slip at your earliest convenience.
Best wishes,
Molly O'Neil
English Teacher & Trip Coordinator

A grin spread across Tommy's face. Zack was on a day trip. Thank God. But almost as soon as it arrived, his grin faltered. Zack was stuck in a prison, and not just any prison. Fairfield Prison. The baddest of the bad.

19

LAURA

Laura was blinded by pain. She couldn't move, couldn't think. She could hear Dave in the bedroom, opening drawers, tossing things onto the floor. The more she heard, the more panicked she became. Her breath was coming too quickly. The way it had, all those years ago, when she'd opened her eyes to find herself lying on the cold hard concrete beside the highway, staring at Alex's upside-down, mangled Mercedes and its smashed windshield.

As something in the bedroom shattered, Laura tried to count slowly from one to ten and back down again. Just as she had when she'd realized that Alex was unconscious, strapped into the driver's seat, bleeding from a head wound.

Staring at him, she had counted to ten to stop the fear in her chest from overwhelming her, and then she had crawled, inch by slow inch, across the ground to get to him.

She had ignored the pain in her back; pain which told her something was very, very wrong. She had ignored it because she needed to get to her husband and get him free. She had ignored it when she crawled through the diesel that had spilled out onto the ground, heaved herself in through the broken windshield, ripping her dress and her skin on shards of glass, and when she had reached up to unbuckle his seatbelt. She had even ignored it as she dragged him free.

It was only afterwards, when she woke up in a hospital bed, that she began to feel the pain properly. She had felt it in every fiber of her body. She had screamed. Loudly. Alex had begged them to give her something for the pain, and as it finally subsided—when morphine was pumped into her veins via an intravenous drip—he had told her what a hero she was.

"Laura, the doctors can't believe it. You pulled me from the wreckage with a broken back. You're unbelievable."

Back then, fuzzy with the haze of the drugs, Laura had smiled and told him she'd do it one hundred times over to keep him safe.

Now, as she lay on the floor of her closet, in agony, unable to move, she wondered—not for the first time—whether she'd still tell him that if he asked her.

Thankfully, he never had.

It was only when Argent stopped barking that Laura' mind began to clear. He was stuck in his crate, and who knew what Dave was capable of; addicts will do *anything* when they're desperate. She knew that first-hand.

Hauling herself into an upright position, she took a deep breath, braced herself for the impact, and slammed her shoulder into the closet door. As pain ricocheted through her body, the door wavered but didn't open. She pushed harder. It still didn't open; Dave had wedged it shut somehow and mere brute strength wasn't going to shift it.

"You should have told me where they were, Laura…" Dave growled at her from inside the bedroom.

"Dave, please. We're friends. Let me help you—" Laura had pressed herself up against the door and was straining to hear his movement. For a moment, there was silence. Through the slats, she could just about make out his silhouette in the center of the room. Still as a statue, as if he were truly considering letting her out. "Dave?" Then the silhouette moved toward the bedroom door, and Dave closed it behind him.

Laura closed her eyes and tried to slow her breathing. She was alone. Trapped. Argent had no way to defend himself, and Dave had free run of her house. Lying down, she peered through the gap beneath the closet doors and inched her fingers along the floor, feeling for whatever Dave had used to jam them shut. Eventually, she came across something, but she couldn't get enough purchase on it to push it free. She lay back, looking up at the coats and dresses hanging above her. One of her evening dresses was hanging toward the back, its hem almost touching the ground.

Laura scooted toward it and began to pull on the skirt, swinging the dress roughly back and forth with an upward motion that, finally, caused it to come tumbling down... along with its hanger. Quickly, Laura grabbed the hanger and shoved it under the closet door, hook first. Whatever was blocking the door was slightly to the right. With all the strength she could muster, she pushed the hanger sideways, and kept pushing until... pop! The object was dislodged.

Tentatively, Laura nudged the door open a few inches. Dave was gone. The room was empty. He had used a book to wedge the door closed. It was one of Alex's favorites, and its pages were now torn. Briefly, Laura told herself that she'd order him a replacement, but then shook her head at her thoughts; of course she wouldn't be ordering him a replacement.

Pulling herself forward, she saw her chair on the far side of the room, next to the bed. When she reached it, she hauled herself back in. Her arms were burning, but at least the sensation was distracting her from the mind-numbing pain in her back. Slowly, she wheeled to the bedroom door and listened. It sounded like Dave was down the hall, in the gym, so she sped down the hall, into the kitchen, and with fumbling fingers freed Argent from his crate.

As the German Shepherd trotted out, tail wagging, she bent down and let him lick her face. Then she remembered Alex's guns. Argent followed her as she headed quickly for Alex's study. It was a room she barely entered—one of the few that hadn't been redesigned with space for a wheelchair to properly maneuver around. Dashing toward the desk, where Alex had left the keys, Laura's chair caught on the table next to his armchair. She didn't stop, but as she moved forward the table toppled over with a crash, sending a pile of books flying across the room.

Shit. Dave.

Looking behind her, she was almost certain she heard the door to the home gym opening and closing as he slammed it behind him. The keys were within reach. She scrambled for them, then turned to the safe. It was next to Alex's desk. She moved toward it but, as she did, her right wheel caught on one of the books that were now lying on the floor. Its front cover was stuck in the spokes. She reached down, trying to tug it free. When she looked up, Argent's ears were pricked, and he was staring at the study door. Footsteps. She could hear footsteps.

Out of time, Laura hurled herself from the chair, landing on her stomach so hard that it almost knocked the breath right out of her and stifling the instinct to cry out as pain gripped her back. Leaving Argent growling at the door, she crawled over the books until she reached the cabinet, then reached up and slammed the key into the lock.

Pulling the door open, she reached inside, grabbed one of Alex's shotguns, and turned rolling into a sitting position. As she released the safety and shouldered the gun, the study door opened. Argent began to bark. Dave stopped in the doorway, looked Laura up and down as she awkwardly faced him, then laughed. "You're not going to shoot me, Laura."

Laura flexed her fingers on the trigger.

"Is that thing even loaded?"

She'd been shooting only a handful of times, none since the accident, and she'd always hated that Alex kept the guns in the house loaded. Now, she thanked God that he had.

"It's loaded," she said, even though her instinct was to put the gun down and try to talk Dave into a different state of mind. He was still looking at her. She thought he might be about to have a change of heart and relaxed her grip, just a little.

Then Argent tilted his head. His body tensed as he stared at Dave.

In the split second that Laura was looking at Argent, Dave lurched sideways, grabbed a lamp and charged for her, holding it above his head as if he wanted to knock her out cold with it. Before he could get even two feet, Argent leapt for him, grabbed his arm between his jaws, and began to tug. Dave turned to Argent. His eyes flashed with something that looked like pure hatred. He lifted the lamp higher, but as he was about to slam it down onto Argent's head, Laura fired.

The force of the recoil, and the noise that bounced off the walls of the study, made her screw her eyes shut. When she opened them, Dave was on the floor, slumped against the wall, dead.

Laura was trembling. She lowered the gun and Argent ran over to her, whining and nuzzling his forehead into her leg. She put her hand on his head, between his ears, unable to take her eyes away from Dave's lifeless body and the pool of blood that was staining the hardwood floor near the bookshelves.

To get around him, she pulled the coffee table out of the way and winced as she pushed the door open, and it pressed up against Dave's shoes. In the ensuite of the guest bedroom, she wheeled straight to the toilet and put her hands either side of the tank, breathing heavily. She started to retch, but nothing came up. Her shoulders were shaking, the shotgun still balanced in her lap. Putting it down on the floor, she pulled the lid off the tank, reached inside it, and pulled out a small white bottle. It was in a sealed plastic bag, and her heart fluttered in her chest as she thought of what was inside.

20

ALEX

Luna's father, Dean, insisted that Alex walk with them until they reached the other side of the bridge. When Alex emphasized that he was in a hurry to get to Erik and Scarlett, Dean simply put a firm hand on his shoulder and replied, "The world's changing, Alex. It's time to slow down. Take a breath."

As much as he wanted to, Alex didn't quite have the nerve to tell him 'no'.

A little way past the bridge, they finally said goodbye. "Good luck," he said, waving to them as he got back onto his bike.

"You too, Alex. You too." Dean waved, and Luna joined in, smiling as if she and Alex had been the best of friends since the moment they met.

"I hope you find your wife," Alex said as he started to pedal.

"I don't!" Dean yelled back. "Me and Luna will do just fine without her!"

Alex was halfway up the steep hill that led away from Southside and toward the highway when, finally, he heard a noise other than his own heavy breathing. An engine… it sounded like an engine! Alex's heart fluttered in his chest. Perhaps it wasn't an EMP after all. Perhaps it really was some freak power outage. He cycled harder, desperate to see the vehicle that was making the noise.

He was near the top of the hill when a huge, ancient farm truck labored over the peak. Alex stopped and leaned one foot down onto the ground. He swallowed hard as the feeling in his chest turned instantly from hope back to despair.

Alex's whole family were farmers, going back generations. Before his father died, he'd spent years trying to convince him to get a new truck because the old one simply wasn't up to the job anymore. Every time he'd tried, his dad had replied with the same words: "Just you wait, when the world ends, all your modern technology will fall apart. This old girl will still be here. Nothing can break her."

Somehow the EMP missed the truck. Alex pressed his lips together and tried not to listen to the voice in his head. *It doesn't matter why it's working. Fact is, it's working. This guy could take me to the prison. Get the kids. Get them home.*

Alex began to wave. The driver saw him but didn't wave back. The truck had slowed down, almost stopped. It began to shudder. It coughed. Then the engine died. From the open window, Alex heard the driver swear loudly. He bent down and was trying to do something. The truck was at the peak of the hill and was still rolling slowly forward.

"Pull the hand brake!" Alex yelled, waving more animatedly now. "Hey! Stop!"

The driver looked up and started waving back. The truck was gathering momentum. "Out of the way!" the driver yelled, sticking his head out of the window.

For a moment, Alex didn't seem to be able to move. The hill was steep, and the truck was getting faster and faster. Alex looked at his bike, blinked at it, then shook himself out of his trance and hauled it to the side of the road. Ditching it on the grass, he turned back toward the truck. The driver had pulled over to the other side of the road, clearly trying to steer as far away from Alex as possible.

"Watch out!" Alex shouted. It was too late. The truck was out of control and heading toward a drainage ditch full of water. Alex watched the driver try frantically to turn back the other way. The wheels spun. The truck began to skid. Then it caught on something and flew into the air. Crashing down, it rolled over and over and over, landing in the ditch.

Alex's heart was pounding against his ribcage. Without hesitating, he raced down the hill, his rifle knocking against his back as he ran. Diving into the ditch, he began to scramble for the door. The truck was upside down, half submerged in water. It was crumpled, creaking and groaning as it sank. The water was up to Alex's chest. He pulled at the door, but it wouldn't budge. "Hold on," he shouted. "I'll get you out, just hold on." There was no reply from inside, so he waded to the front of the truck. Pushing his hands through the water, he found a large rock and was about to throw it at the windshield to break the driver free when he saw the man's face.

Eyes open, blood trickling down his forehead, he was dead. Unmistakably dead.

After climbing out of the ditch, Alex vomited onto the road. Hot, acrid bile burned his throat and he retched until his stomach was empty. The driver's ghostly face flashed in front of his eyes. The way the truck rolled over, the smashed windscreen, the noise it made, began to merge in his head with the day his own car had spun out of control. The truck driver's face was now Laura's face, and Alex was watching himself from up above, as she crawled to reach him where he hung upside down in his seat, held in place only by his seatbelt, as Laura begged him to wake up and move. He could smell diesel and he had no idea whether he could really smell it or if it was his imagination.

To block it out, he screwed his eyes shut. When he opened them, stepping away from the ditch, Alex reached for his pocket, patting it, trying to locate his cell phone. Then he remembered that he'd left it at home, and he remembered why—there were no cell phones. Not anymore. Even if he could have called 911, would there have been anyone there to answer him? Surely, right now, the cops and the paramedics and the fire fighters were scrambled all over the city. If what he'd seen on his way through town was anything to go by, they had their hands full. Why bother attending to a smashed-up truck and a guy they couldn't possibly save?

Shaking, perhaps because he was wet and cold, or perhaps because he'd just seen someone die, Alex picked up his bike and climbed back onto it. At the brow of the hill, he stopped. His wet clothes were weighing him down, so he began to twist the hem of his sweater between his fingers, attempting to wring some water out of it. He was squeezing hard when his rifle knocked against his elbow. He nudged it out of the way, but then a sinking feeling lodged itself in his chest; he'd taken the rifle into the ditch. It was waterlogged. And utterly useless.

Alex was over the crest of the hill when he heard gunshots. Skidding to a halt, he looked back at the town. Had they come from his neighborhood? Or Dean's? As more gunshots broke out, he let the bike fall from under him and walked forward a few paces.

He scraped his fingers through his hair. What the hell was going on? Looting? Wasn't that what happened in the movies? First, the calm. Then, the storm. The part when people realized they could do and take whatever they wanted. He froze, unable to move. All he could think of was Laura. She was alone. Vulnerable. He'd left her *alone*. Sure, she had a gun, but would she use it if she needed to?

Alex grabbed his bike and turned it back toward town. For a brief moment, he put his feet on the pedals, determined to go back for her. Then he hesitated.

In one direction was his wife. In the other was his kids.

He swallowed hard and gripped the handlebars. If something terrible had happened to her, even if he ran back there now, would he be able to help her? Would she want him to? Alex knew the answer; Laura would tell him to go get the kids. She'd be furious that he'd even *thought* about turning around for her.

Alex breathed out slowly. Whatever it was, whatever had caused the gunshots, he couldn't think about it now. He wasn't far from the prison. He needed to keep going. As he started to pedal, a second rumble rippled through the sky. This time, though, it wasn't an explosion; it was thunder.

Without warning, the heavens opened up and it began to rain. Alex hadn't brought anything with him. No backpack. No supplies. No raincoat. He was radically underprepared for this. But he couldn't stop.

He'd gone a couple more miles when ahead, through the dull light and the rain, he saw a figure walking toward him. Half startled, half relieved to see another person, Alex stopped. It was a man, who held out his hand, gesturing for Alex to stop.

Alex slowed down, and another rumble of thunder made the trees at the side of the road shake. Above the sound of the storm, the man shouted, "Hey, man. It's all right. I just need help."

"Help?" Alex was squinting at the guy in front of him. Unlike Alex, he was wearing a jacket. He was on foot, but he was holding something in his right hand. Was that some kind of metal pipe? Alex sat up straight but braced himself to start pedaling.

"My wife is across town. She's got a bad heart. A pacemaker. I need to get back to her. Could I borrow your bike?"

Alex swallowed hard. He'd do the same for Laura. He'd go out in the rain and beg for help if she needed it. But he shook his head. "I'm sorry, I'm on the way to fetch my kids. I can't give you the bike. I'm sorry."

As Alex put his feet back on the pedals, the man yelled and charged forward, waving the metal pipe above his head. Alex pushed down on the pedals and tried to ride away but the man reached for him, swinging the pipe. Alex jerked backwards to avoid being hit, swung to the left, and then tipped off his bike.

Pulling it down with him, he shouted, raising both arms to shield his head.

The man was towering above Alex, ready to strike him. Then Alex heard the screech of tires on the road. He couldn't see through the rain and the dark. The man turned around to look at something, and then he fell.

Collapsing beside Alex and his bike, the man let the metal pipe fall from his hand. Stunned, unconscious, or dead, Alex had no idea, so he scrambled back, pushing his bike off him.

Before he could stand up, a hand appeared. Alex blinked at it. He looked up. A young man, perhaps not much older than Erik, was standing in front of him, one hand stretched out to help Alex to his feet, the other holding a baseball bat. He was wearing a backpack that looked stuffed to the brim and smiled a friendly smile at him.

Alex took the man's hand and stumbled up.

"You okay?" the young man asked.

Alex nodded. "I am now. Thank you."

"I'm Thomas," he said, handing Alex back his bike. "Where you heading?"

Pointing down the road, Alex was purposefully vague. "That way."

"Ah. Me too," said Thomas. "I'm trying to get to the prison to rescue my kid brother. He was on a school trip."

Alex released a whoosh of air from his chest and laughed. "The prison? Me too. My kids are on that same trip."

Thomas nodded, already climbing back onto his bike. "Great. Then we can go together." He started to pedal, waving for Alex to hurry up. "By the way," he shouted over his shoulder. "My friends call me Tommy."

21

DOUGIE

D ougie was back on the couch, next to Zack, trying to make his mind work faster, when the kid interrupted his thoughts.

"So, you know what my brother did to get locked up," Zack said, concentrating on his hands instead of Dougie's face. "How about you? Did you really kill a cop?"

Dougie almost laughed; it was an unwritten rule among inmates that, no matter how curious you were, you never asked another guy what he did to get put away. Never. Yet here was a scrawny high schooler, who looked like he wouldn't say boo to a ghost, asking him straight out: What did you do, Dougie?

"Yeah," he said, matter-of-fact, "I did."

Zack's eyes widened and he sucked in his cheeks. Dougie half expected him to release a low whistle and shake his head. Instead, he turned to Dougie and met his eyes. "Why?" he asked softly. "Why'd you do it?"

Dougie looked over at the teacher, but she was engrossed in conversation with the bus driver and hardly paying him any attention.

"Listen, kid, I had a pretty rough start." Dougie put his arm on the back of the couch and tried to look as though he was totally at ease, even though he hadn't had this conversation with anyone—not even his brief stint with the prison therapist who was only looking to dot his i's and cross his t's instead of caring about the inmates—ever. "Most guys here will tell you the same. Heck, if we came from big white houses with picket fences and porch swings, we wouldn't likely have ended up here, would we?"

Zack offered him a half-smile, perhaps thinking about his own home, which Dougie was almost certain didn't have anything close to a white picket fence.

"My pa was a drunk. A mean drunk. And my ma was...." Dougie stopped to clear his throat and cross his right ankle over his left knee. "She was weak," he said, aware of the disgust in his voice. "A waste of space. Never stuck up for me or my brother. Left when things got too rough, and it didn't occur to her to take us along."

Zack angled himself so he was facing Dougie square on. "Really?" he said before laughing a little and muttering, "Wish my mom would leave me."

Dougie examined Zack's face; he meant it. Which could only mean his mother was an even worse human being than Dougie's was. "Yeah. She walked out. Got a fancy job in Chicago. Forgot all about me and my brother."

"You ever see her again?" Clearly, Zack was under the impression he could now ask as many questions as he wanted to.

Dougie bristled. "Only once. At my brother's funeral," he said, biting back the nausea that always lodged in his throat when he thought of his little brother. Reaching for a bottle of water, Dougie took a long swig, then coughed loudly. "His name was Caleb," he said, concentrating on the writing on the side of the bottle. "He was a good kid."

"What happened?" Zack asked.

Dougie looked at him and laughed. "You sure are asking a lot of questions all of a sudden. You think we're friends now?"

Zack began to blush. "No, sir. I—"

"Our dad was drunk. As usual. Caleb wanted to go to soccer practice. He was only ten, so I'd promised I'd drive him, but I forgot." Dougie glanced at Zack. "Actually, that's a lie," he said solemnly. "I didn't forget. I was too busy driving around trying to impress a bunch of older guys. Trying to be part of their gang. Trying to escape our dark hell-hole of a house."

"Oh," Zack said quietly, probably thinking of his own loser big brother.

"So he went on his own. Walked through the roughest part of the neighborhood. Got himself shot."

Zack audibly gasped.

Dougie shrugged, trying hard to keep his expression blank and his eyes dry. "So I found the guy who shot him, and I killed him."

"A cop shot him?" Zack asked, his mouth dropping open.

"Nah..." Dougie made a *pfft* sound with his lips and waved his hand. "The cop came for me, so I took him hostage. Told them I wanted a helicopter and one million dollars if they wanted him back alive." He laughed and looked down at his prison-issue clothes. "And, well, you can see how that turned out. Soon as I realized I was going to jail for life, I figured I might as well take the asshole down with me."

"So, you shot the guy who shot your brother? *And* you shot a cop?"

Dougie nodded solemnly. "That's about it, yeah."

"Oh." Zack nodded, then rolled his eyes. "Is that it? You didn't go on some kind of revenge rampage like Liam Neeson." Zack's voice changed, and Dougie realized he'd put on a very bad Liam Neeson accent. *"I will find you, and I will kill you...."*

For a moment, Dougie didn't move, but then Zack looked at him furtively from beneath his stupid long hair, and the sparkle in his eyes made Dougie realize that the kid was trying to make him laugh. He was trying to make him feel better.

"Ha!" Dougie let out a thunderclap of laughter and smacked his thigh. "Ha! *Whoever you are...*" he said, pretending to hold up a cell phone and growl into it just like the famous scene from the movie.

Opposite them, the teacher and the others stopped talking and turned in their direction, but Dougie didn't care. He was laughing, properly laughing, for the first time in years, and it felt good.

Dougie was slapping Zack between the shoulders and enjoying the ache in his side from laughing too hard when a commotion broke out in the hallway. The teacher had been muttering something to the bus driver but looked up wide-eyed. Her white shirt was grubbier than it had been at the start of the day, the cuffs flecked with blood from where she'd dragged that dead guard out of the way of the door. He'd been quite impressed by that, actually. As she moved her head to stare at the door, her ponytail swayed from side to side.

"Kids, stay here," she told them, rushing to the door that the two unarmed guards had just bolted through.

Dougie glanced back toward the weapons cage. That guard hadn't moved. Damn it. Then he followed the teacher.

Sticking his head out into the hallway, he heard the guards at the other end shouting.

"What are they doing?" The teacher had grabbed the bus driver's arm and was pointing to the door. "They're opening it?"

Colton pulled her backwards. "Come back," he said, "back in here with the kids."

Dougie stayed put, watching as the guards pulled the door open, ushering someone inside while trying to keep the shouting prisoners out.

Dougie peered past the guards. Who the hell had they risked opening the door for? As the guards parted, helping someone to their feet, Dougie's mouth went dry. He clenched his fists. It was Fox. He was badly wounded, black and blue with blood streaming down his face. Shit. The last time Dougie saw him, Luther was ordering him to be dragged away. And Dougie was stealing Grayson's keys. As soon as Fox saw him here, the jig was up. No more Dougie The Mentor. It would be Dougie The Kidnapper. Dougie The Monster. He couldn't have that....

Slipping back into the break room, Dougie retrieved the shiv from his pant leg and backed away from the door. The teacher was standing in front of the frightened kids. She looked like she was ready to have a fistfight with anyone who tried to hurt them, which made Dougie smile. She might be irritating but she was plucky, and you had to admire that in a woman.

Barely a minute had gone by when the door burst open, and two guards hauled Fox inside. Shouting and hollering was still coming from the hallway. Clearly, the guards hadn't managed to seal the door back up.

Dougie braced himself. *Here we go*....

Fox looked up. His eyes fixed on Dougie. "You…" His voice was barely a whisper, but Dougie wasn't going to give him time to start shouting.

Quick as a flash, he lunged for the guy guarding the weapons cage. In one swift movement, before the guard had even registered what Dougie was doing, Dougie had whipped the handgun from the guard's belt with one hand and stabbed him in the gut with the other.

Someone gasped, maybe the teacher. Someone else screamed. Definitely the goth girl. It didn't matter because Dougie was now holding the gun.

The guard was wavering, clutching his stomach, staring wide-eyed at Dougie. For a second, Dougie felt sorry for the guy. He was only doing his job, after all. As quickly as it had come, the sympathy left. Lifting the gun, he didn't think about it and shot the guard in the head.

As the guard's lifeless body slumped to the floor, the kids began to shout. Dougie ignored them; bending down, he freed the keys from the guard's belt.

A stampede of footsteps in the hallway told him the guards hadn't managed to hold the door and the prisoners had broken through. Waiting for them, he tossed the keys up and down in his hand. When they poured through the door, Luther was at the front of the group. Dougie grinned at him and walked forward, dangling the keys on his index finger.

"My friend," he said loudly. "We have the keys to the castle."

Luther grinned back, and Dougie handed him the keys. "Guns are back there. Save me something good, okay? Because…" he raised his voice, "I am in charge now!"

Behind Luther, the prisoners cheered.

Dougie turned as they swarmed toward the weapons room. Then he remembered the teacher. By the couch, she and the bus driver were inching the kids back into the corner of the room. Dougie walked toward them, gun in hand.

When he reached them, he smiled at the teacher. Shaking, she stepped in front of the kids. "You'll have to kill me first," she spat.

Dougie tilted his head at her, then he waved his gun in the air and laughed. "Ha!"

The teacher didn't move.

"Relax." Dougie reached out and put his hand firmly on her shoulder, pleasantly surprised that she didn't even flinch. "It's time for me to escort you from the building, Miss O'Neil."

22

MOLLY

As Dougie waved his gun at the door, gesturing for her and the kids to file out in front of him, Molly couldn't take her eyes off the dead guard. He was partly obscured by the gang of prisoners who were storming into the weapons room, but she could see the blood pooling beneath his stomach. When Dougie shot him, Molly was certain she and the kids would be next. He had a gun. He was a felon. And he'd hated her from the moment he set eyes on her; she could feel it.

When he told her he was going to help them escape, at first, she didn't believe it. Colton didn't either, taking hold of her arm and whispering, "Are we seriously going to follow this guy?"

Molly had replied, "What choice do we have, Colton?" and when he hadn't been able to think of a reply, he had slowly nodded his head in agreement.

In the corridor, the lights flashed briefly, dimmed and then went out, followed by cheers and boos. Molly froze, unable to move as banging and crashing was heard from rooms nearby. Frank, from the Scared Straight room, whizzed past them carrying some sort of burning home-made torch and waving a can of pepper spray in the air, but skidded to a halt when he saw Dougie. "Dougie, Dougie, can we trash the Warden's office?" he asked excitedly, like a kid asking if he could open his Christmas presents.

Dougie rolled his eyes—as if he were the *real* criminal here, and Frank was simply playing at it. "Yeah. But not now. I need you." He jerked his head. "Come with us."

Frank opened his mouth, perhaps to protest, but when Dougie made a show of lifting his gun a little higher, Frank nodded. "Sure. Okay. Sure."

They walked past a couple of metal trash cans with fires burning brightly and were almost at the door, the one which had been padlocked an hour ago, when a scary-looking guy with a scar on his face stepped out from the shadows in front of them. "Dougie," he said, towering above them. "What's this? You don't share your toys now?" The guy's lips parted into a gap-toothed smile. The teeth he did have were gray and crooked.

Molly gestured for the kids to stay behind her and backed them a little closer to the wall. Colton had straightened his shoulders but knew that now was not the time to start something. He'd just have to let Dougie handle it.

"There are plenty of toys back there." He pointed to the break room. "You better go grab a weapon before they're all gone."

The guy with the scar hesitated. Finally, he moved. As he walked past Molly, she felt him press his shoulder against her, and it made her stomach clench into a knot.

Pulling the door open, Dougie waved them through and pointed in the direction of the front door they'd entered through hours before. "This way."

"Dougie?" Frank ran to his elbow and tugged on it. "What are we doing with them? What's the plan?"

"We're letting them go, Frank."

"But...." Frank frowned at him, confused. "Why? Shouldn't we keep them? You always need hostages in a riot. A teacher and a bunch of kids... they'd make great hostages."

Dougie stopped abruptly and Frank crashed into his back. Turning to him, Dougie grabbed his collar. "You think we need hostages? The power's out, you idiot. There's nothing out there." Dougie waved his gun at the ceiling. "The last thing we need is hostages. Better to throw them out and let them fend for themselves."

Until now, Molly had thought of nothing beyond getting out of the prison. As Dougie spoke, she felt a new type of dread settle in her gut; they had no idea what was going on beyond these walls. They had no idea what they'd find when they were free.

Frank was nodding. "Okay. Okay, Dougie." Then they were walking again.

Every time they passed another inmate, Molly's stomach flipped over, certain that someone bigger and tougher than Dougie would stop him from letting them go. It seemed, though, that Dougie had cemented himself as the one in charge, and most simply nodded at him as they ran past, high on adrenaline and who knew what else.

Soon they entered the main hall, passing the visitor room and heading toward the metal detector, which was dark. This time, they strode into the central lobby without hesitating....

Nearby, a group of inmates wearing disheveled guards' uniforms looked up from where they were leaning against the wall, smoking e-cigarettes.

When she noticed blood on the collar of one of the uniforms, Molly closed her eyes and turned away. It was too late now; she couldn't do anything to help the guards. Whatever had happened to them, she couldn't afford to think about it. She was almost free. Almost safe, with the kids, and with the prison doors locked firmly behind them.

Dougie shot the uniform-wearing inmates a look that said *beat it* and, slowly, they slouched back through the metal detectors, giving them a thump for good measure as they passed through.

Putting her arms around Scarlett and Jenna, and nodding at the boys, Molly whispered, "Come on, guys. Nearly there."

A little way in front of them, Dougie threw the keys at Frank. "Open the doors," he said briskly.

Molly was halfway across the room, the kids almost running to get to the door, when she heard one of them start to laugh. She stopped and turned around. The others had stopped too. Behind them, Zack was standing with his hands on his hips and his head tipped back. As if he was totally losing the plot, he began to guffaw with laughter.

"Zack...." Jenna walked over and tugged on his sleeve. "Knock it off."

But Zack only laughed harder.

"Zack—" Jenna was frowning at him. "What the hell is so funny?"

"Jesus, Zack, shut up and move it." Erik looked at the door, but Zack kept laughing.

"Don't you see?" he said, wiping tears from his eyes. As the others looked at him blankly, he added, "The irony! We came here because we were supposed to be scared into not wanting to come back but, instead, it's the prisoners who want us out!"

Zack was still laughing, the noise filling the room and reverberating off the walls. Molly's jaw twitched. She gritted her teeth but she couldn't hold it in any longer. Something inside her snapped. She'd tried to reach this kid, tried everything she could think of to make him see that he could lead a better life than his brother, and now here he was laughing. Laughing! They'd just watched a man get stabbed and then shot dead, and he was laughing!

"Zack!" she yelled, storming up to him and waving her arms in the air. "Would you *shut up!*"

Instantly, Zack slammed his mouth shut. Scarlett blinked at her and Jenna made an *oh crap* face.

"Shut up! No one wants to hear your opinions. Just because you're smart, doesn't mean we're impressed by your ridiculous, snarky comments. You could use your intelligence for something constructive, but instead you've done nothing this whole time except cause trouble and I'm sick of it! We are moments away from being free of this God-forsaken place and you're choosing to behave like this? It's time you grew up!"

As soon as she'd finished speaking, Molly clapped her hands to her mouth. She had never, *ever*, spoken to a student like that. Not in all her years of teaching. No matter how much they'd pushed her, or goaded her, she had always kept her cool.

It was too late. Everyone was silent, even Dougie and Frank.

"Zack, I—" she started to apologize, but Zack stalked away from her.

Frank pried the doors open and a whoosh of cold air flew into the room. Molly gasped at it, like she'd been drowning and had come up for air. It was dark beyond the doors, a sliver of light bleeding out into the parking lot from the prison entrance. Usually, the darkness would make her shiver, but tonight she wanted to step into it, and it seemed Dougie was happy to give her a helping hand.

"Go on, then," he said, shoving her gently in the back. "Get out."

Molly stumbled forward. Jenna, Scarlett, Erik, and Lucky rushed out beside her, closely followed by Colton. However, when she turned to look for Zack, he was lingering in the doorway.

Dougie walked up to him. "Here," he said, reaching for something that he'd tucked into the back waistband of his sweatpants, beneath his t-shirt.

Molly held her breath, certain that Dougie was about to give Zack a gun. But it wasn't a gun; it was a book.

Zack turned the book over in his hands. It was the one he'd picked up down in the security office. A smile spread over his face, and when he looked up at Dougie, Molly knew exactly what was about to happen. "Dougie," Zack said. "Can I stay with you?"

Dougie was silent for a moment. Next to him, Frank slapped Zack on the shoulder. "Yeah, man!" Then Dougie smiled, and stepped aside.

"Zack, no. Come back—" Molly went to rush forward, but Colton grabbed her arm. Behind Dougie, Zack was staring at her. Frank handed him the keys, and as the three of them stepped back inside, Zack locked the door.

23

TOMMY

Alex Banks looked terrified. When Tommy tried to make conversation, cycling quickly alongside him on the abandoned road that led to Fairfield, Alex answered politely but through thin, worried lips, as if he wanted to focus every ounce of energy on making the journey as quickly as humanly possible.

Tommy couldn't blame him; his kids were in prison and they hadn't even committed a crime to end up there.

"Do you know much about Fairfield?" Alex asked when they stopped to quickly swig some water.

Tommy hesitated. Telling Alex what he knew about the place wouldn't help, so he shrugged and shook his head. "Not much."

Alex was looking at Tommy's tattoos. Was it obvious that he'd been inside?

Feeling self-conscious, he pulled his sleeves down, shoved his water bottle back into his backpack, and put his feet on the pedals. "Ready?" The sun was setting, and something told Tommy that it would be better for them if they made it to the prison before dark.

Alex put his own bottle into his back pocket and began cycling before bothering to say yes.

For about another hour, they kept on the same road. It was long and winding, taking them away from the town and into no man's land. Just trees, scrub, and road. While Tommy's neighborhood had been full of abandoned cars and people milling about, looking for a way to take advantage of the situation they'd found themselves in, this road was empty.

Thinking of the map in his pocket, he wondered how far the Robinsons had gotten. Whether they'd made it to their cabin. What they were doing right now. Probably, they were huddled around a campfire eating some of their well-planned supplies, maybe even playing cards and drinking a beer.

Zack would like the Robinsons. He'd probably find Chris a little weird, but once he got to know him, they'd become friends, Tommy was sure of it.

Already he was picturing a new life. A different life. The opposite of the one that had been handed to them.

Finally, after reaching the brow of a winding hill, Fairfield Prison became visible.

Beside him, Alex Banks stopped and scraped his hands through his hair, releasing a long, low whistle.

Ominous and foreboding, Fairfield was surrounded by a large open field, and then a bank of woods. *Probably how it got its name*, Tommy thought.

"It looks dark," Alex said quietly.

Tommy raised an eyebrow at him. "No power, dude."

"I know." Alex rubbed at his beard with a thumb and forefinger. "It's just that it looks so…."

"Quiet?" Tommy knew that wasn't the word Alex was searching for, and the older man didn't reply.

Behind the prison, the sun was way past setting. The sky was gray, dipping into twilight.

"So, what's the plan?" Tommy asked, leaning forward onto the handlebars of a bike he pinched from his mom's next-door neighbor.

"Plan?" Alex swallowed hard. "I…."

"How are we getting in?" For some reason, Tommy had assumed that Alex had thought this through. Apparently he was wrong.

"I have no idea." Alex breathed out a long, slow sigh and shook his head. "Shit. I have no idea how we're going to get in there. I mean, we can hardly march right on in, can we? They have gates. *Electric* gates."

Tommy bit his lower lip. He'd been locked up for six years. Surely something he knew about prisons would come in useful. He was wishing he'd stopped and tried to locate a gun before leaving, when he heard something.

"What's that?" He spun around, looking behind them, but there was nothing there.

"I didn't—"

"Shhh." Tommy held a finger to his lips. There it was again. He dismounted his bike, took the metal pipe from where he'd strapped it to the back, and weighed it up and down in his hands. Something was moving in the bushes. "Come out or I'll shoot." Tommy raised the piping as if it was a weapon, hoping his silhouette would trick whoever was there into thinking he meant it.

"I mean it," he added, "I'm going to count to three…. One—"

"Wait, don't, please don't." A whimpering male voice was followed by a pair of chunky hands, rising up from the bush in a sign of defeat.

Tommy glanced at Alex, who'd left his bike and was standing next to him.

When he looked back at the bush, a head had emerged. A bald head, followed by a thick neck and a smart but dirty suit.

"Who the hell are you?" Tommy asked gruffly as the man stepped shakily onto the road.

"I... I...."

Tommy looked the man up and down, but before he could say anything else, Alex Banks said, "I know you. I saw you on the news a while back. You're the Warden at Fairfield."

Tommy's eyes widened. *No shit, the Warden ran away. Go figure.*

"Yes," the man stuttered. "Yes, I am. And I'm very glad to have come across you gentlemen. I'm really in need of some assistance...."

"Oh yeah? What about assisting the people stuck inside that place?" Tommy thrust a finger in the direction of the prison and pushed his shoulders back, broadening his chest as he moved closer to the sniveling man in front of him.

"There was nothing I could do," the man said weakly. "Nothing."

"So you left?" Alex frowned at him in disbelief. "There are school-children in that place. *My* children. Did you get them to safety? Did you make sure they got out?"

Tommy put his hand on Alex's forearm because it looked like he was about to knock the guy out.

After blinking rapidly at them, the warden looked down at his shoes and shook his head. "There wasn't time. I couldn't...."

"And your staff? The guards?" Tommy asked.

Again, a headshake.

Letting out a disgusted laugh, Tommy stalked back to his bike and bent to pick it up. "Leave him, Alex. He's useless. Leave him out here to fend for himself."

"How do we get in?" Alex had squared up to the warden. Even though he was slim, he was muscular, and clearly where his kids were concerned, he was willing to get mean if he had to.

"Get in? Well, you can't."

"How did you get out?"

"Through the front door, but I—" The warden stopped mid-sentence, then added, in almost a whisper, "But I pulled it shut behind me."

"So, you sealed them inside?" Alex looked like he was ready to blow, so Tommy grabbed hold of his arm and tugged him back.

Fixing his eyes on Alex's, he said, "Listen. He's a scumbag and we don't have time for this. It's clear he's not going to help us."

"I… I do have this." The warden reached into his pocket and shakily lifted out a folded piece of paper. "A blueprint of the prison. If it's helpful, take it."

Alex snatched it, gave it a quick once-over, then shoved it into his own pocket.

"Wait, don't leave…." The warden hurried over to them as they climbed back onto their bikes. Looking in the direction of the town, he shuddered. "What's it like out there? Is it bad?"

Alex was already cycling away. As Tommy put his feet on the pedals, he tilted his head at the warden, looked him up and down, and said, "Why don't you take a walk and find out? *Sir*."

24

MOLLY

As the doors closed, any light disappeared along with it. It was twilight. The air was damp, the ground slick from a recent rainfall. Before long, it would be pitch dark, but Molly couldn't move. It was eerily quiet, the noise of the prison buffered by its thick, unforgiving walls. She brushed her fingers over her hair and braced her hands behind her head, still staring at the doors. If she hadn't said those things to Zack, he'd have come with them. If she hadn't—

Reading her mind, Colton put his arm around her shoulders. "We have to go," he said. "There's nothing you can do for him now. Let's get these kids back to the bus."

Molly nodded slowly. When she turned around, the other four were watching her. The difference in temperature from the stuffy, airless rooms of the prison to the outside was making Scarlett shiver. "Okay," she said. "Back to the bus. We'll collect your things, then get you all home."

In front of them, opposite the prison's front entrance, the gates that were usually sealed shut and guarded by a small glass security booth were open. Not far, but far enough for them to squeeze through. Colton went first, then the kids, then Molly. Once they were on the other side, he pushed the gates shut and they sealed with a loud clunk.

Out in the parking lot, it was even darker, but they could see the yellow school bus in the distance.

As they ran toward it, Molly's breath began to catch in her throat. At first, she thought it was because she was tired. Exhausted from what they'd been through. Then she realized it was because she was crying.

Before the kids could see, she wiped the tears from her face and came to a stop next to the bus. All around them, it was quiet. Too quiet. Of course, Colton didn't have the keys to the bus. He'd left them with security when they entered the prison. Even if he'd had them still, it wouldn't have helped.

After ripping the bandages from his hands, Colton began to tug at the door, trying to get a purchase on them with his chunky fingers. Molly tried to help him. Erik did too. Finally, the door opened enough for Colton to get a good grip, and he heaved it fully open.

Quicker than she'd ever seen them move, the kids raced onto the bus and dove into their seats, grabbing hold of their possessions as if they were discovering old friends. Colton tugged the door closed behind them and leaned against it. Molly picked up her empty coffee flask and held it to her chest. It seemed like another lifetime ago that she'd sat there, sipping coffee, staring out of the window at the traffic.

"I can confirm our phones are dead," Erik shouted from down the bus.

"Yep," Jenna agreed, rifling in her backpack for something else. "At least we've got snacks." Surprisingly, she slid over to the Banks twins and offered them each one of her stash of protein bars.

"Thanks," Erik said, nodding appreciatively at her.

"You know," Scarlett added, mouth already full of potato chips, "you were unbelievably awesome back there."

Jenna shook her head. "Not really. When that guy with the knife got hold of me, it was Miss O'Neil who tricked him into letting me go."

"Yes," Molly said, leaning on the back of one of the seats, "but you beat him to the ground, Jenna. You'll have to teach me some of your moves someday."

"You can teach Erik too," Scarlett said, laughing at her brother.

As the kids continued to relive the events of the day, Molly let herself smile. Already they were talking about what had happened as if it was all some crazy, fun part of the trip. As if it were a tale they'd continue to tell when they went back to their normal lives and remembered that day when the power was out for a few hours.

Thinking about what would happen next, a twinge of sadness came to her chest, but she pushed it away. For now, the kids were okay. At least, most of them were okay....

"Miss O'Neil?" Lucky was standing in front of her. She smiled at him.

"Yes, Lucky? Are you all right?"

The boy nodded. "I just wanted to say... thanks. For looking out for us back there. And..." He scraped his shoe on the floor of the bus, then laughed. "I'm pretty sure the Scared Straight trip worked. I don't *ever* want to come back to this place." He reached into his pocket and held out the lighter that he'd pocketed back in the prison. "And I swear I won't burn down any more barns."

Molly tilted her head. She reached out to take it but, instead, she curled Lucky's fingers around the lighter and said, "You know what? I think you earned this one. Keep it as a memento." She gestured to the others. "Now go grab one of those protein bars before they're all gone."

Lucky grinned at her, then stomped his foot on the floor and offered her a Boy Scout salute. "Yes, ma'am."

As he walked away, Molly slumped into the seat next to her and exhaled loudly.

"You did a good job back there," Colton said, sitting down opposite her and rubbing his leg. "You kept them safe."

"Not all of them." She wrapped her arms around herself and rubbed her arms against the chill that lingered in the air. She looked back toward the prison. Zack was in there. She should have seen what Dougie was doing. She should have done something to stop it.

"Zack will be okay." Colton was watching her, his eyes bright in the gloom of the bus.

Molly stood up, trying to ignore the voice inside her head that whispered, *Will he be okay?* The sun had finally disappeared. To the right, the prison was giving off a muted glow from its small square windows. To the left, however, darkness was pressing up against them. More darkness than she'd ever seen in her life. Then there was the silence. "Do you think the whole city's out?" she asked Colton.

"If we're talking EMPs, probably the whole country," he said grimly.

Molly shuddered. Right now, for miles and miles, there would be nothing but darkness. In a weird way, Zack was right, wasn't he? The prison was the only place where there was light. Except, light or no light, it was filled with men who could, at best, be described as unhinged and, at worst, as dangerous psychopaths. She sat down opposite Colton and leaned forward onto her thighs. "It's my job to protect these kids."

"You have." Colton fixed his eyes on her. "You stepped in front of a guy holding a gun for these kids, Molly."

"I know. But I came here with *five* students, not four." She looked down the bus at where the twins, Jenna, and Lucky were sharing food and bottles of soda. As she watched them, Zack's face floated in front of her. The way he'd looked when she yelled. The heartbreak on his face when she treated him exactly the same way everyone else had ever treated him—like dirt. When she did what she swore she would never, *ever* do to a student: tore him down instead of building him up, just because *she* was scared.

When she looked back at Colton, he was shaking his head. "No. Molly—"

"We have to go back for Zack. We can't leave him in there."

Colton shook his head. He was looking at her as if she'd lost her mind.

Molly reached for his hands and clasped them between her own. "We're responsible for him. We can't abandon him. People have been doing that to him his entire life." She breathed in, her nostrils flaring a little, and sat up straighter. Defiantly, she said, "We need to go back in there and get him out."

"And put the others in danger again?" Colton's voice was a little too loud and, down the bus, Molly noticed the others slide into silence.

"Miss O'Neil?" Erik had stood up.

"You're not thinking of going back?" Jenna was looking at her with wide eyes.

"I—" Before Molly could answer them, a loud knock on the side of the bus made her gasp. She gestured for everyone to be quiet. Another knock. Then another, more frantic this time.

"Kids? Are you in there?! It's Dad!"

25

MOLLY

S carlett bolted down the aisle. "Dad!" she was yelling as loud as she could. Colton opened the door and Scarlett hurled herself down the steps, embracing a man with a neat beard and a very damp sweater. A moment later, Erik was up too, pulling Scarlett and their father into the bus.

Mr. Banks tucked his children under his arms and kissed their heads. Molly noticed tears in his eyes and felt as if she should look away. Behind them, a second man stepped into the bus and lingered by the door, looking toward Jenna and Lucky.

"Hi." Mr. Banks held out his hand to shake hers. "I'm Alex Banks. Scarlett and Erik's dad. Thank you so much for keeping them safe."

Molly smiled thinly at him; if he knew even half of what his kids had witnessed, he might not be so grateful to her.

"We were inside when the power went out," Scarlett said quickly. Then, in unison with Erik, "We think it's an EMP, Dad."

Alex Banks nodded grimly. "I think you're right. I got an emergency alert on my phone and then the power went out. Nothing's working. Phones, cars…."

Scarlett looked behind her father. "And Mom?"

"She's fine. Just fine. At home with Argent safe and sound." Alex ruffled Erik's hair. "She sent me to fetch you. But I had to bring the bike, so it took a little longer than I'd hoped."

Erik laughed. "You biked all the way here? From home?"

"Course I did." Alex puffed out his chest a little. "Your old man's still fit." He almost smiled, but then frowned as he looked at Erik's face. "Erik… what happened to your eye?"

Behind Alex, the younger man cleared his throat. "Excuse me," he said, moving further into the bus. "Where's my brother?"

Molly blinked at him, glanced at Colton, then back at the man.

"Sorry," he said, smiling and offering to shake her hand. "I'm Tommy. Tommy Hargrove. My brother Zack was supposed to be on this trip."

A fierce nausea sprang into Molly's throat. *Tommy?* But how? He didn't look anything like the way Zack had described him. Certainly not like a murderer—unless she'd been surrounded by prisoners so long that anyone outside those walls seemed friendly.

Molly took Tommy's arm and moved him down the bus away from the others. She gestured for him to sit down and knew the others were straining to hear their conversation. "Tommy, I'm so sorry."

Tommy was holding his breath and was suddenly very pale. "Oh God, did something happen? Is Zack… is he…?"

"Zack is still inside," she said, forcing the words out quickly. "He's safe and well. But he made friends with one of the prisoners and he refused to come with us."

"Refused?"

Molly expected Tommy's face to grow red and angry, perhaps for him to punch something, but he simply looked confused.

"He refused to come out?"

She nodded solemnly. "Yes, but we're going to go back for him." She stood up and put her hands on her hips. Using her best teacher voice, she said loudly, "Kids, I'm going to help Tommy get Zack back. I'll need all of you to stay here." She glanced at Mr. Banks. "Or go with Mr. Banks."

"We should leave together," said Alex. "We'll be much safer in a group."

Molly noticed Scarlett look up at her father, as if she wasn't sure why they needed to be kept safe now that they were out of the prison. She didn't have time to deal with that question now.

"Okay. Then wait here." Molly trotted down the steps, back into the darkened parking lot, Tommy following close behind. At the gates, she stopped. Colton had pushed them shut. They were sealed and far too tall to climb over.

Through the darkness behind her, she heard Colton's heavy footsteps. "You'd need a key card to get back in." He pointed to the card reader next to the gate. "We don't have one and, even if we did, the power's out."

"We could probably get it working." Erik's voice through the dim light made her jump. "Me and Scarlett... if you found a key card and we got access to the generator—"

"Erik. No." Mr. Banks was standing next to his son looking extremely unhappy. But Molly had already started to jog away from the group. If anyone could get a generator working, it was the Banks twins; since the power first went out, it had been clear Erik and Scarlett knew more about EMPs than the rest of them put together.

Tommy followed her. "These cars," she said. "If they belong to members of staff, there might be a spare card in one of them." She stopped at the nearest car, stooped down, grabbed a stone, and threw it at the driver's side window, then reached inside to open the door and began rifling through the glove box.

"Cool...." Lucky was next to them and didn't need any persuading to copy her. Quickly, he jogged to the next car and did the same. Stone. Window. Search.

Tommy followed suit, and then Molly heard Alex Banks shout at the twins as they too began to smash car windows with rocks, each of them searching for a card.

As Molly broke the window of an expensive-looking VW, Colton appeared at her side. "Molly," he said, looking appalled, "this is madness. We can't go back in there. It's a suicide mission."

Molly stood up straight and looked at him. She was about to tell him to get off his high horse and help them when Scarlett shouted.

"Miss O'Neil! I found something!"

Molly, Erik, and Alex ran over to her. She was standing behind a large black car. Its trunk was open, and she was pulling out a large metal case. Setting it on the ground, she tried the lid, but it wouldn't lift.

"It looks like a laptop case." Scarlett looked up at Erik and he grinned.

"Scarlett, we need a keycard, not a laptop," Molly said softly.

"I know, but it's a metal case, Miss O'Neil. So, if there's a keycard in here, it means it might actually still work."

When Molly frowned, Erik added, "The metal offers a layer of protection from the—"

Molly interrupted him with a nod. "I get it, I get it."

"But it's locked." Scarlett tried the lid again. "Looks like it needs a key."

She had sighed and was pushing the case aside when Tommy stepped up, angling the case into the light of the moon. Squinting at the lock, he nodded, then swung his backpack onto the ground and opened it up.

"Here, kid." He passed an odd-looking flashlight to Lucky. "Crank the handle and point it at the lock."

Lucky frowned at it. "It won't work," Lucky said, shaking his head.

"It's wind-up." Tommy turned the handle on the flashlight's side, and it flickered to life.

Lucky's eyes widened. "*Coool.*"

"A friend gave it to me," Tommy explained. Then he dove back into his backpack and drew out a miniature tool kit. Using a tiny screwdriver, he started to fiddle with the lock. As Tommy stuck his tongue out of the corner of his mouth and leaned closer to the lock, concentrating, the others all watched in awe.

Finally… a faint but distinct clunk and the lid popped open.

Tommy pushed it toward Scarlett, smiling and allowing her to open it. Catching the exchange of glances between them, Alex Banks stepped up and picked up the case, balancing it on the hood of a nearby car. Scarlett stepped up beside him, lifted the lid and took out a slim black laptop. After looking at it longingly, she tossed it to one side and searched the rest of the case, then triumphantly looked up, grinning. "Ta dah!" She was holding a key card.

"Well done." Molly patted Tommy's shoulder.

"Now all we need is access to the generator." Erik looked triumphant, but their father was not happy.

"Absolutely not, Erik." he said. "It's far too dangerous. Someone else will have to…." Alex looked from Molly to Colton, but Molly pursed her lips.

"I'm sorry, Mr. Banks. Erik really is the only one who can help us."

"Come on, Alex. It's my *brother*." Tommy had strode over and was looking at Alex as if he owed him something.

"Look," Erik said loudly. "Zack is a jerk." He glanced warily at Tommy. "No offense, man… he's a jerk. But he's one of us. So, we're going back for him."

26

MOLLY

"Where's the most likely place for it to be, Erik?" Molly was ignoring Colton's and Alex's worried frowns and focusing on making a plan.

"It'll be on the perimeter of the building somewhere, probably fenced in. So, we might need some—"

"Wire cutters?" Tommy interrupted and produced something from his backpack. As he held up a large red pair of wire cutters, Molly nodded approvingly.

Erik grinned. "Yeah, they'll do."

"Okay then, we stick together, start at the front entrance and work our way around the building." Molly was about to stride back across the moonlit parking lot when Alex Banks coughed and stepped forward.

"Will this help locate it?" He handed her a piece of paper, which had been folded several times.

"We came across a blueprint," Tommy said, as if it was no big deal. "It should show you where the generator is, and how to get back inside too."

Molly wanted to ask how on earth they'd 'come across' a blueprint for Fairfield Prison, but there wasn't time. So she unfolded what looked like a map and peered at it.

"There," Erik said, pointing to something that looked like a box on the outside wall near an exercise yard. "That's it."

"Okay then, let's go." Molly handed Erik the map and let him lead the way.

Quickly they moved past the cars they'd raided, and then around the opposite side of the building. "Can you hear that?" Erik called out. "Come on." They passed two doors that looked like fire exits, each with a keycard entry system, a fenced-in and sparse exercise yard with tiered seating at the back that reminded Molly of the high school playing field, and a loading zone that seemed like it might lead to a kitchen.

Finally, Molly saw Scarlett tug on Erik's sleeve and point to a large white metal box that looked like an oversized air-conditioning unit.

"That's it," Erik said excitedly, shoving the map into his pocket, charging toward the wire fence that enclosed it and gesturing for Tommy to follow him.

At the fence, Tommy expertly used the wire cutters to snip a slash that they could peel back and climb through. As they approached the generator, Molly noticed Erik's eyes widen. It was big. Probably bigger than he'd expected, and it seemed, at first glance, to be totally sealed.

Slowly, Erik began to snake his fingers across its surface. Behind him, Molly and the others watched, unsure what to do to help.

"Okay, so this is the access door." Erik turned to them and, this time, he wasn't smiling. "But it needs a key."

Molly inhaled sharply. Their plan was failing already.

"A key like this one?" Lucky was holding a small round key, offering it to Erik.

"Where'd you get that?" Scarlett asked, taking it on Erik's behalf and squinting at it in the darkness.

"The security office," he said, shrugging. "Thought it might be useful."

Erik breathed out heavily, making a *pfft* sound with his lips that reminded Molly of a horse neighing. "Right, then. Let's do this."

As Erik moved closer to the generator's housing, his father put a firm hand on his shoulder and leaned in. Not so quietly, he whispered, "Erik, do you know what you're doing here, son? I don't want you getting hurt trying to save some kid who decided of his own volition to stay behind."

Molly looked at Tommy, expecting to see anger on his face, but his expression was unreadable—as if he were thinking of something else entirely.

"Yeah, Dad. I know what I'm doing," Erik said, moving his dad's hand. Looking at the others, he added, "Who's got a flashlight?"

Molly looked at Jenna, who still had the working flashlight in her back pocket. When she turned it on, the light caught Molly's eyes and the brightness made her blink hard. She gestured for Jenna to point it at the lock.

At first, when Erik turned the key and pulled at the door, it didn't budge. The casing looked ancient; weatherbeaten, rusted at the edges, and no longer the bright white it would be if it were newly installed. "It looks like it hasn't been so much as looked at it since it was installed," Molly said as worry niggled at her stomach.

"This thing looks about thirty years old, which means it shouldn't have any modern electronics," Erik replied, grinning. "Also this," he banged his fist on the metal casing, "offers an element of protection, so hopefully, if I can figure out what's wrong...." His grin wavered; that seemed like a big 'if'.

Turning away from the others, Erik began to tug at a section of the casing that looked like it should open up. The metal, warped from being outdoors so long, was stuck firm and when it finally moved, it made an almighty screeching noise. Erik pulled it back and Scarlett stepped up to hold it open for him.

"Okay, then, son, what's the plan?" Molly almost smiled as Alex Banks moved up next to his son and peered at the generator. As he did, the two of them exchanged a knowing look, a look that said they didn't agree but would work together anyway.

Erik folded his arms and stared at the insides of the generator. To Molly, it looked utterly unintelligible. A panel with switches and buttons. Wires. More wires.

Confidently, Erik began to shift the wires aside. "So, it's been stopping and starting, which means it's not completely dead," Erik mused.

"But it did stop altogether before you escaped?" Alex countered.

"Yeah. It did." Erik started inspecting each component in turn. "The batteries were protected from the EMP, or it wouldn't have worked at all," he said, looking up at his dad. "So, it's not that."

"What about filters? Like aircon units? Does it have those? The aircon in your mom's studio needs to be serviced regularly with new filters or it stops working."

Erik pursed his lips and considered the idea. "Possibly. If that's the case, then this will take a while. We've got no fresh filters, so we'll have to try and clean them."

"What else could it be?" Molly interrupted. She sounded impatient but was painfully aware that every second they used the flashlight was a second they wouldn't have in the future if they needed it, and every second they hung around out here was a second they risked being discovered.

Sensing her nervousness, Colton nudged her elbow and nodded. "Let the boy think, Molly. He looks like he knows what he's doing."

"Are you disappointed?" She half-smiled at him as Erik went back to muttering with his dad.

Colton tilted his head. "No. I can't say I'd have made the same choice, but *leave no man behind* is hardly something I can disagree with."

Molly nodded. Knowing Colton didn't think any less of her for insisting they return eased the tension in her stomach.

"That's it!" Erik shouted, before being shhh'd by his sister. Looking at his dad, he raised his eyebrows questioningly and Alex shrugged his shoulders.

"It's worth a try."

"Okay, so…" Erik's fingers hovered over the control panel. "Grandad's tractor had a similar problem once. Do you remember, Scar?"

Scarlett looked blankly at him.

"It kept stopping and starting because the fuel gauge was faulty. It thought the engine was empty when it wasn't. But it wasn't consistent. It kept, like, resetting itself. I think that's what's happening here."

As Alex stared at his son, looking both impressed and confused at the same time, Erik began to quickly unplug and re-plug a selection of wires.

"How do you fix that, Erik?" Colton asked, stepping forward and peering over Alex Banks' shoulder.

"With a bit of luck," Erik replied, grinning.

Finally, after what felt like minutes but was probably seconds, Erik stood back and wiped his hands. Gesturing for Jenna to turn off the flashlight, he took a deep breath, reached forward, and flipped a switch.

Nothing happened.

For a long moment there was silence, but then the generator made a clunking sound. It started to whirr, louder and louder, and then BAM, light streamed from the prison windows, casting long strips of orange and yellow across the ground outside.

Erik whooped loudly and high-fived his sister. Alex patted them both on the back and kissed their foreheads. "Great job, you two," he said proudly.

"Really great...." Molly breathed out a sigh of relief and slipped the flashlight into her back jeans pocket, hiding it with the hem of her shirt.

"After you...." Erik pointed to a door in front of them. Muted light was coming from a small glass pane above it, and next to it was a keycard reader.

Molly took the keycard from her pocket and walked nervously to the reader. This was it. If this didn't work, they'd have no choice but to leave the prison—and Zack—far behind them.

She held her breath. A small green light on the reader was blinking. She smiled. Pressing the card on top of it, she waited. Clunk. The door was unlocked. They were going back in.

27

DOUGIE

Dougie was sitting on a plastic chair, tipping it back and forth, and staring at a trash can. He had instructed Frank to fill it with papers from the Warden's desk and set it on fire; now it was pitch black outside and with the generator conked out, they needed light.

Frank, of course, had willingly obeyed and was now setting more trash cans alight in the hallways and wherever inmates were congregating. Dougie began to chew a loose piece of skin on his thumb; his eyes were watering from the smoke from the trash cans but they needed the light from the fires. In front of him, a group of prisoners were setting out their weapons, prepping them, examining them. Another group was playing cards. Other than the low murmur of voices, for the first time that day, everything was quiet.

Luther was on guard duty. Dougie knew he'd jump at the chance to finish rustling out any remaining guards still in hiding, and Dougie didn't much care what Luther did to them when he found them. The only one he wanted was Fox. He wanted to know where he was because something about that guy got under his skin, and he didn't know how he'd managed to escape when the prisoners stormed through the barricaded door.

Next to him, Zack was quiet, nose in his book. Dougie had never been much of a reader, but he knew the book would do the trick as soon as he saw the look on Zack's face as he offered it to him. He still hadn't figured out whether he wanted Zack to stay because he recognized some of himself in the kid's pathetic life; or if he simply had known from the moment he set eyes on him that he'd be useful. Either way, he'd gotten what he wanted. So he supposed his motivation didn't really matter.

Dougie stood up and began to pace up and down. He should be feeling relaxed, but he wasn't. He was on edge and it was starting to piss him off.

"Right! Listen up!" He stopped and yelled at the others. "I think it's time we celebrated the new world order around here."

For a second, no one moved, but then they started banging on tables and cheering.

"Raid the kitchen. We're having a feast!"

"I can think of somewhere better to raid!" A guy whose name Dougie had never bothered to learn got up and walked over to him. He was bigger, but dumber. A meth-head with yellow teeth and sunken cheeks.

"Oh yeah?" Dougie sat back down and leaned onto his thighs, pressing his fingertips together. "Where's that?"

The guy scratched at the skin on his forearms. He was jonsing, and that was one road Dougie had never allowed himself to go down. "The pharmacy, man, but we need a key."

Dougie saw his fellow inmate's eyes go to the keys on Dougie's belt—a belt he'd prised from a dead guard—but didn't attempt to hide them.

It was a tricky moment to navigate; he needed the inmates to have their wits about them, but he also needed them to respect him and do as he said. He couldn't have an uprising so soon after taking command, and if the meth-heads decided to create a fuss, well, everyone else would join in.

"Come on, Dougie, it's a party," someone else called up at him.

"Yeah, man, let us have some fun."

Dougie pretended to be thinking about it, then slowly stood up and took the keys from his belt. Dangling them in front of him, he gave them a wiggle. He could feel Zack watching him, could almost feel the kid's anxiety seeping from his pores. His big brother might be hard as nails, but Zack wasn't.

"Okay," Dougie said. "I'll go check it out, and I'll bring you some goodies at dinner time."

The inmate opened his mouth to speak but Dougie, not so subtly, flexed his fingers on the trigger of his gun.

"Okay, inmate?"

A flash of annoyance crossed the guy's face; Dougie was talking to him the way the guards did, but for now he let it go. "Okay, boss."

Dougie gestured for Zack to come with him. "Let's go, kid."

Half an hour later, every morsel of food from the kitchens had been spread out on the large trestle tables. Someone had fetched a batch of contraband home brew from their cell, and someone else was passing around cigarettes stolen from the guards' lockers. Dougie smiled to himself. *Keep them happy and they'll keep you safe*, he thought, stepping dramatically into the middle of the room.

After taking what he needed from the pharmacy, Dougie had allowed the others to have their fill. But he had a little something extra up his sleeve.

"And finally, gentlemen," he shouted with a flourish. "For your entertainment...." He gestured for Zack to come forward and the kid walked nervously up beside him. He was holding a huge bowl, full to the brim with thick, bright pink liquid.

Painstakingly, the two of them had emptied boxes and boxes of different pills into it. Dougie had then handed Zack his gun and instructed him to use the butt on the grip to crush them. With the kid's spindly arms, it had taken a while, but when they were finally nothing more than a powder, Dougie had grinned widely.

"Okay, now the fun part..." he'd said, enjoying the look of awe on Zack's face as he'd added coffee and Kool-Aid to the mix and it turned pink.

Before Zack put the bowl down on the table closest to him, Dougie gave it one last stir with his index finger, raised it up high so everyone could see it, then licked the mixture off and let out a loud crass laugh.

The room instantly erupted into whoops and hollers. Inmates banged their fists on the tables, and as Zack approached them, he looked like he might be about to piss his pants.

Finally, he set the bowl down at the head of the longest table. Dougie watched with interested eyes as a pause descended. He'd expected the men to rush forward, clamor for it, push and shove and probably even start fighting, but they didn't.

Instead, one of the guys near the front shouted, "Bring your mugs, fellas," and stood up to start dishing it out. "There's enough for everyone!"

Well, well, well, thought Dougie, *there's still some surprises to be had, after all.*

Beside him, Zack tugged on his sleeve. "Dougie?"

"Yeah, kid?"

"I—"

"What?" Dougie walked back to his chair and picked up the chocolate pudding he'd saved for himself.

Zack cleared his throat and pushed his hair over his shoulder; sooner or later, Dougie would get him to shave it off. It really was absurd for a dude to have hair like that. "It's just... perhaps we shouldn't eat *all* the food."

Dougie put down the pudding. At least Zack wasn't whining about the pills. "Why's that?"

"An EMP will mean there's no more supply chain beyond these walls." When Dougie looked at him blankly, Zack continued, "Food is now a finite resource—"

Dougie narrowed his eyes. "Finite. As in..."

"As in... it'll run out," Zack answered.

"Right." Dougie looked up at the crowd of inmates who were loudly downing their mugs of medicated Kool-Aid and had already devoured nearly half of the food on the tables. Then he snapped his fingers and stood up.

No one noticed.

He motioned for everyone to be quiet, but still no one noticed, so he took his gun and fired it at the wall. *Bang!* That got their attention.

"Shut it! The kid has something to say...." He waved his hand at Zack. "Tell them what you just told me, but louder, and in plain English."

Zack looked horrified. For a moment, he simply stuttered. He'd begun to sweat. Finally, he spoke. "It's just...." He tried to raise his voice. "What's in the prison is our only food supply right now. There'll be no more deliveries. Nothing coming in the next days or weeks. Eventually, we'll have to venture out and find more but, for now, we should probably eat the perishable stuff first." Zack pointed to Dougie's pudding. "Like the pudding, that's great." He smiled weakly. "But the canned stuff and the dried stuff... we should keep that. For later."

Dougie nodded slowly. Zack had killed the mood. A couple of guys looked like they wanted to throttle him. Before Dougie could say something to rectify the situation, however, there was a whirr and a click, and the power snapped back on.

The room erupted into cheers, but Dougie instantly silenced them.

"Go check it out!" he yelled, jumping to his feet. "You!" he pointed at a prisoner near the door. "Go!" Then he leaned down and put his hands down firmly on the table in front of Zack. "What does this mean?"

Zack shook his head. "I don't know."

"You don't know?"

"I don't think it's good. Either the EMP wasn't as bad as we thought or...."

"Or?" Dougie moved his face closer to Zack's.

"Or someone else is here and has fixed the generator."

28

MOLLY

C olton pushed the service door open and slowly stepped through it. Alex was at the back of the group, Tommy and Molly behind Colton.

"It's some kind of storage room," Colton said, looking around. Even with the power back on, the room was dimly lit, but Molly could make out workbenches, cupboards, and tools hanging on the walls.

"Colton," she said, pointing at the tools, "will your keys open those cupboards?"

For a moment, he looked at her as though he'd forgotten that he had keys with him. Then he took them from his pocket and tried the one nearest to him. "Bingo," he said, as the doors swung open.

"Okay, kids, grab whatever you can to fashion a weapon. The guys up there are armed. If we can get to Dougie, I think he'll listen to us. He seemed to genuinely care for Zack, but we need to get to him first."

The kids nodded. Alex Banks pointed to a workbench nearby and they began to empty the cupboards, lining up the tools and trying to decide which would be most useful if they came across a group of vicious felons.

"There are no weapons here," Scarlett said, picking up a hammer. "Not real weapons."

"Times like these," Tommy said grimly, "we have to use what we find. We don't have the luxury of *real* weapons. But something like this...."

Molly watched as Tommy picked up a wrench and weighed it up and down in his hand.

"This could be deadly if you use enough force."

As Scarlett looked at Tommy with wide, impressed eyes, Molly stepped up beside him and picked up a screwdriver. Glancing at him, she narrowed her eyes and examined his face. He didn't look anything like what she'd pictured when Zack described him.

Sensing that she was watching him, Tommy turned to her and said, "Everything okay?"

"You don't look much like your brother," she said, trying to smile. "And you don't look half as scary as he said you were."

Tommy tilted his head to the side and chuckled. "Yeah, well Zack was a little kid when I got put away. I haven't seen him for years." He paused and bit his lower lip. "I'm a very different guy now."

"He said you... killed someone?"

Tommy raised his eyebrows, as if he were impressed that she'd dared to ask the question. Slowly, he nodded. "I stole a car and crashed it into a guy on the sidewalk. He died."

Molly pursed her lips.

"I've got no excuse for it. I was a dumb kid."

"It must be hard knowing that Zack got himself into trouble after you went away."

Tommy frowned. "Trouble?" He laughed a little. "Zack's never been in trouble. Not as far as I know. Unless not doing his homework counts."

Molly leaned back onto the bench. "But… he was kicked out of military school."

"Military school?" Tommy lowered his voice and added, "Nah. That was a stupid rumor. Zack's never been anywhere like that."

"I see."

"Listen…." Tommy turned to her and met her eyes. "Zack is a good kid. I left him alone with our waste-of-space mom, and he didn't deserve that. So I get why he never came to visit me and why he'd make up a bunch of shit about me. That's why I had to come get him. To show him that he can count on me."

Molly was about to tell Tommy that she knew it would mean a lot to Zack when, across the room, Jenna screamed.

"Miss O'Neil!"

Molly and Tommy rushed toward her.

"It's the guards from the Scared Straight room." Jenna pointed to the floor and Molly looked down to see one of the guards—Fox—slumped against the wall. He was bleeding but alive.

Quickly, Molly bobbed down in front of him and shook his shoulder. "Mr. Fox? Can you hear me?"

The guard's eyes fluttered open. He inhaled a slow, rattly breath. "Emma," he whispered, "Help Emma."

Molly leaned closer. "Emma? Mr. Fox, who's Emma?"

Before Fox could answer, Colton put his hand on Molly's shoulder. "It's the other guard, Molly, there."

A few yards away, half beneath the workbench, Molly spotted a pair of women's feet. Alex had run to her and was bending down, leaning under the bench. Scarlett was next to her dad. She looked back at Molly and shook her head. "It's Grayson. She's—"

Finally, Alex reappeared. Pushing his fingers through his hair, he shook his head. "I'm sorry," he said, "she's dead. It looks like her throat was…" he trailed off, almost choking on his own words.

Scarlett pressed her eyes closed and backed away.

At Molly's feet, Fox let out a loud anguished cry and tried to wave his arms. "Run," he said. "Get the hell out of here and save yourselves before it's too late."

Molly shook her head. "Absolutely not. We're not leaving you. I'm very sorry about your friend, Mr. Fox, but we can still help you. Can you stand?" She tried to help him up, but he stumbled and cried out in pain, so Molly beckoned for Colton to help too. Together they helped him to his feet. "We can't leave him here alone," Molly said, thinking quickly. "Jenna, Lucky, take Mr. Fox back to the bus. There's a first aid kit. Patch him up as best you can and give him some water." She handed Jenna the keycard and told her to put it in her pocket.

"Are you sure?"

Molly nodded firmly. "If the cops do show up, they'll need a way in."

Jenna nodded, already slotting her strong frame under the guard's arm. Lucky took the other arm and nodded at her; whether he was pleased he'd been trusted with a job of significance or simply pleased to be excused from the rescue mission, she couldn't tell.

"Take this too." Molly held out the working flashlight, but Lucky shook his head at her.

"No, Miss O'Neil, we tried like every flashlight we could find and were lucky to find that one. You might need it."

"Lucky, we've got the generator now. You and Jenna—"

"Take this one." Tommy stepped up and gestured for Lucky to take the small red wind-up flashlight he'd used to pick the lock outside.

Accompanying them to the door, Molly instructed them to go straight to the bus and pull the doors shut behind them. Jenna nodded. "We'll be fine, Miss O'Neil." As the two of them helped an injured Fox out into the darkness beyond the prison, Molly was already beginning to wonder if she was doing the right thing.

"Okay, everyone." She turned back to the others and nodded at them. "I think it's time—"

Behind Alex, the door to the rest of the prison slammed open, bouncing on its hinges as it whacked back against the wall. Silhouetted in the doorway were Dougie and Zack.

Molly noticed Tommy move toward his brother. Before he could get more than a foot, Dougie raised his arm and pointed his gun into the room. "Whatever you're holding, put it down!" he shouted, looking around at the group's makeshift weapons. "Put it down or I start shooting!"

29

LUCKY

The guard's arm was like a block of lead resting on Lucky's shoulders, but Jenna didn't seem to be struggling, so he kept his back straight and carried on walking. Slowly, they headed back through the wire fence and across the eerie parking lot.

As they passed cars of all makes and sizes, Lucky was struck by the thought that—in all likelihood—none of these cars would ever be used. Ever again. They'd just sit here and rust for all of eternity. Unless the power came back. Although, at this point, he was pretty convinced that Erik and Scarlett were right; an EMP had destroyed the planet. There was no going back.

Snapping his thoughts back to the present, Lucky nudged the guard and asked him if he was okay. No answer.

It was dark in the parking lot. The moon was bright, but obscured by clouds, and it seemed to take forever to make the short distance to the back of the lot where the bus was parked.

While holding onto the guard, it was impossible to wind up the flashlight, but as soon as they reached the bus and deposited his lumpy body into one of the seats, Lucky stood back and began to crank the handle.

"The first aid kit's under Colton's seat," Jenna instructed, pointing to the front of the bus.

Lucky retrieved it and tossed it to her. "You know first aid?" he asked.

"No," she replied snippily, a hint of panic in her voice. "I'm sure I can figure out how to put a bandage on him." Tentatively, Jenna pointed to the guard's shirt. It was soaked with blood. "Sir, sorry, could you lift your shirt so I can see?"

Mr. Fox nodded and winced as he raised his shirt to expose his belly. "My name's Victor," he said through clenched teeth. "Call me Victor."

As Victor lifted his shirt, Lucky puffed out his cheeks and released a heavy breath. There was a large gash in the man's chest, which was bleeding heavily, and a smaller one beneath it, as if whoever had stabbed him had gone back for a second go. "Oh, man. What happened to you?"

"I think it was a shiv," Victor said gruffly. "Possibly a knife."

"Shit, mister. I'm not sure we can—" Lucky's chest was beginning to feel a bit panicky. He was a kid. He didn't know anything about first aid. The most he'd ever done was stick a bandage on his own knee when he fell off his bike. All he really knew how to do was burn stuff. And a fat lot of good that was now!

"Here…." Victor beckoned for the first aid kit. "I'll do it myself."

Jenna handed it to him and sat back in her seat, looking a little helpless as the guard placed a large gauze square over his wounds and then started to awkwardly wind a bandage around his middle. Already, blood was seeping through it.

The procedure seemed to take an age, during which Lucky and Jenna waited silently. When he'd finally finished, Victor looked from one to the other and shook his head. "Listen," he said, his breath catching in his chest, "what the hell were you all thinking coming back inside? You should have run for the hills the second you got out of that place."

"Our teacher," Jenna said proudly. "She wanted to go back and rescue Zack. He decided to stay with the prisoners but—"

Victor shook his head and accepted the bottle of water Jenna was offering him. "That's the dumbest thing I ever heard," he said after taking a few large swigs. "You two should go back there right now. Get the others out and leave this place." Victor looked from Jenna to Lucky, then widened his eyes. "I mean it. There are dangerous men in there. Very dangerous men, and don't think just 'cos you're kids they won't touch you. Those guys...." Victor tipped his head in the direction of the prison. "They're pure evil."

"But Zack...."

"Sorry, but if he decided to stay, that was his choice. No point getting yourselves killed, or worse, just because he made a stupid decision."

Lucky stopped winding up the flashlight. It stayed lit, so he passed it to Victor. Jenna's lips had set into a thin, pursed line. "We're going back?" Lucky asked her, almost sighing.

"We're going back."

Leaving Victor with the first aid kit and Tommy's flashlight, Lucky and Jenna ran back across the parking lot toward the rear entrance of the prison. The generator was still whirring away, and they passed it quickly, pausing outside the door and straining their ears.

Jenna brandished the keycard and was about to use it when a gunshot rang out from inside. Lucky flattened himself against the wall and pulled her back with him. "What do we do?" he whispered.

"I have no idea. Run?" Jenna was staring at the door.

"We can't," Lucky said in a loud whisper. "We can't leave them."

"There are *guns* in there, Lucky. What the hell can we do to help?"

On any other occasion, Lucky might have made a joke about Jenna fighting them with her bare hands, but right now, it didn't seem appropriate. He closed his eyes. It was cold. He shoved his hands into his pockets and began to fiddle with the lighter Miss O'Neil had allowed him to keep. He began to turn it between his fingers. Then suddenly, it came to him. Without looking at Jenna, he took off running, back toward the parking lot.

"Lucky," Jenna had followed suit and was grabbing his arm, "what are you doing?"

"We," said Lucky, "are going to light a few fires."

In the middle of the parking lot, Lucky stopped running. Jenna was looking at him as if he'd lost his mind, so he quickly explained his plan. "Get as much fabric as you can find. Anything. Search all the cars in the lot."

"Okay," she said hesitantly. "Why?"

"I'll explain in a bit, just do it," Lucky said, already racing toward the nearest car and preparing to smash the window and gain access. "And check the trunks too."

"What for?"

"Ammo or anything flammable. But don't take them out. Leave the trunks open so we know which ones to go back to."

"Go back to?"

"Just *do* it," Lucky said, trying not to sound impatient.

For a few minutes, they worked quickly, not speaking, just smash, search, grab. Smash, search, grab. When they had gathered enough to form a small pile, Lucky nodded.

"Now what?" Jenna asked, hands on hips.

"Now," he said, wiggling his eyebrows at her, "we need fuel."

As they ran back to the bus, Lucky told Jenna to go get the flashlight from Victor. Popping the hood, he heard Victor ask Jenna what was going on. She ignored him, said, "No time to explain," and rushed back out.

"Right, crank the handle and give me some light," Lucky instructed, feeling a little like a bomb disposal expert in one of those cop shows his grandmother watched.

Peering at the bus's engine, he tentatively poked at some wires and cables.

"What are you doing?" Jenna hissed.

"I need a hose. Something we can use to get fuel from the tank."

"I think I saw one over there." Jenna pointed in the direction of a fancy-looking BMW.

"Great. Show me."

Together they ran over to it, and Jenna rifled through the contents of the trunk. "Here. God knows why you'd want to keep this in your car."

"Who cares?" Lucky grabbed it and ran back to the bus. Behind him, Jenna yelled. "Lucky, please, tell me what the hell you're doing?"

Lucky paused, hose in hand, panting from running. "Okay, we need to do two things: cause a distraction so that whatever's going on inside, the others have a chance to escape. And try to attract help from any cops who might be nearby and still give a damn whether people are okay or not."

Jenna narrowed her eyes at him. "Ok*aaay*...."

"How many cars did you find with ammo?"

Pointing, Jenna gestured to five cars with the trunks left open.

"Great. And I found two, which should be plenty...." He forced himself to take a breath and slow down a little. "We set fire to the cars. Worst case scenario, all that happens is lots of black smoke and some decent flames. Hopefully enough to attract attention. *Best* case scenario, the ammo gets so hot it starts pinging like firecrackers and whoever hears it thinks it's gunshots."

"Ohhhh." She grinned and thumped Lucky on the shoulder. "Well, that's freaking brilliant." Then she paused. "Wait... firecrackers?" Jenna's eyes had widened.

"Yeah—"

"I saw some."

"Huh?"

"Not firecrackers. Fireworks." She turned and started scanning the cars. "Over there. The blue one. It had a whole bunch of party stuff on the backseat." Her eyes brightened as she finally began to share Lucky's vision. "Including a box of fireworks."

"Oh," Lucky smiled. "That'll do nicely."

Running to the back of the bus, he tried to reel through his memory and figure out what to do next. Hastily, he opened the fuel cap and shoved the hose into the hole. Okay, how did this work? His cousin had done it once, when his motorbike ran out of fuel and he decided to steal some from their grandad's tractor, and Lucky had watched a couple of YouTube videos. He'd never actually done it himself, though.

Waving at Jenna, he told her to bring the fabric over and she came with a bundle of hoodies, sweatpants, gym towels, and blankets. "Put them there," he told her, pointing to the ground next to the back tire of the bus. Then, bending down, he put the hose in his mouth and began to suck.

"Don't swallow any," Jenna warned.

Lucky rolled his eyes, but as the greasy, acrid taste of diesel filled his mouth he gagged. He nearly choked on it, but then spat it out onto the ground and directed the siphon to the pile of clothes. Heavenly-smelling fuel poured out, soaking the fabrics as he'd intended.

When they were drenched, Lucky picked them up and handed the pile back to Jenna. "Shove a couple of pieces in a bunch of these cars. But more in the ones with the ammo." Wiggling his eyebrows at her, he added, "I'll follow and do the setting on fire part… but save the fireworks until last."

His chest began to flutter. It was brilliant. And it was going to be the coolest thing he'd ever seen. As Jenna deposited the fabric, he leaned in behind her, flicked his lighter, and waited patiently for the bundles to catch fire.

Finally they came to the trunk with the fireworks. "We'll need to be quick with this one," Lucky said solemnly.

Jenna nodded and tossed the diesel-soaked clothes onto the backseat, then stepped away.

Quickly, Lucky leaned in, held the lighter beneath a corner of cloth until it caught fire, then slammed the door closed, grabbed Jenna's hand, and ran to the other side of the parking lot.

"How long before they…?" Jenna asked as they pressed themselves up against the wall of the building.

"Not too long," Lucky said, rubbing his hands. "It's going to be epic."

30

LAURA

For a long moment, Laura didn't move. She stared at the bottle in her hand, rubbing her thumb over the shiny clear plastic of the bag she'd sealed it in, and tried to convince herself to put it back where it had come from. Eventually, she opened the bag and tossed it into the trash can beside the sink. Now that the bottle was in her hand, the urge to pop it open and tip the pills into her palm gripped her shoulders. Her throat twitched as she recalled the feeling of swallowing one, two, three… and the release that came after. The sweet, sweet release.

That tiny white bottle had remained in its hiding place for months. She put it there before rehab because she knew Alex would empty her drawers and sift through her purses as soon as she was gone, weeding out anything that might hinder her recovery when she returned. She'd never allowed herself to think about whether it was because he was simply doing his bit to help her or because he didn't really believe rehab would work.

When she did return home, she checked—just once—to see if he'd found it. At first, when she saw that the bag was still taped to the inside of the tank, she wondered whether Alex had left it there as some kind of trap. No, not a trap—a test. If he had, then it was a test she passed with flying colors. All that time since, she'd never touched it. Never even been tempted to, because knowing it was there had been enough. A fail-safe. A back-up plan.

Looking at the fading light beyond the bathroom window, Laura swallowed hard. The world was falling apart. In the weeks and months to come, who knew whether they'd be able to find medication if they needed it. If one of the kids got hurt. If Alex got hurt.

Laura nodded, pursed her lips, then reached around to shove the bottle into the back pocket of her jeans. She would keep them with her. In case someone else needed them.

After picking up the gun and gently wheeling herself down the hallway, heart still thudding loudly against the sudden quiet of the house, she headed to the kitchen. Drawers and cupboards had been flung open, cutlery and cereal boxes scattered over the worktops. Laura shook her head; did Dave really think she'd hide pills in the kitchen?

She placed the gun on top of Argent's cage and reached for a bottle of water. As she took a long drink, she realized that her hands were still shaking. She leaned forward and rested her head in her hands. She was exhausted. Her muscles felt twitchy and sore, like they did if she worked out too hard for too long, and a dull ache was gripping her skull.

When she looked up, Argent was sitting in front of her. He tilted his head to the side, and as Laura reached out to cup his head with her hands, tears sprang to her eyes. "I'm glad you're okay, boy," she whispered. "I don't think I could do this without you."

Argent allowed her to rest her forehead against his for a moment, but then stood up, walked into the middle of the living room and looked towards the study.

Laura swallowed hard. The door was ajar, but she knew what lay behind it.

Slowly, she wheeled over to the living room window and looked out at the street. She'd fired a gun; on any normal day, a neighbor would have come running, checked that she was okay, called the cops. But the street was eerily quiet. It wasn't yet pitch dark, but it was getting close. From a couple of houses, muted lights flickered in the windows, but there were no people; it was as if the entire neighborhood had gone into hiding.

Trying to think methodically, like Alex would, Laura went to the front door and bolted it shut, then went from room to room closing the blinds and checking that every window and door was locked. Finally, she returned to the front door to double check that it really was sealed shut. After rattling the handle three times, and finally feeling satisfied that no one could open it, she paused, staring at the coat rack beside the front door. From the corner of her eye, she could see Alex's study. The room beyond the crack in the door looked darker than the rest of the house, but Laura was certain she could make out the shape of a lifeless arm splayed across the floor. Dave's arm. The arm of the man she killed.

A knot of nausea began to form at the bottom of Laura's throat. She killed someone. There was a dead man in her husband's study. She wanted to rush back to the bathroom and vomit. She wanted to go to bed, wrap herself in her duvet and pretend that none of this was happening.

Instinctively, she looked at her smartwatch for the time. Of course, the screen was black. Shiny and useless, it was now nothing more than an ornament on her small, tanned wrist. It was light when Alex left, and now it was nearly dark, but she had no real idea of how many hours had passed.

He might be gone until morning, but he might also be back any minute now with the kids in tow. And how the hell would she explain it to them? Alex would probably tell her she did the right thing; she was protecting herself, what choice did she have? But the kids? They'd be terrified.

Laura breathed in sharply through her nose and looked at Argent. "Okay, boy," she said. "I might need your help with this one."

As Laura pushed the door, it butted up against something hard, which she knew was Dave's dead body. She didn't look at him until she was fully inside, and when she did, she gripped the arms of her chair so hard that her knuckles whitened with the pressure.

A short while ago, he'd looked like a dangerous psychopath, trembling with rage, eyes wide and jittery with the itch for whatever drugs he could find. Now he looked peaceful. He looked like the man she'd spoken to at group, a man she'd found to be funny, kind, normal. A man who, like her, had stumbled upon hard times but was pulling his life back together.

Laura exhaled a shaky breath and blinked back tears; then she straightened herself up and looked away. She began to examine Alex's study in a way she hadn't before. Usually when she came in here, it was to look for old coffee cups her husband had forgotten to wash up or candy wrappers he'd left scattered on his desk. Now she was looking for something she could use to help her move a man's body.

She needed Dave out of the house before the kids got home or before neighbors came knocking to check on her, but she had no idea how to do it. She was strong, but she couldn't walk. Looking down, she noticed the rug she'd bought to liven the place up a little. Alex's preference was for dark wood furniture and sparse walls but, even though it was *his* space, she hadn't been able to resist injecting a bit of brightness.

The rug was wool, terracotta orange with yellow tassels. Dave's feet were touching the edge of it, and it was held in place by the coffee table. Laura pressed her lips together, then wheeled closer to Dave, put the brake on her chair, and grabbed him by the ankle.

Argent was sitting by the door, watching her closely, and when he saw what she was doing, he walked over to her.

Laura gestured to Dave's other foot. For a moment, she thought Argent was going to walk away— confused by this strange game she was asking him to play—but he didn't. Dutifully, he took Dave's lower leg in his mouth and together they began to pull.

Unable to move the chair and Dave at the same time, Laura was forced to twist awkwardly as she and Argent heaved him further onto the rug. A rod of pain shot from the base of her spine all the way up to her neck, so sharp it took her breath away, but she ignored it and kept pulling.

A couple of times, she stopped to reposition the chair and get a better grip on Dave's leg. Eventually, his entire body was on the rug. Panting, Laura braced her hands on her hips and sat back. Argent was panting too, but almost looked as though he was enjoying himself—as if she were teaching him a fun new job that he could add to his repertoire.

After allowing herself to rest for a minute, Laura moved the coffee table out of the way and—once again fighting the urge to puke—used the footrest of her chair to roll Dave's body into the center of the rug, as she nudged the chair forward.

"Okay," she said softly, whether to herself or to Argent she wasn't sure. "Okay, we can do this."

With each movement feeling more labored than the last, Laura folded each half of the rug so that they met across Dave's stomach. Then she pushed the door wide open and headed to the garage. With no outside light, it was horribly dark, but Laura could make out the silhouette of their car, a modified Honda Odyssey with a retractable ramp to allow her easy access in and out, and a roof rack for Alex's bike.

Behind the car was Alex's disorganized DIY shelving. Toolboxes that he barely used, items he kept because they might be useful one day.

Straining her eyes, Laura began to rifle through them. She was looking for rope, string, anything she could use to tie around the rug. In the first few boxes, she found nothing, but then she came across some large strips of nylon that she recognized as the tie-down straps Alex used to secure extra luggage to the roof rack. She picked one up and pulled it taut between her hands, then nodded; that would do.

Back in the study, her arms still shaking from the effort of dragging Dave onto the rug, Laura lowered herself out of her chair and onto the floor beside him. Tucking the straps under the feet-end of the rug, she pulled and wriggled them until they were positioned half-way up. Then she knotted them together, reached up, and secured them to the back of her wheelchair.

Without looking behind her, she heaved herself back into her seat, breathed in, took the brake off her chair, and tried to wheel herself forward. The effort of moving just a few inches made her release a guttural cry, and Argent began to whine.

Gripping the doorframe, Laura pulled and pulled until finally she was in the hallway. Here, the flooring was easier; shiny hardwood that Alex installed because the grooves between their previous tiles had caused her chair to bump too much and had made her back hurt. Even with the smoother floors, and with Argent pulling on the top of the rug to help her, the weight of an extra person was cripplingly difficult.

Laura had no idea how long it took her to travel the small distance from Alex's study to the back door in the kitchen, but by the time she got there, it was completely dark outside. As she opened the door, cool air hit her face and she realized she was drenched in sweat.

She wanted to stop. To rest. Instead, once again, she got out of her chair. This time, she unhooked the straps from the back of it, and then rolled Dave towards the door. Just outside, on the patio, a gentle slope led down into the garden—another of the alterations Alex had made for her after the accident.

Laura pushed the rolled-up rug, and kept pushing, until Dave was positioned at the top of the slope, then she gave one final heave and watched him tumble down it, ending with a soft thud on the dewy grass of their neatly mown lawn.

Pressing herself up against the wall of the house, she scraped her fingers through her damp hair and tried to catch her breath. The pain in her back was now vibrating through her whole body so strongly that she couldn't tell where it even started from. Her chair felt too far away, and if it hadn't turned so cold, she might have been tempted to lie down and go to sleep.

She braced her hands in the small of her back and tried to wriggle into a position that would ease the discomfort but, as she did so, her fingertips brushed against the bottle in her pocket. Without even thinking, Laura pulled it free and clasped it tightly in her fingers. If there was ever a time when she deserved to take some, it was now. No, not *some*. One. For the pain. One pill would stop the pain and get her back on track. Without anything at all, it would simply continue to get worse. Her muscles would be inflamed and sore and it would build and build until it rendered her utterly useless.

Laura sucked in her cheeks and breathed slowly through pursed lips. Then she opened the bottle and spilled the pills into her clammy hand. She nudged the pills with her thumb. She closed her eyes and pictured the sweet release she'd feel after she took one. When she opened them, Argent was sitting in front of her. He blinked slowly, looking at her hand, then nuzzled the tips of her fingers.

Laura shook her head. "I'm sorry, boy. What am I doing?"

Argent replied with a sigh.

"You're right," she said. "Enough." Before she could think any more about it, she tilted her hand to pour the pills back in and snapped the lid back on. She then raised her arm and, using every ounce of power left in her, threw the bottle into the bushes at the bottom of the garden. As she heard it meet the leaves, and lost sight of it, she wiped her eyes with the back of her hand.

Finally, after all this time, she was free.

31

DOUGIE

Shit! What the hell was he supposed to do now? He couldn't let them get away with this kind of idiocy. He'd let them go and they'd *come back*? What kind of morons was he dealing with here?

"Kneel on the ground!" Dougie yelled, pointing his gun at each person in turn and trying to keep his cool.

"Boss, you need to kill them," Frank said, bouncing up and down. "You can't let them go, you can't—"

"I'm not letting them go!" Dougie snapped. "Shut up and let me think."

He didn't want to kill them. He didn't know why; it hadn't bothered him when he killed the guard. Nothing he'd done had ever bothered him. Sure, he'd told the guards, his cell mates, pretty much anyone who'd listen, that he was sorry for the cop he killed before he was locked up. But that was because he wanted to get out of this goddamn place. Really, he wasn't sorry one bit.

His lack of remorse had actually made him wonder, once or twice, whether he might be what was now fashionably termed a *psychopath*. He'd researched it a little, as much as his reading skills would allow, but had come away pretty convinced that, no, he wasn't a 'psycho'. He was just pragmatic. People died. It was a fact of life. It was also a fact that you couldn't change the past. So why waste energy feeling guilty about it?

For some reason, though, he couldn't quite bring himself to shoot Miss O'Neil *or* her students. Was it because she was the first attractive woman he'd had contact with in years? Maybe. Was it because he'd always considered that kids were where he'd draw the line? Perhaps. Although that hadn't mattered to the bastard who shot his brother, had it? Dougie braced his hands behind his head and looked up at the ceiling. He gave them their freedom and they threw it away. They came back. Presumably for Zack—because he was one of *them*. Because they thought he needed rescuing from Big Bad Dougie.

Well, Dougie thought, *he's not one of you anymore. He's with me now. And he's not going anywhere.*

"You should take them as hostages," Zack said, sidestepping in front of Dougie and trying to get his attention.

Dougie slowly looked down at him. "Hostages?" he said in almost a growl. "A few minutes ago, you were reminding me that our resources won't last forever, and now I'm supposed to share them with a bunch of *hostages*? We agreed hostages were pointless."

Zack frowned and looked confused. "You don't have to feed them," he laughed. "Just keep them. You know, in case."

"In case what?"

Zack looked up at the lights overhead. "We don't *know* what's happened out there. Even if the power's gone, the cops might still show up."

Dougie shuddered as he thought of the cops; cops and hostages were what had got him locked up in the first place.

"Just keep them for a couple of days, until we're sure. In case we need them to bargain with. And then—"

"Then we shoot them," Frank said, glowering at the bus driver and enjoying every second of it.

"Or—" Zack cut in. "We use them. Scarlett and Erik are smart, I bet it was them who got the generator working. Colton's strong as an ox and a good fighter."

Dougie was listening, trying to process what Zack was saying. "And the teacher?" he said, allowing his eyes to linger as he looked at her, surprised by the fact that she *still* looked the picture of calm. "What's she good for?"

"I can think of a thing or two!" Frank guffawed and wiped his mouth with the back of his hand. At this, finally, Molly O'Neil flinched.

Ignoring him, Zack waved his hand in the air and said, "Well, she's good at getting people to work together, isn't she? Organizing stuff. You've got to have some kind of order here, Dougie, or the prisoners will do whatever they like. You've got to show them you're in charge."

"Exactly!" Frank tugged at Dougie's arm. "Which is why you need to shoot them, boss. You can't—"

"QUIET!" Dougie didn't just yell, he screamed, and as he screamed, he fired a quick sharp shot into the ceiling. He knew his face would be flushed and his eyes wide, and he aimed his anger at Frank; the kid was useful, the way a puppy dog was useful, loyal and stupid, but he was annoying too.

Dougie turned to Zack and narrowed his eyes at him. "Are you trying to protect this lot, Zack? Is that what you're doing? Trying to save their skins by persuading me they're useful?"

He watched carefully as Zack processed his words.

"No, Dougie, I swear. I was trying to help you." At first, Zack looked worried, but then his features settled into a distasteful grimace. "They mean *nothing* to me." He shrugged and waved his hand at them. "Kill them if you like."

Dougie examined Zack's face. Maybe the kid was trying to protect his teacher, but he did have a point; she was an impressive woman. Dougie was weighing up the pros and cons of keeping her around, rather than having Frank shoot her just to shut him up for ten minutes, when his eyes came to rest on two faces he didn't recognize.

His muscles tensed. The man he was looking at was older than him, bearded, pale. The type who probably went to work in a suit and spent weekends taking long hikes with his wife and kids. Next to him, a younger guy. Shaved head. Tattoo on his wrist. Dougie pointed from one to the other with the barrel of his gun. "Who. The fuck. Are you two?"

The man with the beard swallowed hard and began to stutter, but the younger guy simply shrugged and said, "Does it matter? We're not cops."

"They were passing on bikes. They saw us trying to get back in and came to help," the teacher said quickly.

Dougie studied her face. Something was off, but before he could start asking questions, a series of deafening gunshots rattled the walls and the ceiling and made the kids shriek.

"What the hell is that?" Frank looked torn between being excited and terrified and had put his hands over his ears.

Another bang. And another.

"It's coming from outside. Is it the cops? Have the cops come?" Frank was now bouncing up and down on the balls of his feet, looking as if he were about to run.

Bang, bang, bang-bang-bang.

The noise went on and on, as if they'd suddenly been dropped right in the middle of a war zone.

Dougie put his hand in front of Zack and pushed him back against the wall. He could feel the kid's heart beating ten to the dozen and Dougie closed his eyes as he realized his own was doing the same.

As the noise battered his brain, he breathed heavily, fighting the images he knew were coming.

It was no good.

As the shots grew louder, Dougie's body started to shake. He saw Caleb, peppered with bullet wounds, falling to the ground and bleeding out on the sidewalk. He saw the killer's face as he realized Dougie was about to take his revenge. He saw the cop. His hostage. Terrified. Pleading with him that his wife was pregnant and that he didn't want to die. He saw all the faces of the men he'd killed, and it made his knees fall from beneath him.

As he wavered, the kid held him up.

"Dougie? You okay?"

When he opened his eyes, Zack was looking at him as if he might have been shot.

Bang. Bang, bang, bang.

In front of them, the teacher and Colton had put their arms around the brother and sister, keeping them sandwiched between them. The two men Dougie didn't recognize had ducked their heads as if they thought a bullet might whistle past their ears at any moment.

"I'm fine, kid. Fine." Dougie stood up.

Bang. Bang. Wheeeeeeeeeeee.

Dougie did a double take. "That's not gunfire," he muttered, running over to the window. "It's fucking fireworks!"

As he peered out, he looked up at the sky. Fireworks were fizzing like the Fourth of July. Lighting up the sky above the prison and the trees in the distance.

"Cool!" Frank thumped the worktop.

Finally, it stopped. Dougie's ears were ringing and his heart was pounding. "Open the door," he said to Zack, "See what else is out there." Zack hesitated, then nodded and inched forward, staring at the short-haired new guy as if he was afraid he would jump up and grab him. When he reached the door, he pushed it open a crack and peered outside.

"Well…?" Dougie was beginning to feel jittery. The smell of sulfur tickled his nostrils. "What do you see, kid?"

Zack turned back and closed the door. "Smoke and a bunch of fires."

"A bunch?"

"Like… like the cars in the lot are on fire," Zack replied hesitantly.

"What the hell?" Frank was looking from Dougie to Zack as if Dougie should have some kind of answer. He was becoming a bigger pain in the ass with every passing moment. "Fireworks and bonfires?"

"People? Do you see people?"

Zack shook his head. "No. I don't see anyone."

"Okay, you lot. Get up." Dougie waved his gun at the group, then looked at Zack and told him to barricade the door. "You know what I think?" He fixed his eyes on the teacher.

The emotion surging through his veins was hardening, turning to anger.

"I think your little friends did this to attract the attention of the cops. To get you rescued. Well, they'll have to do better than that."

"Dougie, if there are cops still in the city, a bunch of fires and gunshots will bring them here," Zack said quietly.

"Yeah, kid. It will. And if they come... well, you're right. We might need some bargaining power." Dougie fixed his gaze on their new hostages.

When he looked back at the kid, a flash of pride crossed Zack's face knowing that Dougie agreed to his plan.

"Up against this wall." Dougie made the teacher and the others stand with their hands behind their heads, facing the wall, while he instructed Zack and Frank to grab anything that looked like a useful weapon.

"What are you going to do with us?" Scarlett, one of the goth twins, whined as Dougie shoved her into the hallway and instructed her to walk behind her brother.

"Well," he said, "for now, I'm going to lock you away in some cells. Later... who knows? Depends on how generous I'm feeling, I guess."

32

MOLLY

As Dougie marched them back into the bowels of the prison, Molly looked at Colton and tried to interpret what he was thinking. He was eyeing up Dougie's gun, and Molly sincerely hoped he wasn't thinking of doing something reckless. Sure, their group outnumbered Dougie, Frank, and Zack, but they had no weapons and wouldn't know how to use them even if they did. If it came to a fight, right now, Dougie would win. Hands down.

With the generator working, it felt strangely bright inside the prison. Odd sections of corridor were better illuminated than others, and when they came across one, it made Molly blink uncomfortably.

As they exited a stairwell that Molly recognized, she wrapped her arms around herself and shuddered. Whether it was fear or exhaustion causing her to feel suddenly chilled, she had no idea, but she knew that now wasn't the time for weakness to creep in. She needed to stay alert, figure out what Dougie was planning, and get the kids out of there. All of them—including Zack.

Behind her, Frank nudged the small of her back with his gun. He was enjoying his slice of power far too much and, unlike Dougie, he seemed too volatile to be trusted with a weapon. Molly shot him a narrow stare and said tightly, "There's no need for that, Frank."

Momentarily, Frank looked the way he might have if he were a naughty pupil in one of her classes—as if he were afraid of being told off. He soon rallied, though, and simply curled his lip at her as he snarled, "I'm the one with the gun, lady, so *I* say if something's needed. Got it?"

Next to her, Molly saw Colton's jaw twitch, but she shook her head at him. *Don't get involved, Colton. Not now.*

"Right. Here we are." Dougie had pushed open a gray metal door and was ushering them inside a small room full of individual cells. "Pick a room. No bunk mates."

Molly saw Scarlett and Erik look wide-eyed at their father, but he nodded at them and, taking the lead, walked to the nearest cell and stepped inside.

"See, *that's* what I like," Dougie grinned, "a hostage who pays attention and follows orders. If you all behave like that, well, then we'll get along fine, won't we?"

As if it was physically painful for them to be separated, Scarlett and Erik peeled away from one another. Colton was next, then Tommy, but Molly stood stock still. She'd never been particularly claustrophobic but, suddenly, the thought of being sealed inside a cell, alone, made her blood run cold. What if the power went out again? What if Dougie simply left them there? Locked in. What if he and the other prisoners left?

"Miss O'Neil, I've been very nice to you today, but it's time you started doing what you're told." Dougie had stepped up beside her and was gripping her elbow.

Molly turned her head and blinked at him. "When will you let us out?" she asked as Frank began to lock the others away.

Dougie narrowed his eyes, then allowed a smile to come to his lips. "Well, if I told you that, it'd ruin the fun, wouldn't it? Don't worry, though, princess. I promise I'll be back for you."

He let go of her and gestured to the cell next to Tommy's. With trembling legs, Molly walked toward it, trying to look more confident and less afraid than she felt. She'd barely set foot inside the cell when Frank gleefully slammed the door closed behind her and waved flamboyantly as he ran off behind Dougie shouting, "See ya later, bitches!"

Dougie was at the door when he stopped, gestured for Frank to give him the keys, and stalked back into the room. For a brief second, Molly thought he'd changed his mind, but then she saw him approach Alex Banks' cell. Her breath caught in her throat as she heard Scarlett and Erik shout, "Hey... what are you doing?"

"Seeing as you're such a good hostage..." Dougie paused.

"Alex. My name is Alex."

"*Alex*... I think I'll take you with me."

"Why? Why d'you need him?" Scarlett shouted.

"Why do you care?" Dougie asked her calmly.

When Scarlett didn't reply, Molly heard Dougie unlock Alex's cell and say, "Off we go. Don't be shy, now."

She watched Dougie lead Alex from the room with a sense of pure dread crawling across her skin. This wasn't good, and if something happened to their father, how on earth would the twins cope?

Molly listened as Dougie and Alex's footsteps faded down the corridor outside. Alone, with no one watching her, she sank down onto the floor and rested her back against the wall. The cell was sparse. Just a cot bed and a urinal with a sink next to it, and no signs that anyone had been resident in it before the riot.

"Does anyone know where we are?" Erik's voice called from the far end of the room.

"Holding cells by the look of it," Tommy answered.

"Not far from the guard's station," Colton added, "and the front entrance."

Molly bit her lower lip. She wanted to join in. She wanted to think of something constructive to say or something they could do to get themselves out of this mess, but her breath was coming thick and fast and the only thought circulating in her brain was, *We were free, and I made them come back. We were free, and I did this to them.*

Leaning her forehead against the bars of the cell, she closed her eyes. "I'm so sorry, everyone," she said loudly. "I'm so, so sorry for bringing you all back in here."

"We wanted to come, Miss O'Neil," Erik answered quickly before settling back into silence.

Molly wondered whether he was holding back from saying what she was thinking—that they'd risked their lives to rescue Zack, but that Zack didn't seem very keen on being rescued.

Eventually, as if he knew what they were all thinking, Tommy said, "Zack was protecting me. He'll have a plan. There's no way he'd hook up with that scumbag."

Molly angled herself so she could see through the bars. The cells opposite were empty, but she could see Tommy's hands, fingers laced together, sticking out through the bars of the cell next to hers. Everyone was silent. From what they knew of Zack, and the way he'd behaved since he met Dougie, joining his gang was exactly something Zack would do.

Breaking through the silence, Scarlett's shaky voice said, "It must have been Lucky who started those fires, Miss O'Neil. Perhaps the guard's helping him. Maybe he and Jenna…."

"Maybe—" Erik cut in. "But Zack locked the door. So, even if it was

Lucky—trying to get the cops to come and help us—how will they get in? Dougie's turned this place into a fortress."

Molly pictured Scarlett opening her mouth to reply, realizing she couldn't think of anything, and closing it again.

"Let's wait and see what happens," Colton said gruffly. "No one try anything stupid, but stay alert. Watch everything and every *one*. And if we get the chance to run, safely, we take it."

"I'm not leaving my brother behind," Tommy said gruffly.

"And we're not leaving our dad."

Even from her cell, Molly could sense the tension rising. From his EMP drills in the Marines, Colton knew that it was very unlikely the cops would show up, and he'd also be weighing up the merits of sticking around to try and find Mr. Banks and Zack versus getting the remaining kids out safe if the opportunity arose. "Guys, now isn't the time to argue," Molly said shakily. "Let's just try and recoup some energy, okay?"

A sharp pain had lodged in the center of Molly's forehead and she rubbed it with her index finger. It was preventing her from thinking clearly, and she badly wanted a drink of water. Looking up at the ceiling, she traced a long winding crack in the tiles above her. It started in the far corner and came to an abrupt stop at the edge of the tile above the bed. She frowned at it, then stood up, climbed onto the plastic mattress, and prodded it with her fingers. The tile moved; the tiniest bit, but it moved.

Turning so that she could quickly sit down again if she saw Dougie or Frank come back into the room, Molly pushed harder. On the third push, the tile dislodged and popped upwards. A shower of dust covered her face as she stretched up and moved the tile sideways. She started to cough, and heard Colton ask, "Molly? You okay in there?"

"Fine," she replied, sticking her hand up into the hole, "I'm fine." She hesitated, unsure what she'd find, then began to snake her fingers along the inside of the ceiling. If it seemed like a big enough space, perhaps she could crawl up into it? Free the others that way too? Wasn't that something that happened in TV shows? People escaped through air ducts or pipes?

At first, she came up against nothing but air, and was about to try and haul herself up to see inside when she nudged something that didn't belong. Something that moved. It was almost out of reach, but she managed to hook it with her index finger and pull it closer. It was small, plastic maybe.

Molly grabbed hold of the object and pulled it out. As she sat down on the bed, she opened her palm. She was holding a small, clear plastic bag. Inside it was a handful of red capsules. Pills of some kind. She counted them. Twenty-one. What they were, she had no idea, but she knew that in prison, pills of any kind were the kind of thing inmates would kill to get their hands on.

She was about to put them back, for precisely that reason, when she stopped. She had no idea whether Dougie was the kind of guy who'd perform favors in return for drugs, but she was fairly sure Frank would. If either of them came back, maybe, just maybe, she could use these somehow to persuade them to set them free.

Quickly, Molly slipped them into her back pocket, then climbed back onto the bed. She was about to continue her exploration of the ceiling when she heard the door open. As fast as she could, she pulled the tile back into place, jumped down, and brushed the dust from her clothes. Looking up, she saw Zack sneaking back into the room and closing the door softly behind him.

Molly rushed to the door of her cell and grabbed hold of the bars.

"Zack!" Erik was whispering, but loudly, "Let us out, man. We came back for you. We came to help you. So, help us, okay?"

Zack paused in front of Erik's cell, tilted his head at him, then completely ignored him and kept walking. When he reached Tommy, he stood stiffly, facing him, hands behind his back. "What are you doing here?" he said in a low voice.

"Don't tell me you're not pleased to see me, bro? Good acting back there, by the way. Making that douchebag think you're on his side." Tommy sounded genuinely happy, convinced that Zack was about to set them free. Molly bit her lower lip and held her breath as she waited for Zack's reply.

After looking at his brother for a moment, Zack tucked his hair behind his ear, then folded his arms. "I asked what you're doing here, Tommy?"

Molly winced as Tommy fell silent. Finally, he cleared his throat and replied, "When the EMP hit, I went home to find you. Mom was there but she was out of it, as usual. She didn't even realize the power had gone out."

Zack's eyes twitched and Molly noticed him suck in his cheeks at the mention of his mother.

"Eventually, she told me you'd gone to prison. I thought you'd been locked up. Then I found a letter from the school about the Scared Straight trip."

"So, you came here to find me?" Zack's expression had softened, although he was clenching and unclenching his fists.

"Course I did. I know these places. You think I'd leave my baby brother trapped inside one when the world's ending?"

"What do you know about EMPs?" Zack took a step closer to his brother's cell, then stopped.

"Does that matter right now?" Tommy asked, but when Zack didn't reply, he added, "I was staying with a friend. His family knows about this stuff. They gave me a big list of stuff I'd need, said that however bad things are now, they'll get worse—much worse—and that we needed to get organized." Tommy laughed a little. "Scared the shit out of me, to be honest."

"So, what? I'm supposed to believe that you give a damn about me all of a sudden?" Tears had sprung to Zack's eyes and he looked away from Tommy.

"Zack, dude, of course I give a damn. I never left because I didn't care about you. I had no choice. I had to serve my time."

"If you hadn't done something dumb in the first place, you wouldn't have gotten locked up, would you?"

As Molly watched Zack's face crumple, the emotion he'd been holding inside for so long bubbling to the surface, she leaned her forehead on the bars of the door and breathed out slowly. Like everyone else in Zack's life, she'd gotten him wrong. He was just a kid. A kid with a rotten home life who felt utterly abandoned by the one person in the world he trusted—his big brother.

"Come here...." Tommy gestured for Zack to come closer to him. At first, Zack stood firm, but then he folded. Rushing forward, he shoved his arms through the bars of Tommy's cell and let his brother embrace him. "I'm sorry," Tommy said softly, "I'm sorry for everything. Right now, we need each other. We've gotta put the past behind us and team up. Okay?" Tommy pulled back and ruffled Zack's hair.

Zack nodded. Wiping his eyes, he said, "Yeah. Yeah, okay."

"So, then," Tommy said, "how about getting us the hell out of here?"

As soon as Tommy suggested that Zack help break them out of their cells, the younger boy's expression changed. His shoulders stiffened and his hands, which had been loose at his sides, began to flex. "Is that what all that was about?" he asked bitterly. "Persuading me to help you?"

"What?"

"Sweet-talking me, so I'll get you out?" Zack laughed loudly and shook his head. "You're no different from the rest of them, are you? Using me when it suits you. Being my friend when it suits you. Being my *brother* when it suits you. But you weren't much of a brother when you left me alone with Mom, were you?" Zack was visibly shaking, staring at Tommy as if he had a million more things to say, things that had been building up inside him for far too long, and couldn't possibly stay caged any longer.

Before Tommy could speak, Molly stuck her hands through the bars and waved to get Zack's attention. She needed to de-escalate this, and quickly. "Zack... your brother insisted we come back in here to find you. He loves you."

Zack stalked over to her and folded his arms in front of his chest. "Oh yeah?" he said bitterly. "What do you know about it?"

Molly deliberately met Zack's eyes and took a deep breath. "I know that I'm sorry for the things I said to you, and for the way I treated you. I got you all wrong, Zack. Tommy never did. He always believed in you, and he came here to help you." Molly paused, praying Zack believed her.

From further down the cells, Erik called, "It wasn't just your brother, Zack. Miss O'Neil wanted to come back for you. We all did."

As Molly held her breath, waiting for Zack's response, Scarlett added, "Miss O'Neil is telling the truth. It was her and your brother who made us all come back for you." Softening her tone, she added, "So, stop being a douche and let us out?"

Zack didn't look in the twins' direction. His eyes were fixed on Molly's face as if he were trying to work out whether she was sincere or not. She expected him to say something, to be sarcastic or pessimistic, but instead he simply turned on his heels and walked toward the door.

"Hey! Where are you going?" Erik and Scarlett began to shout.

Colton joined in. "Come back here. We need your help. Your friends need your help."

"Zack? Come on, buddy, don't leave." Tommy was reaching through the bars of his cell as if he might somehow be able to grab hold of his brother and pull him back.

But Zack didn't turn around. He kept heading for the door, stormed through it, and allowed it to close with a thud behind him.

33

ALEX

When he saw his children's faces, Alex's heart throbbed with joy. He didn't think he'd ever felt so happy in his life, except maybe when Laura came safely out of surgery after her accident, or home from rehab looking truly rested and like her old self. Instantly, he wanted to scoop them up and carry them home like he did when they were babies and he nervously brought them out of the hospital in matching car seats.

When they told him they thought it was an EMP, though, the happiness faded. Since he left home, he'd been telling himself it might not be. The power might come back. If Erik and Scarlett believed it was; well, that was different. That was bad news.

He had almost put his foot down when they'd insisted on going back inside the prison. Erik's face was badly bruised and they'd clearly been through quite an ordeal getting out, although neither of them told him the full details. He could have told them he was worried about their mother. That would have convinced them, for sure. For some reason, he couldn't bring himself to use their mother as leverage. Laura was fine. She was home with Argent, safe and sound with food, water, and candles. She had the neighbors to look out for her. Sure, she'd be getting nervous because of the long wait for them to return, but she was *okay*, and it felt wrong to pretend that she wasn't just to get his own way.

So, still trying to make up for dismantling their computers, even though they had no idea he'd done it in the first place, Alex had agreed. Or at least, he hadn't tried to stop them. He had to admit, he'd felt a huge rush of pride when they fixed the generator, although it was quickly followed by a tsunami of sadness with the knowledge that their skills would now be wasted in a world where electricity had ceased to exist, and that he hadn't recognized their talent as such when it actually mattered.

Now, as he was marched down the corridor by a felon he was finding impossible to gauge, he prayed to a God he was fairly sure he didn't believe in not to take him from his family. The kids needed him. Laura needed him.

"Dougie, can I grab some more water from the cafeteria?" A kid Alex recognized from when he dropped the twins off at the bus that morning jogged up to Dougie's elbow and waited for his response.

"Sure. Get me some chips while you're there. And a soda." Dougie nodded back in the direction they'd come from and the kid, Zack, sped off. "While you're there," Dougie shouted at him, "tell them to secure all the exits. Tell them if the cops do turn up, we need to be ready, then come straight back. We need to make a plan."

Alex resisted the urge to scoff. They'd risked their lives coming back for that kid, and he was kissing Dougie's ass and running around eating chips and drinking soda as if he were at a frat party.

The other prisoner, Frank, who gave off the same energy as a bouncy but vicious puppy, grinned at Dougie, almost bouncing as he walked. "What you gonna do with him, boss?"

"Like I said. Talk," Dougie replied.

Frank looked disappointed.

"And I don't need you here for it," Dougie added. "Go help the kid."

"Fetch water?"

Dougie's jaw twitched. "No, you imbecile. Go help him tell the inmates what happened outside. Tell them the cops could be coming and that we need to man all the exits. Got it?"

Frank nodded. "Got it, boss."

They had reached the visitor's entrance to the prison. Alex could see it and could see that it had been barricaded from the inside. He tried to calculate how long it had taken them to get here from the holding cells, and while Dougie ushered him through a door that led past the guard's station and down a narrow corridor, Alex counted every door, every person, every lock. Because there was no way he was being separated from his kids again. No way. Whatever it took, he would get back to them.

"I don't think we've been properly introduced." Dougie pushed Alex into what looked like a guard's break room and gestured for him to sit down on a brown leather couch. "I'm Dougie," he said as he perched on the coffee table in front of Alex and extended his hand. "Nice to meet you. Alex."

Half expecting to be slapped with handcuffs, Alex returned the gesture. Dougie's hand was rough, his nails yellow and bitten down to the quick.

"Likewise," Alex said curtly.

Before continuing, Dougie looked up. "You lot," he shouted at the other inmates in the room. "Take any spare weapons down to the cafeteria. Now. The cops could be on their way. Reinforce all exits while you're at it."

Alex watched as the other men immediately did as they were told; somehow, Dougie had ended up in charge of this show.

"So...." Dougie leaned forward and pressed his fingertips together. "Who *are* you, Alex? And where did you come from?"

Alex willed his expression to remain unchanged. "I was passing by, saw the others struggling to get in, offered to help."

"Why would you do that?" Dougie tilted his head to the side.

"I'm sorry?"

Dougie laughed. "The world's fallen to shit out there and you stopped on your way to—"

"My uncle's cabin," Alex answered quickly. "I was on my way to—"

"Right. You stopped on your way to your uncle's cabin to help a teacher, a bus driver, and some school kids get *into* a prison?"

Alex exhaled slowly. "Yes."

"And your friend?"

"My friend?"

Dougie rubbed his shaved head and grinned. "The ex-con. Where does he fit in?"

"Ex-con? I don't know what you're talking about."

Leaning closer, Dougie made an exaggerated sniffing sound. "The thing is, Alex, us criminals, we can *smell* other bad guys a mile off. He's one of us."

"If he is, I know nothing about it. He helped me on the road. Someone tried to steal my bike. We decided to travel together as we were going in the same direction. That's all I know." He'd once heard that the best way to lie was to stick as close to the truth as possible. Seemingly, it worked.

"Okay," Dougie said slowly. "Okay." He'd opened his mouth to say something else when Zack came running into the room, panting, and not holding chips or soda.

"Dougie, it's kicking off in the cafeteria. You better come."

Dougie sucked in his cheeks and narrowed his eyes at Alex, then looked at Zack. "Stay here and watch him." Dougie stood up, pulled Alex up too, and shoved him over to the wall. Then he reached into his pocket. Ah. There they were. The handcuffs.

Handing them to Zack, Dougie nodded. "Chain him to the radiator and don't take your eyes off him. Something's not right with this guy. I want to know what it is."

"Sure thing," Zack said as he seamlessly took the cuffs, slapped one on Alex's left wrist and the other onto the radiator. "You better hurry, Dougie."

For a moment after Dougie left, Zack watched Alex with steely eyes, but then they changed. He walked to the door and stuck his head out into the corridor.

"Quick," he said, running back over to Alex, "we don't have much time."

Alex was speechless. Zack had taken a key from his pocket and was undoing the cuffs.

"How'd you—"

Zack shrugged. "One good thing my brother taught me—pick-pocketing," he said.

As the cuffs sprang open, Zack rushed over to the table in the middle of the room and grabbed a backpack. "Here," he said, chucking it at Alex, "grab anything useful, but hurry."

"Is there really something going on in the hall?" Alex asked as he loaded some water into the bag.

"Nah. But there will be by the time he gets there." Zack met Alex's eyes. "I might have told one of them on the way out that I heard another call him a little bitch." When Alex didn't react, Zack added, "Big no-no in jail. Guaranteed to start a fight, and they've got guns, so it should be good."

"But why…?" Alex followed Zack to the door.

"Because you guys came back for me. So, the least I can do is get us the hell out of here."

34

MOLLY

When Zack left them, snippets of noise from the rest of the prison had drifted inside. With the door closed, they were muffled, but there was clearly a lot of movement going on. The fires Lucky had started—if it really had been Lucky who started them—had seriously unnerved Dougie. Molly could tell by the way his demeanor changed as he marched them back into the prison. He was less assured than he had been, on edge, rattled by the prospect of the cops arriving.

Molly tried not to think about what the other prisoners might do if they found out that Dougie had locked away some hostages and left them unguarded; if Dougie was distracted, and if big-mouthed Frank spilled the beans, anyone could come find them. Unlock the doors. Start waving guns in their faces… or worse.

"We should have guessed he'd abandon us. I can't believe I actually thought it was a good idea to come back for him!" Erik yelled and rattled the bars of his cell.

In the cell next to Molly's, Tommy remained silent.

She was pacing up and down, desperately trying to think of a way she could use the drugs she'd found to aid their escape—perhaps by bargaining with a prisoner, bribing them, offering them in exchange for their freedom—when the door swung open on its hinges. Zack was back, with Alex right behind him, and rushing toward his brother. He lifted his hand. In it was a big bunch of keys. He grinned widely as Tommy whooped, then hurriedly unlocked his cell.

Tommy put his hands firmly on Zack's upper arms and met his eyes. "I knew you'd come through," he said proudly. "I knew it."

Zack pursed his lips. He looked like he might begin to cry, but then Erik shouted for him and he turned away from his brother. Running down the line of cells, Zack unlocked each in turn. When he reached Erik's, he paused, then turning the key in the lock, said, "Just so you know, I still think you're an idiot."

As Erik rushed out, he nodded thankfully at Zack and replied, "Ditto. But thanks."

Finally, Zack returned for Molly. Without flourish or drama, he unlocked her door and pulled it open. Molly's legs were trembling as she stepped out and, even though she knew he'd hate it, she grabbed Zack's hand. Looking straight into his eyes, she said, "Thank you, Zack. Really, thank you."

"You did a good job, son," Colton added, "but where is Dougie? What's going on out there?"

Zack glanced at the door then back at Colton. "He's worried about the police turning up. They're making stronger barricades at the doors and looking for extra weapons."

"I can't see the cops turning up, can you?" Tommy asked Colton. "Surely they'll have bigger things on their mind than a bunch of prisoners blowing each other up."

"Depends if they think there are guards and civilians here, I'd guess," Colton said, "On the whole, I'd say no. We can't rely on them coming. We need to get out of this ourselves."

"How?" Alex Banks had his arms around his children and was looking at Colton.

"Well," he said, "I think that's where Zack comes in. What do you think, Zack?"

As if he couldn't quite believe that anyone was asking his opinion, Zack straightened himself up and cleared his throat. Adjusting the strap of the bag on his shoulder, he blinked hard, then swung it onto the floor and opened its neck so they could see inside. "These might help," he said, reaching inside and holding up a can of tear gas.

"Haha!" Tommy clapped Zack hard between the shoulder blades. "That's my bro. Where'd you find this stuff?"

Zack nodded toward the door. "Dougie and the other prisoners were so excited about the guns they forgot about this stuff. Just left it sitting there. So... I borrowed it."

Molly began to smile. "Okay," she said. "That could work."

"And..." Zack reached further into the backpack and pulled out a folded sheet of paper. "I found this." He crouched down and spread it out on the floor.

When Molly looked at Colton, he was rubbing his neatly shaved head with such a look of relief it was as if someone had handed him a teleportation device that would take him straight out of the prison. "Alex's map," he breathed.

"Yep." Zack grinned and smoothed out the blueprint. "I pinched it when we found you guys."

"Zack, this is fantastic," Colton said, patting the teen on the shoulder. When he looked at Molly, he almost smiled. "This means we're not working blind. It means we have a real chance to get out."

"Zack, you know the lay of the land better than us. Is there an exit nearby?" Molly was poring over the map, eager to get the hell away from the cells they'd been locked in, but aware it would be reckless to simply charge out into the prison without a plan.

Zack bit his lower lip and used his thumb to turn the tear gas can over in his hand. "Okay, so this is where we are, here's the main exit and here's the guard's station." He pointed to their holding cells and then to the spot where Dougie had initially released them back into the parking lot. "Back here…" he traced his finger along the corridor from their cells to a section indicating a stairwell. "This is the stairwell we used to get to the lower floor, but there's no point going that way. Dougie sent some guys back to secure the door you got in through."

Each of them was scrutinizing the map, desperately searching for further exits.

"I think our best bet is here…." Zack pointed to a small square at the end of a corridor that didn't look much like anything, let alone an exit. "It's one door they might not have thought of."

"Yeah?" Erik Banks was looking at Zack with a newfound respect and was clearly as keen as Molly was to get going.

"What is it?" Colton asked, tilting his head so he could make out the map key.

"The pharmacy," Zack said bluntly. "Dougie and the others raided it, but while they were in there, I noticed a door at the back. I'm pretty sure it leads outside. See, if you look here, this looks like a loading bay."

Tommy put his hand on Zack's shoulder and nodded quickly in agreement. "Yeah, that sounds right. They never bring drugs through the main body of the prison. Makes sense they'd come from outside straight into the pharmacy."

"There's a door at the back of the kitchen that goes into the same area," Zack added. "I think they'll have secured that one. This one, though… it should be clear. They took everything they could get their hands on. So, if we can get there, I think we can get out." He waved the large bunch of keys at them. "Assuming one of these opens it."

Molly looked around the group. "What do we think?" she asked, unsure whether she should take the lead after her disastrous decision to bring them all back into the prison.

"It's as safe a bet as any," Colton said. "There are a few other fire exits but they're all in easily accessible areas, so I think we should assume the prisoners haven't got to this one."

"I agree," Alex nodded. "If they were too distracted by the drug haul to notice a door in the pharmacy, that's our best option." He turned to Molly and raised his eyebrows at her. "You agree, Miss O'Neil?"

Molly reached into her pocket, nodding. "I sure do," she said. "And *I* just so happened to find these in my holding cell." She dangled the small pouch of pills in front of them and grinned. "So if we come across an angry prisoner in the pharmacy, I'm pretty sure I have the ideal bargaining chip to get us free."

"If we can *get* to the pharmacy," Erik said, pointing at the map. "Isn't this the cafeteria?"

Solemnly, Zack nodded. "It is. And last time I was in there, there were plenty of prisoners in there getting high on some Kool-Aid thing Dougie concocted. So they could either be passed out or extra dangerous."

"Not a problem," Colton said confidently. "We have the ideal tools to cause a distraction with the tear gas. So," he added, standing up and gesturing to the door, "we take a left out of here, head down the hall, then another left at the end."

"Great." Tommy was up too and marching toward the door. "Then let's do this, okay?"

35

MOLLY

G lancing at the door, Molly told Zack to pull out the tear gas.

As he weighed one of the cans up and down in his hand, she looked him straight in the eyes and said, "You got this, Zack?"

Zack nodded slowly. A smile twitched at the corner of his mouth. "Yeah, Miss O'Neil. I got it."

"Not so fast." Tommy gestured for Zack to hand him his backpack and took out a second can. A smile broke across his face. "We're in this together," he said, making a 'cheers' gesture with the can.

"Will two be enough?" Alex asked, looking at Colton.

"Start with one. It's powerful stuff." Turning to the others, he added, "Remember what this stuff does to you? We need to move fast, but if we run, we'll breathe harder and inhale more gas. So, we stick low, form a line with one hand on the person in front, and *stick together*.

Okay?" He looked at Molly, and she caught the glimmer of worry in his eyes.

Molly took a short sharp breath. "Okay," she said, gesturing for Tommy and Zack to lead the way, "let's go. Zack, Tommy, you guys go up front. Erik, Scarlett and Alex in the middle, Colton and I behind. Right?"

Silently, the group nodded at her and moved toward the door. Zack paused with his fingers around the handle, then he shook his shoulders, looked at his brother, and pushed it open.

In the hallway, everything was eerily quiet. If they turned right, they'd end up back near the front entrance and the guard's station, but Zack gestured for them to follow him left. As they began to walk, not for the first time that day, Molly's boots clip-clopped loudly on the floor beneath her feet. She paused and looked at them and then, without thinking, bent down, unzipped them and left them behind.

Straightening herself up and breathing a little easier now that her presence wasn't so loudly marked, she glanced at Colton. She half-expected him to have raised his eyebrows at her, but he simply smiled thinly. *Smart move.*

They were a few feet away from the room Dougie had left them in when Colton grabbed Molly's arm. "I heard something. Behind us—"

Molly turned, but before she could tell the others, a figure appeared at the end of the hall. A figure she knew instantly was Frank. For a moment, he stopped stock-still, but then he yelled, "Hey! You're not supposed to be out here!" and ran toward them.

"Run!" Molly yelled at the others and they sped ahead, but Colton had stopped dead-center of the hallway, like a human barricade waiting to be battered.

"Colton...." Molly grabbed his arm and tried to pull him with her, but he stood firm.

Frank was holding a weapon, but as he lunged for Colton, Colton grabbed him by the throat and slammed him hard into the wall, ripping his gun from his hand and pointing it straight at Frank's head.

Trembling, Frank pressed himself up against the wall and screwed his eyes shut. "Don't kill me, man. I wouldn't have hurt you. I'm nobody. Take the gun. Take it."

Colton stood back, still pointing the gun at Frank. "Get out of here," he growled. "Now."

As Frank fled down the hall, stumbling over his own feet as he ran, Molly examined Colton's face and couldn't help wondering whether it had been wise to spare Frank's life. If she'd been holding the gun, would she have let him go?

"We should catch up with the others." Colton began a slightly awkward jog down the corridor and Molly followed suit but, before they reached the end, a gunshot rang out from somewhere up ahead. Then another, and another, and people yelling, and more gunshots.

Tommy, Alex, and the kids were out of sight, so Molly hurtled forward, toward the sound of the gunshots and around the corner where she smacked into a frozen-in-place Tommy. Quickly, he grabbed her by the arms and pulled her to the wall. Zack, the twins, and Alex were pressed up against it, staring at the doorway ahead.

When Colton arrived, limping but with his gun poised, he whispered loudly, "I'm guessing the pharmacy's through there?"

Zack nodded, his face pale.

"Who's firing?" Colton edged to the front of the group, speaking to Tommy.

"Looks like prisoners shooting at each other," Tommy replied.

"Then we need to find another way." Alex Banks looked back in the direction they'd come from.

"There is no other way," Zack said bluntly. "Dougie had all the other exits barricaded and there are prisoners everywhere."

Stepping up next to Zack, Molly put her hand on his arm and nodded at him. "Then I think it's time we use what we've got at our disposal. Don't you?"

Zack looked at the can of tear gas he was holding, then at Colton, Tommy, and Molly. "Yeah," he said, "I think so."

"Right." Molly quickly moved to the front of the group, almost laughing at herself because she sounded exactly like a teacher organizing a bunch of students on a school trip. "Everyone line up, single file. Tommy and Zack up front, then Erik, Scarlett, Alex, Colton, and me. Tommy, keep your can for later if we need it. Zack, the door we need is on the right. So that's where you throw the gas. Got it?"

"You want me to throw the gas in the exact spot we're heading for?" Zack frowned at her.

Immediately catching her logic, Colton added, "The prisoners will head away from the gas. Away from us."

"Right." Zack swallowed hard, then tightened his grip on the can. "Okay. Throw it in front of us. I can do that."

Slotting into a line, just as she'd directed, and still flinching at the sounds of guns and yelling from the room ahead, the group silently did as she asked.

"Ready?" Molly looked at Colton, who nodded. "Okay, go!"

Zack and Tommy charged forward and, barely a whisper into the room ahead, Zack popped his canister and threw it in the direction they were headed. Almost immediately, a billow of gray smoke plumed out from the can. Prisoners stopped shooting and began to yell at each other. Someone spotted Zack and tried to shoot but missed.

"Move! Move! Move!" Colton hollered as they ran around the edge of the cafeteria.

"This way!" Molly heard Zack shout but couldn't see him. Her eyes were scratching, stinging, filling with tears, but she kept moving, trying to keep her breath shallow and steady despite moving at speed.

Hanging onto Colton's shirt so she didn't lose him through the acid fog, Molly began to cough. Bullets were whizzing through the room, and she felt certain that any second now one would rip through her skin.

"Nearly there!" Zack shouted, and then suddenly they were through the smoky cafeteria and in a narrow corridor. As the others kept running, Molly paused at the door, pulled it closed and fumbled for a lock while Colton used his body weight to pin it shut. At the top, she found a bolt and slid it across, sealing them inside the corridor.

"Here," Zack said. "Here it is." He was panting, bending over and resting his palms on his knees, but Molly could barely see through the tears that were streaming down her face.

She felt Colton pulling her arm and followed him. As her eyes cleared, just a little, she realized the door to the pharmacy was hanging off its hinges. The room was empty. Not one box or bottle of pills remained. Even the shelves had been ripped off the walls and left lying on the floor, but at the back was the unmistakable silhouette of a door.

"This is it." Zack had stopped panting. "We did it."

"We didn't do it yet," Tommy answered. "We're not celebrating till we're—"

"Safe?"

Molly's heart tripped over in her chest. A whoosh of cold air, and the unmistakable smell of smoke, had wafted into the room, and she recognized that voice. As Scarlett shrieked, Molly narrowed her eyes and realized what she was seeing: Dougie. Standing in the doorway. With a gun.

"You thought I wouldn't figure out what you were up to?" Dougie growled.

Instinctively, Tommy and Colton moved to the front of the group to shield Zack. Colton's hand was behind his back, clutching his gun, but Dougie squared up to him.

"No!" Molly gasped as Dougie raised his gun and pressed it to Colton's forehead.

"Get out of my way," Dougie spat. Then, without even blinking, he kicked Colton in the knee. His bad knee.

Just like that, Colton fell to the ground, writhing in agony. While Tommy pushed Zack further back into the room, Molly dashed forward and reached for Colton. Ignoring her, Dougie stepped over them and pointed his gun at Tommy. "Move. This is between me and the kid."

Molly was about to jump up and lunge at Dougie when Colton groaned and tugged at her arm. Catching her eye, he gave her the briefest nod and she realized that he was trying to create a distraction. Angling herself so Colton was shielded from Dougie, Molly held out her hand as Colton slid his gun into it, then she slowly stood up.

"You think I'm dumb?" Dougie was yelling now, peering over Tommy's shoulder at a quivering Zack. "You think I didn't know you'd betray me? Oh, I knew it. When I found your sweet, sweet teacher's boots in the hallway," he said, tossing Molly's boots to the floor in front of them. "And I knew exactly where you were headed."

"He's a kid," Tommy said, his jaw twitching with anger. "You got something to say, say it to me."

"You! Who the hell are you?"

"I'm his brother. That's who." Tommy raised his fists—as if, somehow, they'd be a match for Dougie's gun—and gestured for the others to slip back out of the room.

"Don't fucking move!" Dougie yelled. "I don't care if you're his brother. His uncle. His priest. That kid betrayed me. Now you're all going to pay for it. So..." he said, pointing his gun at each in turn. "I'm gonna make this real simple. Who wants to die first?"

36

DOUGIE

A rage Dougie hadn't felt in a long time was coursing through his veins. Every muscle in his body was quivering with it. He wanted to scream. He wanted to start shooting and to keep shooting until every single one of those Scared Straight bastards were dead.

Not because of the teacher or the bus driver. Not because of the fake gunfire that had clearly been designed to distract him. No. He was angry because of the kid.

Zack.

Because, for the first time in a long time, Dougie had felt a connection to another human being and had acted on it. He'd let the kid stay. Taken him under his wing. Treated him like a brother. And, just like every other goddamn time in his life that Dougie had allowed himself to care for someone, he'd been betrayed.

"I asked who wants to die first?" He wasn't yelling, but he knew his eyes were almost black with fury.

Zack was trembling. The thick-necked guy who claimed to be Zack's brother, although they looked nothing alike, had clenched his fists ready for a fight. Dougie wasn't going to make this easy on them. He was going to make them suffer.

He wasn't sure when it had happened—when he'd started *liking* the weird, long-haired loner of the group. Maybe when they'd been in the guard station, when Zack had been talking about his brother and had gotten Dougie to talk about his own; something he hadn't done since Caleb died. Maybe when Zack made him laugh—really laugh—for the first time in forever, or when Zack proved how smart he was by teaching Dougie all that EMP crap and showing him how valuable the prison would be in the coming months. Or maybe right from the beginning—from when Dougie had looked into Zack's eyes, told a sad story about a kid with a loser-mom and realized it was true.

Whatever the answer, it had undoubtedly happened. Dougie had begun to picture himself and Zack ruling the roost. Lords of a new prison empire. Comrades in the new world order. In just a few hours, Dougie had grown fond of Zack. But now... he had to kill him. And that made Dougie even angrier.

"I tell you what, Zack," he spat. "To show my gratitude for all you've done, I'll let you live a little longer." He allowed a snarl to creep across his face. "I'll kill your big brother first...."

Dougie raised his gun and aimed it at Tommy's chest.

Bang!

Dougie blinked. He looked at his finger, which hadn't yet pulled the trigger, then watched his gun fall to the floor.

"Shit...." He stumbled, fell sideways into the wall, then slid to the floor.

When he looked down, he realized he was sitting in a pool of blood. His blood.

Zack stepped around his brother and crouched in front of Dougie, but Dougie looked past him, rolled his eyes up, then began to laugh.

The teacher was holding a gun. The bitch had shot him in the back, and she was still pointing it at him, her finger on the trigger.

"I'm going to make this real simple," she said softly. "Goodbye Dougie."

Bang!

Dougie chuckled weakly and closed his eyes.

Killed by the hot teacher. Now that was a funny fucking joke.

37

LAURA

When Laura opened her eyes, she looked out of the bedroom window at the sky and realized it was nearly dawn. She had no idea what time she'd gone to bed, but she knew she'd barely slept. Every time she closed her eyes, she saw Dave's face. Every time she was about to drift off, a noise from outside on the street cut through the new, eerie quiet of the house and made her jump. Even Argent seemed twitchy, his usually unruffled demeanor now alert and switched on. Like her, unable to relax.

After throwing away her pills, Laura had gone back down into the garden and, painfully, continued to move Dave's body. The garden was small and unremarkable—not many places suited to hiding a corpse. In the end, she'd settled for underneath the outdoor dining table and, once Dave was in situ, still wrapped in the rug from Alex's study, she had pulled the winter tarpaulin over it and returned to the house.

Trying to erase the last few hours from her mind, she had lit some candles and made her way from room to room, straightening the mess

Dave had made when he was searching for her hidden oxy stash. She had left the study until last and, with no energy left for scrubbing the bloodstain from the floor, had simply repositioned Alex's armchair to cover it.

After that, she had realized that she was utterly exhausted and, while she hated the idea of going to bed as if everything were normal—when it was so very far from normal—she also knew that she would need strength for what was to come in the next few days. So, reluctantly, she had climbed into bed, laid the shotgun beside her, and tried to sleep.

Now, staring at the muted light outside that was inching slowly toward daylight, she realized she needed to shower. The effort of moving Dave's body had been more than even the most intense workout, but their hot water heater was electric. So, of course, it wouldn't work. Plus, she wasn't sure how much longer they'd have running water.

Instead, Laura washed with cold water from the bathroom sink, and then changed into jeans and a loose-fitting sweater. Her hair needed washing too, but it would have to wait. Spritzing it with dry shampoo, she rubbed her fingers through it and scraped it into a ponytail. Usually she would put makeup on at the start of the day but, somehow, spending time applying foundation and mascara felt ridiculous; there were more important things she could be doing with her time.

Wheeling through the house, gun resting barrel up on the footrest, Laura lit some more candles and smiled at the soft light that danced on the walls of the living room. Under any other circumstances, the quiet and the candles could be quite beautiful. Romantic even.

She'd started to remember the time when Alex had surprised her with his first and only homecooked meal—when they were fresh out of college and still madly in love—when a knock on the door sent her heart racing. Immediately, Argent's ears pricked up and he headed for the hallway. Laura looked at her hands and realized they were shaking. What if Dave had told someone he was going to her house? What if someone was looking for him? She glanced at the kitchen window and her throat pulsed uncomfortably as she pictured Dave's dead body, hidden beneath the outdoor table, wrapped in a blood-soaked rug.

She held her breath, as if whoever was outside might hear her and start knocking even louder.

"Laura, it's Jerry. I just wanted to check you're okay?"

Before, hearing a familiar voice might have helped Laura relax. Now, after Dave, it did nothing to stop the thud of her heart against her ribcage. Slowly, she wheeled to the door and spoke through it. "Jerry, yes, fine. It's pretty early. I'm not really dressed for visitors."

"Oh, sure. That's fine. I couldn't sleep," Jerry chuckled, as if their conversation was completely normal. "Took a walk and saw some light from your windows, that's all." He paused, clearly not ready to leave and go back to his own house. "Did you hear the gunshot last night? Barb thought it came from your place, but I said no way. I would have come and checked on you, of course, but Barb didn't want me to leave her. Had to wait until she was asleep before I snuck out."

Laura closed her eyes. Jerry's wife Barb had been sick for as long as they'd lived next door. She suffered from anxiety and depression, and Jerry was incredibly attentive to her, but it meant he liked to talk. Every morning, on his way to work, Alex tried to leave the house as stealthily as possible in case Jerry came outside and caught him up in one of his too-long chats. Laura, too, found that she sometimes pretended she hadn't spotted him or that her headphones were blasting loud music into her ears and preventing her from hearing him shout hello.

"Thanks, Jerry. Thanks for checking on me. Are you and Barb okay?"

"Oh, sure. We're fine. Just waiting it out."

Laura felt her nose wrinkle. She leaned her forehead on the door, then took a deep breath and opened it, just a crack. "Jerry," she said softly, "if it's an EMP that's taken out the power, it means it might not come back. So maybe you and Barb should think about gathering some supplies? Food? Water?"

Jerry's forehead crinkled into a frown and he folded his arms in front of his rotund stomach. "You think it's that serious, do you?"

"I do, yes." Laura didn't offer further explanation but met his gaze and held it. "Do you have a gun?"

As she asked the question, Jerry's eyes flitted to the shotgun that was balanced between Laura's legs and he swallowed hard. "Ah. I do, yeah. My father's rifle. Not been used for years but I—"

"Good. Maybe keep it close by? okay?" Laura had begun to close the door. Although part of her felt she should take Jerry and Barb into the house, look after them, keep them safe, a bigger part knew that she had to look out for her own family first. "I'll talk to you later, Jerry, if that's okay? Let me know if you need anything."

Jerry was still frowning when Laura shut and locked the door.

Somehow, speaking to Jerry filled Laura with a new sense of purpose. How many others, like Jerry and Barb, were sitting at home right now, content in the belief that in a few days the power would be back on and that everything would be back to normal? Hundreds, *thousands*, across the city, she'd bet. Which meant that people like her, people who started to get organized, would have a better chance of survival.

If she were wrong, if the power did miraculously return, there'd be nothing lost. But there was everything to gain in being prepared.

Returning to the kitchen, she studied the supplies she'd emptied onto the worktops. She had food and water covered, but after having to defend herself from Dave, she felt the sudden need to have more tools at her disposal. A few hours ago, she'd considered this something that could wait; Alex could deal with it when he returned. After all, he was far more practical than she was. Now, though, she knew that was a foolish attitude to have. Partly because every time she thought of her husband and her kids, a thud of anxiety gripped her chest, partly because she was trying to distract herself from the pain that still throbbed in her lower back, and partly because what had happened with Dave had filled her with the sense that danger was lurking right around the corner. She had to *do* something. Something useful.

With a candle in her hand, Laura headed back to the garage and—in several trips—took every bit of DIY equipment, camping gear, and potentially useful items into the house. All the while, Argent watched her as if he couldn't make out for the life of him what was going on. First an intruder who turned out not to be very nice, then a fun game with the rug, and now his mom was bringing all sorts of weird and wonderful stuff into the living room and spreading it out on the large glass coffee table.

Instinctively, before she began to sort through what she'd gathered, Laura reached for her cell phone. It was sitting on the desk, and she had the impulse—as she usually did when she was attempting a methodical task—to play some music. When she picked it up, though, the screen remained blank.

Laura stared at it for a moment, holding the phone in her hand as if it might jump back to life if she wished hard enough. By the time she put it back down, she realized her cheeks were wet with tears. Before she even had time to think about the reasons why, she began to sob. Her shoulders shook. Loud, ugly cries escaped her lips, and she braced her hands on the arms of her chair.

With wide eyes, Argent padded over to her and rested his chin on her lap. As he looked up at her, he whined. "It's okay, boy, I'm okay." Laura tried to reassure him, but she was struggling to breathe. The weight of what had happened in the past twenty-four hours had hit her, almost as strong as the force from the car crash. An EMP had wiped out their electricity supply, and every electrical device along with it. She looked at her phone, now lifeless on the desk, then at the television. There would be no more music, no more movie nights with the kids, no more turning up the radio as she cooked dinner for Alex. Perhaps even no more food when supplies ran out.

"Oh God...." Laura sobbed even harder, and the sobs kept coming. For many, many minutes until she had no more tears left to cry.

Finally, as her breath returned to normal and she wiped her eyes, she began to feel better. *Okay, Laura. You had your meltdown. Now it's time to pull yourself together. Alex will be home soon with the kids.*

Outside, the sun was higher in the sky. Dawn was approaching fast, which meant Alex had been gone a very long time. The prison wasn't far, even by bike, but with the kids in tow they'd have had to walk all the way back, so Laura didn't allow herself to slip back into a panic. They might even have stopped somewhere, sheltered overnight. Perhaps on the school bus with the other kids and the teacher. Miss O'Neil.

Laura nodded to herself. Yes, that was it. Miss O'Neil seemed sensible. She'd have made sure the kids were all right, and any time now Alex would be back with them. Safe and sound. The Banks family, together again.

Laura looked at Argent. "You hungry, boy? Why don't I fix some breakfast?" She headed for the kitchen and smiled to herself. At least if she could make the kids feel something close to normal when they got back, she'd feel like she'd done something useful. They'd talk, refuel, and make a plan. Together.

Argent followed her as she took his dish from his cage, filled it with his favorite kibble, then wheeled back out onto the back deck.

She didn't want to be close to Dave, but she did want to feel the sun on her face and listen to the birds singing. To pretend, just for a few minutes, that this was a normal morning on a normal day.

She was thinking about lighting a fire and boiling water for coffee when she realized the birds had stopped. Seconds later, a loud BOOM shook the deck and a plume of dark black smoke filled the sky.

Laura headed for the edge of the deck and wheeled down the ramp. Somewhere beyond the end of their garden, something was on fire.

She put her hands over her mouth, watching as smoke soared into the sky. Was it coming from the train tracks?

"Argent," she called, suddenly feeling as if she *needed* him by her side.

Before he could obey, a second BOOM rang out. This one was louder. As Laura put her hands over her ears, the ground vibrated. She lowered them, and then heard something else... a creak. A snap.

She turned and, as if in slow motion, realized that the big old ash tree near the fence was falling toward her. There was no time to move, so Laura threw herself from her chair and covered her head with her hands. As it came crashing down, she braced herself for it to smash into her, to pin her to the ground. But it didn't.

When she finally looked up, the tree branches were barely a foot away from her. Blinking tears from her eyes, she tried to focus. Argent was whimpering, but she couldn't see him. She tried to push herself up, but she couldn't move. A branch was on top of her legs, and she knew she was bleeding.

38

MOLLY

S till shaking, but trying to hide it, Molly slipped the gun she'd used to shoot Dougie into the back of her jeans and closed her eyes. A few hours ago, when he first set them free from the prison, she had convinced herself that deep down he was a good person. Had she been wrong? Or had his good nature simply been buried so deep that he couldn't get to it?

Either way, it didn't matter anymore. Now, Dougie was nothing but a lifeless shell—slumped on the floor of the prison in a pool of his own blood.

If someone had told her, just yesterday, when she left her cozy suburban apartment for the Scared Straight trip, that she would end the day by killing a man in cold blood, she'd probably have vomited into her kitchen sink. She certainly wouldn't have wanted to believe it. Instead of feeling nauseated, though, she simply felt… numb.

She closed her eyes and breathed deeply.

It was him or us, she whispered to herself, *and I chose us.*

When she opened her eyes, Erik and Scarlett had reached the door at the back of the pharmacy. Behind them, Alex was supporting Colton as he walked on his damaged knee, and Tommy had his arm around Zack. The twins paused for just a second, perhaps worried that another prisoner was about to jump out from behind it; then together they pushed it open.

They stepped across the threshold, looked around them, then beckoned for the others to follow. "All clear," Erik shouted gleefully. "We did it!"

As the others stepped outside, Molly grabbed her boots from where Dougie had dropped them, pulled them back onto her feet, and followed behind them. Cool early-morning air hit her face and she breathed in a long, deep breath. She let it fill her lungs, even though it was tinged with the reminder of smoke from the fires in the parking lot, and allowed herself to smile.

Before walking away from the prison, she turned and pulled the door closed. "Colton, you still have your keys?" she asked, holding out her hand.

"Sure." He passed them to her, wincing as he moved, and Molly tried three large silver keys before finding the one that locked the door.

"Okay," she said, allowing herself to relax a little. "Okay."

When she turned back to the group, she was surprised to see that Zack was grinning. A true, happy grin. A smile she hadn't ever expected to see on his pale, sullen face. If he was upset about Dougie, he didn't show it. Instead, he seemed elated to have his brother at his side.

Trying to orientate herself, Molly spotted the outer edge of the parking lot to their left. Wherever they were now seemed like a drop-off zone for the pharmacy and the kitchen, and Alex had helped Colton over to a nearby van so he could rest on its hood.

While Colton rubbed his knee and flexed his leg, Alex embraced his children, patting them as if he needed to physically check they were all right and telling them that they were incredibly brave. Molly smiled. She agreed; the kids had managed to hold it together. Every single one of them.

Looking toward the parking lot, she realized that wispy plumes of smoke were drifting into the sky. *Lucky and Jenna....*

She was about to hurry the others on, back to the bus, to find their classmates and Mr. Fox the guard, but stopped herself; they needed a moment. Just a moment. To be still.

Walking over to Colton, Molly scraped her hands through her hair and released a long sigh.

"You did it," he said, meeting her eyes, "you got them out. All of them."

Molly nodded and glanced at Zack. "Yes. All of them."

"It might take time to sink in, you know," Colton said quietly. "It's not easy, the first time...."

Without even asking, Molly knew exactly what he was talking about; she took a life. At some point, that would hit home, but not now. Not today. "I know."

"When it does... I'll be here."

"Will you?" Molly asked, leaning on the hood beside him and crossing her arms in front of her. "Won't you want to be getting back to your family?"

Colton looked away, fixing his eyes on nothing in particular in the distance. When he looked back, he rubbed the back of his neck and said, "My wife and I divorced a few years back. She lives in Florida now. No kids."

Molly offered a slight smile and nodded. It was the first truly personal thing Colton had told her about himself, and she appreciated him opening up to her. She also appreciated the idea that he might stick around; she'd seen him fight. Bad leg or no bad leg, he was a good ally to have.

After pausing for a moment longer, finally, she clapped her hands together and stood up. "Okay, guys, I think we need to go find Lucky and Jenna."

No one disagreed, and so they walked, close to the building, in the direction of the smoldering cars.

As they rounded the corner into the parking lot, Molly narrowed her eyes. Two small figures were running toward them. She reached for her gun, but then Scarlett shouted, "It's Jenna and Lucky!"

The Banks twins waved their hands in the air and jumped up and down as their friends approached. In the distance, the cars in the lot were smoldering ruins, and when Lucky reached them, the grin on his face told her instantly that he was responsible.

"I guess you had something to do with this?" Molly asked, waving at the carnage.

Lucky stopped and scraped his foot on the ground, looking up at her sheepishly. "Maybe," he said.

Molly held his gaze for a moment, then allowed a smile to creep over her lips. "Well done." She patted him on the back and laughed. "Well done, both of you."

"Did it work?" Lucky asked. "Did it cause a distraction? Did it make them think the cops were coming?"

Erik and Scarlett launched into telling Lucky and Jenna what happened, but before they could get very far, Colton cleared his throat and said loudly, "I don't think we should hang around here. We're not far from the exit near the generator. If the prisoners realize the police aren't coming, and if they find Dougie...." He hesitated, glanced at Molly, then continued, "well, they might decide to leave their castle and seek revenge."

Tommy, who was still holding on tight to Zack, nodded. "Agreed. So, now what?"

"I need to go home. Check on my folks," Lucky said, almost coyly.

"We need to get back to Mom," Scarlett said to her father.

"Okay then," Molly said firmly. "We go back to town, check on our families. Then decide what to do next."

"*We?*" Zack had shrugged free of Tommy and was standing in the middle of the group. "So, we're sticking together?"

Before Molly could answer, Jenna thumped Zack on the arm and laughed loudly. "Of course, we're sticking together, you idiot. You think we'd go through all this just to go our separate ways? We're stronger as a group, right, Miss O'Neil?"

Molly looked at Colton and, although she couldn't interpret his expression well enough to figure out whether he agreed, she nodded resolutely. "Yes. We are. So, let's go get our things from the bus, then get out of here."

As they crossed the parking lot, the sky still brightening, Molly saw Colton stumble and slipped her arm around his waist to steady him. "You should head on without me. I'll only slow you down," he said earnestly. "My leg—"

"Your leg will be just fine. And if it's not, well, we'll fashion a stretcher and tie it to Alex's bicycle." She laughed and nudged him with her elbow. "Leave no man behind, right?"

Colton didn't smile, but he did bite his lower lip and nod, ever so slightly, as if to say, *All right. If you insist.*

From a little way ahead, Lucky called back, "I found a cane in the back of one of the cars. Took it to use as a weapon. It's in the bus...."

Molly examined Colton's face. He was scowling, but he didn't say no.

247

"Perfect," she said to Lucky. "Can you go on ahead with the others and fetch it?"

Dutifully, Lucky nodded and charged off ahead while Molly stuck by Colton's side.

By the time they reached the bus, the kids had fetched down everyone's bags and dished them out. "What are we going to do with Mr. Fox?" Molly asked, looking up at the bus. "Is he okay?"

Jenna exchanged a look with Lucky. "He's gone, Miss O'Neil," she said. "No sign of him apart from some bloodied bandages."

"Gone?"

"He's not on the bus," Lucky added. "He was in pretty bad shape when we left him. I didn't think he'd be able to walk, but it's like he just—"

"Vanished," finished Jenna. "Into thin air."

Molly pursed her lips. If a prisoner made it out of the building and came across a guard, she doubted it would have ended well. They could have taken him back inside or, worse, taken him somewhere else to deal with him. "He must have felt better and decided to make a move," she said, trying to sound as if she believed it, and slung her bag across her shoulder. "Whatever happened, we don't have time to figure it out. I'm ready to be as far away from this place as possible. Aren't you?"

In unison, the group *mm*'d in agreement, and together they started back across the parking lot.

As they neared the exit to the prison, Molly looked up at the sky. It was brightening. Dawn was almost upon them. She could even hear birds singing. Singing as if nothing in the world had changed.

With Alex and Tommy pushing their bikes, they walked through the open gates and headed up the gentle slope that led from the prison down to the main road.

They were walking slowly past a copse of trees when Jenna glanced back at the prison and said solemnly, "The cops never did show up, did they, Miss O'Neil? Even when me and Lucky set off the fireworks and the ammo."

Molly felt Colton tense beside her. He was using her, as well as the cane Lucky had given him, to steady himself, and was clearly having the same thoughts she was... what the hell kind of a world were they walking back into?

"No," Molly said gravely. "They didn't."

On the brow of the hill, they stopped. Behind them, Fairfield Prison looked unassuming, quiet, no different from the way it had looked when they'd arrived there yesterday, with the exception of some persistent plumes of smoke from the car fires. Ahead, the town too seemed as it always had. The same buildings, the same skyline, the same slightly orange sky as the sun crept up over the horizon.

It won't be the same, though, will it? Molly thought as the group walked on. *Nothing will be the same, ever again.*

She was about to ask the kids where each of them lived, so they could plot out a route between the houses, when something made her look up. In the distance, something rumbled. A moment later, an enormous cloud of thick black smoke filled the air and the Banks twins gasped loudly.

"Dad..." Scarlett had grabbed hold of her father's arm. "Isn't that our neighborhood?"

Alex Banks' face had turned deathly pale. "Yes, Scarlett. I think it is."

"What about Mom?!"

EPILOGUE

For an entire day, almost, Santi had managed to stay out of the way of the trouble. While the prisoners raged around him, he'd stayed in his cell and prayed. Occasionally, he'd thought of the teacher and her five wet-behind-the-ears kids. He wondered briefly if Dougie had gone back for them but didn't trouble himself with whatever the answer might be, simply added them to his prayers and focused on blocking out the sounds around him.

Mostly, the others left him alone. A couple tried to get him to join in tracking down the guards, but he wanted nothing to do with it, and he'd served enough time to earn their respect. When he said no, they simply nodded and moved on. Perhaps there was something in his voice which told them that, although he was done with violence, they probably didn't want to test what he was made of.

When the lights went out, close to nightfall, Santi closed his eyes and breathed purposefully and slowly. He thought of his wife and his kids. His youngest had been due to visit with his very first grandbaby next week. He was guessing that now it would be a few more weeks before that happened.

He didn't believe the rumors that had been shouted through the walls. "The world's ending! The power's gone! Down with the hierarchy!"

If the power was gone, why had the generator continued to work long after the first outage?

When it flickered back on, an hour or two later, he'd smiled to himself. Any time now, they'd be locked back up in their cells and everyone but him would be getting time added to their sentences. Not him. He'd been in Fairfield thirty-five years and, next month, he was getting out. Home to his family. Home to his beautiful wife and his grownup kids. Santi had plans for his old age, and he wasn't going to blow them all up for a few hours of fun.

As night fell, though, something began to niggle at him. He'd heard no sirens. No sign that reinforcements had arrived. Nothing. Surely, by now, there should be something.

So, taking advantage of the fact that for the first time in years, he had the freedom to walk unencumbered from one section of the prison to another, he headed for the yard. Just for some fresh air.

Outside, he looked up. The sky was bright with stars. Was it always this bright? It had been years since he'd looked properly at the night sky; perhaps he'd forgotten it, dulled it down in his memory.

It was quiet too. Weirdly quiet. It was only when he saw a strange orange glow in the direction of the parking lot, and realized that the cars were on fire, that he decided something was definitely off. *Okay,* he thought, nodding his head, *if that's a sign, consider it heard.* Looking up at the stars, he smiled. God was telling him to leave, and he was going to listen.

When he reached the back exit and saw a hole in the fence, he smiled. Another sign. Without hesitating, Santi ducked through the hole and walked past the burning carcasses of the cars. He didn't stop. He didn't look back. He kept on walking.

By the time he reached the top of the nearby hill and stepped into the woods that lined the road, the smoke from the burning cars was nothing more than tendrils in the sky. It had been a long time since he'd seen trees. He stopped and pressed his palm against one. He could almost feel it breathing beneath his fingers.

Santi moved a little deeper into the trees. On the other side of the woods, he could dip down toward the town and catch a ride. Home was more than one hundred miles away, but he'd get there somehow. Now that he was free.

When he stumbled on something, he looked down. A man was lying on the ground. At first, Santi thought he was dead, but then he groaned, and it became clear he needed help. *Ah*, Santi whispered to himself, *So, this was your plan? You sent me here to help.*

Santi bent down and helped the man sit up. "Mr. Fox?" Santi ducked his head. Yes, it was definitely him. "Are you all right? Can I—"

Santi blinked hard. Victor Fox had hit him with something. A tree branch. He was holding a tree branch. Santi reached up and touched his head as a surprisingly hot trickle of blood pooled around his temple. Santi wobbled and fell to the ground. He blinked up as the guard towered over him. Now, he was holding a rock.

"One down," he spat.

Santi tried to speak, but Fox put a finger to his lips.

"Shhhh," he said. "There's a war starting out here, and I'm gonna make sure that guys like you don't win it."

END OF ESCAPING ANARCHY
DARK NATION BOOK ONE

Escaping Anarchy, February 9th 2022

Enduring Anarchy, March 9th 2022

Surviving Anarchy, April 13th 2022

PS: Do you love EMP fiction? Then keep reading for exclusive extracts from Enduring Anarchy (Dark Nation Book Two), Fractured World and Emerging Chaos.

THANK YOU

Thank you for purchasing Escaping Anarchy
(Dark Nation Book One)

Get prepared and sign-up to Grace's mailing list
to be notified of my next release at www.GraceHamiltonBooks.com

Loved this book? Share it with a friend, www.GraceHamil-
tonBooks.com/books

ABOUT GRACE HAMILTON

Grace Hamilton is the prepper pen-name for a bad-ass, survivalist momma-bear of four kids, and wife to a wonderful husband. After being stuck in a mountain cabin for six days following a flash flood, she decided she never wanted to feel so powerless or have to send her kids to bed hungry again. Now she lives the prepper lifestyle and knows that if SHTF or TEOTWAWKI happens, she'll be ready to help protect and provide for her family.

Combine this survivalist mentality with a vivid imagination (as well as a slightly unhealthy day dreaming habit) and you get a prepper fiction author. Grace spends her days thinking about the worst possible survival situations that a person could be thrown into, then throwing her characters into these nightmares while trying to figure out "What SHOULD you do in this situation?"

You will find Grace on:

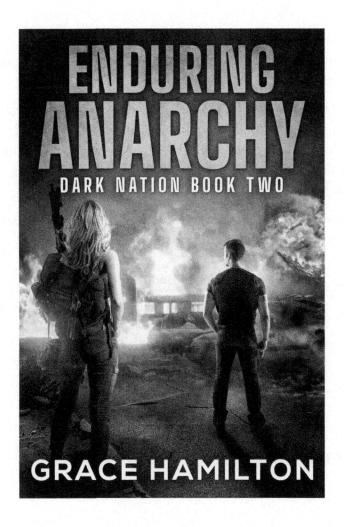

BLURB

They survived annihilation. But the real danger has only just begun...

When Molly, Colton, and their group of high school students narrowly escape a field trip gone wrong, they return home to find their town in shambles. An EMP has devastated the world. And life has been reduced to a daily battle for survival....

After a derailed train throws what's left of the town into chaos, Diego, the father of one of Molly's students, quickly takes charge. At first, he seems determined to help the survivors and clean up the train's wreckage. But it soon becomes clear that he has a sinister motive of his own for taking over. And Molly is certain he can't be trusted...

Things become much worse after a failed attempt by the local police has Diego seizing control and drawing a line in the sand. It isn't safe for anyone and Molly is ready to head to the woods, but not without all her students. Colton might be the Marine, but she isn't leaving anyone behind.

Molly will do anything to protect her students. But can she lead them to safety when the entire world has fallen into chaos?

Get your copy of **Enduring Anarchy**
Available March 9th 2022
(Available for Pre-Order Now!)
www.GraceHamiltonBooks.com

EXCERPT

CHAPTER ONE

MOLLY

Despite the distant sunrise, the trees lining the road remained eerily dark. With every step, as her foot met the road, Molly's heart pounded. Shadows looked like people. The innocent snap of a twig in the undergrowth sounded like the loading of a gun. The wind on her back felt like movement; the movement of a body walking too close behind her, following her, preparing to attack. Someone who was armed. Dangerous. Looking for revenge for what Molly did in the prison or looking to steal whatever the group might be carrying that could be useful in this dark new world they'd found themselves in.

Molly shuddered. The image of an imaginary attacker wavered and bled into her memories of Dougie. Although her eyes were open, she could see him in front of her; the way his body had slumped onto the ground after she shot him. The glassy look in his eyes as his last breath left his body.

She'd had no choice but to do it. It was the only way to get the kids out of Fairfield. It was the only way to get them safely back home. But that didn't mean she was okay with it. She had taken a life and there was no way—even if circumstances had allowed it—that she could go back to her old life. She was different now and, although the kids didn't seem to have noticed it, she sensed that Colton understood.

Beside her, the retired Marine stopped walking and grimaced as she looked at him. He was resting on his cane and looked extremely pale. Despite his injury, he'd made it out of the prison and had—until now —gritted his teeth through his obvious pain. The last thing he wanted was to become a burden, but they'd started this thing together and Molly was sure they were going to finish it together.

"Guys?" Molly called to the others. "I think we need to stop. Take a break."

Shortly after leaving the grounds of Fairfield Prison, Molly had given Tommy her gun, hanging back to help Colton while Tommy and Alex led the group on their journey back to town. The two of them had already traversed the empty roads once—they knew what to expect— but she was beginning to regret handing it over. She'd felt safer with the gun, even though she'd been praying she wouldn't ever have to use it again, and she'd felt safer when she was the one up front.

Molly tried again. "Guys, we have to stop. Colton needs a break."

"We can't," Erik Banks looked over his shoulder and shouted at her. Too loud. Walking faster instead of slower. "Our mom could be...." He trailed off, glancing at his sister Scarlett, then returning his gaze to the horizon.

An hour ago, as they trudged up the hill away from the prison, they'd witnessed a plume of thick black smoke mushrooming up into the sky and had heard what sounded unmistakably like an explosion. It had come from the south side of town, but whether it was from the Bankses' neighborhood or the less affluent area on the other side of the train tracks, it was impossible to tell.

Either way, Erik and Scarlett Banks had immediately started running. Until their father Alex pointed out there was no way they could run all the way back home and that they needed to stick together until they figured out what was going on; it wouldn't do anyone any good—especially their mother—to charge into danger.

While the Banks twins had looked almost sick with worry, the others in the group—Zack and his brother Tommy, Jenna, and Lucky—had remained quiet. All four of them came from Southside. All four of them were probably worrying about their own parents, but Erik and Scarlett were the only ones who let it show.

"I'm sorry, Erik, but Colton needs to rest for a moment." Molly glanced at Colton and noticed his jaw twitch. "We *all* do," she added.

Lingering between her classmates and her brother, as if she wasn't sure whether she should charge ahead with Erik or listen to Molly, her teacher, Scarlett braced her hands behind her neck and shook her head. "Miss O'Neil, maybe you and the others should slow down? Wait with Colton? Me, Erik, and Dad will go look for Mom."

Up ahead, Alex Banks stopped and turned around. He'd been pushing his bike and continued holding it with one hand while gesticulating with the other. "We're not separating from the group, Scarlett," he said gruffly. "We already decided we're stronger together." Alex rubbed his beard and swallowed hard. Ever since they'd witnessed the smoke and heard that deep, unsettling rumble that made the ground vibrate, Alex's face had been ashen. Gray around the edges. Etched with worry.

He was worried about his wife, of course, but Molly could tell there was something else he wasn't saying. He was extremely keen for them not to separate, despite the fact that he had a bike and could have traveled much more quickly if he'd used it.

This reluctance was troubling, and Molly was willing to bet it had to do with what he'd seen in town when he left home yesterday. While Molly and the kids had been stuck in Fairfield Prison, Alex had traveled through Fairfield to reach them. He'd met up with Tommy and they'd seen what the EMP had done. The start of it, anyway.

"Molly...." Colton tugged at her elbow, and she turned to look at him. "I'm slowing you down." He met her gaze and held it.

"Then *we'll* slow down," she said. "We are *not* leaving you." Putting her hands on her hips, Molly looked at the others. "He just needs a few minutes, that's all."

Alex looked at Tommy, who was also in possession of a bike. "It's your call, man," Tommy said. "If you want to take the bikes, we can catch up with you but...." He lowered his voice and said something to Alex that Molly couldn't catch.

After glancing at the skyline and the whispers of smoke that were filling it, finally Alex said, "Five minutes." When Erik began to protest, Alex held up his hand and told his son bluntly, "Five minutes, Erik."

Molly didn't realize she'd been holding her breath, but as she released it, she smiled at Colton. From the backpack Lucky had given her, she took a bottle of water. "Here," she said.

Colton took it, staggered to a nearby tree, leaned against it and took a long slow drink. "Thanks."

"You'll be fine when you've had a chance to rest."

Colton raised his eyebrows at her. "Oh, yeah? And when do you foresee that happening?"

Molly bristled. Nearby, Lucky and Jenna were talking with Erik and Scarlett in hushed whispers, pointing toward the town and to the Bankses' neighborhood. Between them, they'd decided the smoke was something to do with the trainline, but Molly was trying not to hear what they were saying. She was trying to focus on one thing at a time;

escape the prison, get the kids home to their families, and then... well, she hadn't quite figured out the next part.

"I don't know," she admitted, chewing her lower lip. "I have no idea, Colton. All I know is that we've got a better chance if we stick together." She looked back in the direction of the prison. "We survived the jail. We made it out. None of us could have done it alone."

Colton nodded and took another sip from his water bottle. "I hear you," he said, pushing himself away from the tree and allowing the cane to support his weight once again. "In which case, we better get moving."

"You've barely rested for a second." Molly folded her arms in front of her chest and gave Colton her best teacher-stare.

"I'll be fine."

As Colton straightened himself up, Molly put her hands on her hips. Her fingers brushed against her back pocket, and she sucked in her breath as she remembered what was hidden there. Angling herself away from the group, she took out the pills she'd found when she was locked in that dark, awful cell and nudged Colton's elbow.

"I found these," she said quietly. "I don't know what they are but I kept them in case we needed something to bargain with. Perhaps you could...?" She shrugged and her eyes widened as Colton stared at the pills.

After a long moment, he closed his eyes and shook his head. Reaching out, he pressed Molly's fingers back against her palm, hiding the pills from view, and said, "No, thank you. I'll be all right."

"Are you sure?"

"You should get rid of those," he replied gruffly. "Ditch them."

"You don't think they could be useful? They could be prescription pills. Painkillers? I'm sure we can find someone who could tell us...."

Colton's hand was still pressed against her fingers. As he spoke, he held her gaze. "Prescription or not, I don't mess with pills, and neither should you. Get rid of them, Molly."

Molly pressed her lips together and swallowed hard. She was trying to interpret the look in Colton's eyes—a dark, watery look she hadn't seen before—when she heard Jenna's voice behind her.

"Miss O'Neil, I'll hang back with Colton for a while if you want to head up front with Alex and Tommy." Jenna was standing with her hands in her pockets. She looked tired. Her short hair was tucked behind her ears, and she smiled as Molly looked at her.

"Sure. Thanks, Jenna." Molly smiled back and patted Jenna's shoulder with one hand as she slipped the pills back into her pocket with the other. The girl clearly wanted a change of pace, and Molly was happy to take the lead for a while.

Casting a quick glance at Colton, Molly nodded to tell him she'd understood what he'd told her. As soon as she had chance to ditch the pills safely, so they wouldn't be found by a child or an animal who could be harmed by them, she would.

As the group started moving, they formed a cluster with Alex and Tommy up front, the Banks twins with Zack and Lucky in the middle, and Jenna and Colton at the back. Molly wove through them until she was standing between Alex and Tommy.

"Do you really think it's your neighborhood?" she asked Alex.

He nodded solemnly. "Looks like it. But it could be Southside. It's rough. The other side of the train tracks."

Molly cast a quick glance at Tommy. Like Jenna and Lucky, Tommy and Zack were from Southside. She remembered the address from Zack's school records and thought Tommy might take offense at what Alex had said. Instead, he was nodding.

"You can say that again." Tommy shrugged his shoulders and looked away from the horizon as if he didn't want to think about what might be happening in his neighborhood.

Lowering her voice, Molly leaned a little closer to Alex. "When you left home yesterday...." She pursed her lips, unsure how to ask what she needed to. "What was it like? The town? Is there anything we should be prepared for?"

Alex looked at her. Beneath his beard, his top lip curled into a sad sort of smile. "It was okay," he said bluntly. "But it'll be worse by now."

"The calm before the storm," Tommy added. "Yesterday, some folks would still have been convinced the power was coming back. Some of them were probably kicking back, relaxing, pleased to have a few days off work, waiting for everything to get back to normal."

"And today they'll be realizing that it won't," Molly finished solemnly.

Tommy nodded. He patted the gun Molly had given him. "It'd help if we had a few more of these."

"I'll add 'guns' to the grocery list, shall I?" she quipped.

"Guns and coffee," Tommy replied. "I'd give my back teeth for some coffee about now."

Fractured World (EMP Aftermath Book One)

BLURB

No power. No law & order. No safety net. The world as everyone knows it is over.

Laurel is stabilizing a patient in the ER when the power goes out. As she struggles to keep her patients alive, she faces an ugly truth—the world as everyone knew it is over. The smart thing to do is run and try to survive, but Laurel refuses to leave her patients behind—least of all her sick mother. There's only one choice to make. She'll have to stay and fight.

Bear is done fighting. War and PTSD have cost him everything—his job, his self-respect, and his wife - Laurel. But when he can no longer deny the old world is gone, he gains a new purpose. Laurel is hundreds of miles away from his mountain cabin, but he knows she needs him.

After so long being a lost solider, he finally has something worth fighting for. The highways are clogged with dead cars. Frantic survivors want his truck, his tools, his supplies. He'll face treachery, desperation, and endless miles of unforgiving wilderness, but he's going to find his wife. Together, they can survive anything.

He just has to reach her.

Grab your copy of Fractured World (EMP Aftermath Book One)
Available July 13th 2022
(Available for Pre-Order Now!)
www.LeslieNorthBooks.com

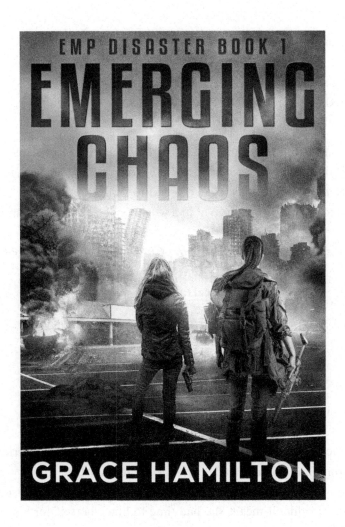

BLURB

The power is out, and the world is in chaos...

When a Coronal Mass Ejection causes an EMP catastrophe and shuts down the power worldwide, Melanie Pearson is determined to reunite with her husband and daughter. But to cross dangerous territory and earn a spot in a well-fortified safe haven, she'll need to help her boss find his own son first. As tension between Melanie and her boss escalates and he shows his vicious side, it becomes clear she may have made a deal with the devil.

When the lights go out, it's Mark's job to keep his daughter Shona by his side and find a way to reunite with his wife, Melanie, when the lights go out. There's no way to turn the power back on, and Knoxville is quickly descending into chaos. His only goal is to find a way to get his family to safety.

With a destination in mind, the fractured family will face off against a world that is quickly becoming unrecognizable. And when even greater tragedy strikes, they will need to find a new way to survive. But what is the cost of survival in a world on the brink of collapse?

Grab your copy of *Emerging Chaos* (EMP Disaster Book One) from www.GraceHamiltonBooks.com

EXCERPT

Chapter One

His voice always preceded him, like the storm surge of a hurricane, a deep rumbling sound that hit just the right resonance to carry all the way down the hall and into the break room. Melanie Pearson was grateful for this. It meant she had time to brace herself for his arrival. And when Hurricane Derrick entered a room, it always brought trouble. Fortunately, it was a long walk from his big upstairs office at the back of the building to the break room where they'd had the Christmas party, and she'd left the door open.

"Sounds like a storm's brewing," Lizzy said. Currently, Melanie's best friend was on her hands and knees, an open trash bag on the ground beside her. Melanie heard the soft clatter of plastic cups, as her friend dug party residue out from under the table.

"What does he possibly have to complain about now?" Melanie grumbled. She had a plastic grocery store bag in her left hand, and as she worked her way down the long counter, she picked up debris and tossed it into the bag. "We volunteered to clean up after the party on our own time."

"Well, he didn't have to have the party in the first place, let's not forget," Lizzy said, imitating Derrick's voice as she strained to reach a corner where someone had dropped a paper plate with globs of red and green cake frosting still on it. "He's just keeping the Platt family tradition alive."

"Not without making sure we all know he resents it," Melanie added.

The break room at Beaton's Food Factory was a big, dingy space with ugly gray carpet that was frayed in spots, a big plastic table in the middle, a chipped counter, and a bulletin board covered in outdated information. Still, the employees had made a valiant effort to spruce up the place for the Christmas party. Red and green curled streamers hung down from the drop ceiling, a small Christmas tree stood at an angle in the corner, drooping with mismatched ornaments, and there'd been plenty to eat and drink, some of it halfway delicious.

Derrick's voice had stopped somewhere down the hall, diverting into one of the offices along the way, where the boss seemed to be chewing someone out about "deadlines." Good. Maybe he would forget about them long enough that they could finish cleaning and get out of there. Indeed, Melanie heard said office door close, the boss's voice becoming muffled. Poor soul. Someone was really getting it now.

"Let's pick up the pace," Lizzy said. She was done under the table and folding up the stained paper tablecloths now. "There's still time to get away without seeing his face again."

But Melanie was trying to scrub away the dried residue of a sloppy casserole. "These people are such pigs," she said. "How do you get this much of a dish onto the counter? Was it intentional?"

"Was it the ham and cheese casserole?" Lizzy asked. "The one Helen made. It was pretty good."

"I can't tell," Melanie replied. "It dried like concrete, though." She had to set down the rag and use the side of a metal fork to get some of it up. Even then, it was like chipping away old paint, and in the process, she left a small but notable scratch on the plastic countertop. Not that anyone would notice. She swept the crumbs into the bag, then turned to head back the other way.

When she did, she was startled by the person standing in the open doorway, totally silent and suddenly there. She hadn't heard him approach. Nathan Platt, the boss's son, was a gawky teen, awkward in his own body. He was wearing an oversized, faded t-shirt covered in comic book characters, and his pants were a bit too short, showing off his mismatched socks. His black hair mostly stuck straight up in a big, crooked poof, which accentuated a long, lean face, a somewhat prominent nose, and pointy chin.

Still, despite his awkward appearance, Nathan couldn't have been more different from his father. At first, he was staring up at the streamers, which were dancing in the current from the air conditioner. However, he seemed to realize Melanie was looking at him after a couple of seconds, and he turned and gave her a big, earnest smile.

"I could...I could help clean, if you want," he said.

"Are you actually *offering* to clean?" Lizzy said. "Do teens do that?"

"Yeah, it's kind of boring out there," he said. "I don't have anything else to do."

Melanie beckoned him, and he came trotting toward her. She held out the damp rag. "If you wouldn't mind, finish wiping down the counter for me. I'm going to work on removing the streamers."

He took the rag from her like she'd offered him a new toy for Christmas. "What do I do? Is there a trick to it?"

"No, just wipe in big circles until the whole counter is clean," she said. "Can you do that?"

"Of course. Whatever you say." He went to work, bent over the counter with a serious expression on his face. Again, Melanie marveled that this was Derrick's kid.

She went to retrieve a small stepladder from the corner and used it to begin pulling the colored streamers down from the ceiling.

"So tell me, Nathan," she said, as she reached up to grab the torn end of a loose green streamer. "Are you looking forward to Christmas?"

He paused in his work for a second, staring at the wall, and his serious expression seemed to dissolve into something sad. "I don't know. I guess I should be. It's a break from school, so that's something." And then he went back to his work.

"Does your family have plans?" Melanie asked. She wadded up the streamer and stuffed it into the bag. "A big dinner maybe?"

"Probably," he said. "Or maybe just takeout of some kind, if any restaurants are open." He glanced at her and attempted a smile. She could tell he was really struggling to make it stick.

For Melanie, it all hit a little close to home. Maybe home life wasn't something he wanted to talk about. She tried to think of some other subject, anything to keep him engaged. Working in silence was uncomfortable. Lizzy was sweeping up crumbs from the table and filled in the conversation.

"What about Christmas presents?" she asked. "Every kid looks forward to presents. What are you hoping for? I don't even know what fifteen-year-olds are into these days. Some app I've never heard of, probably, but you can't put an app under the tree. Or maybe you can. I don't know."

"I don't care about presents, really," Nathan said, and Melanie noted he was slinging the rag just a little too hard onto the countertop. "I don't want anything, to be honest. I mean, whatever…"

He bent over the sink, frowning deeply. An innocent attempt to engage him in conversation had clearly gone awry.

"Okay, I'll be honest. I'm not looking forward to Christmas at all," he said, as he resumed wiping a part of the counter that had already been thoroughly cleaned. "It's going to be super uncomfortable. Mom and Dad got into a huge fight about some dumb thing Dad is doing, and everything is uncomfortable right now. I wish I had somewhere else to go over the break—school or camp or just about anywhere else."

"I'm sorry to hear that," Melanie said. "Do we need to...?" She was going to offer to change the subject, but she became aware then of the imposing form filling the doorway.

Somehow, Derrick Platt had managed to approach the end of the hallway without being heard, which was a rarity. He stood there now in his short-sleeved shirt and red tie, his thumbs hooked under his black leather belt. He was tall like his son, but that was where the similarities ended. With his jowly face, thick neck, and watery eyes, he looked a bit like a human-bulldog hybrid. A beer gut strained at the buttons of his shirt and hung over the top of a shiny brass belt buckle. His hair was slicked back with too much product, shiny and greasy in equal measure, which made his big ears seem even more prominent.

When he frowned, as he did now, creases ran from the corners of his mouth, framing his little bump of a chin. "Why don't you ladies leave my boy alone and get back to work?" he said, in that rumbly voice of his.

"We never stopped working," Lizzy pointed out. Melanie's best friend was dwarfed beside the boss. Small, thin, with blondish hair tied back in a loose ponytail, she had a round face, bright blue eyes, and was prone to easy smiles. "Look at this." She held up the big bag of trash in her right hand.

"I'm just helping out so the work will get done faster," Nathan said. "Nobody forced me to do anything."

"Yeah, well, this is not your job," Derrick replied. "Why don't you go back upstairs to my office and play a video game or something?"

"I played plenty of video games," Nathan replied, bending over his work even more intensely. "I've got my phone with me, but it gets boring after a while just being up there by myself."

"He's not hurting anything," Lizzy said.

"I didn't say he *was*," Derrick replied, "but I want him to stay out of the way. Nathan, get back upstairs. Now." He jerked a thumb over his shoulder.

"Why does it matter?" Nathan replied. "I'm not bothering anybody."

"You're bothering *me*. Get upstairs. Now!" Derrick barked the final word. It hit just the right note to make Melanie's ears hurt.

Nathan screwed up his face in a hateful scowl and flung the dirty rag into the sink. "Fine, Dad. Whatever! I'm actually doing something productive, but I'll just go back up there and sit and do nothing."

The poor kid seemed on the verge of tears, but Derrick was unmoved. He stepped to one side and motioned his son through the door. Nathan, his lower lip jutting out so far he could have tripped on it, stormed across the room and passed through the door without looking at his father. When he was gone, Derrick stepped back into the doorway and shook his head, as if to say, *Kids these days.*

"Do me a favor and don't humor him," Derrick said to Melanie and Lizzy, giving them a stern gaze. "He knows he's not supposed to be wandering around the building."

"Whatever you say," Melanie replied, then ripped down another streamer and jammed it into the bag. *Just go away and let us finish up.* Oh, how badly she wanted to say it, but she bit her tongue.

Grab your copy of *Emerging Chaos* (EMP Disaster Book One) from www.GraceHamiltonBooks.com

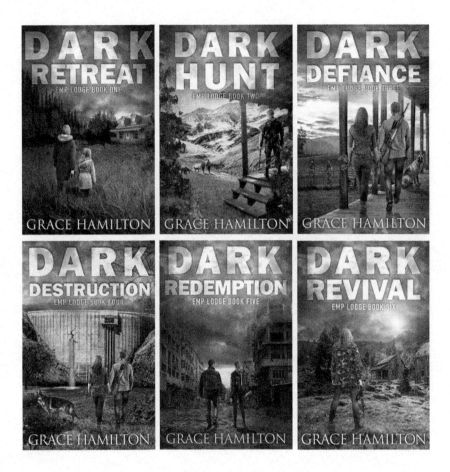

Made in the USA
Coppell, TX
13 February 2022

73516061R00164